ALL DWARF'ED UP

ALL DWARF'ED UP

DWARF BOUNTY HUNTER™ BOOK THREE

MARTHA CARR

MICHAEL ANDERLE

DISRUPTIVE IMAGINATION®

LMBPN Publishing
PMB 196, 2540 South Maryland Pkwy
Las Vegas, NV 89109

First Version, December 2020
Version 1.02, January 2021
ebook ISBN: 978-1-64971-344-5
Paperback ISBN: 978-1-64971-345-2

THE ALL DWARF'ED UP TEAM

Thanks to our JIT Team:

Dave Hicks
Allen Collins
Diane L. Smith
Jackey Hankard-Brodie
Thomas Ogden
Deb Mader
Dorothy Lloyd
Peter Manis
Kelly O'Donnell
J.R. Caplan
Paul Westman

If I've missed anyone, please let me know!

Editor
SkyHunter Editing Team

CHAPTER ONE

"Before this ceremony draws to a close, please join me once more to thank our generous benefactors. Ms. Leira Berens, Mr. James Brownstone, and Mr. Johnny Walker."

The field outside the main building filled with applause. Most of the enthusiasm came from the adults who stood around the perimeter of the neat rows of chairs on the grass. The kids— ranging in age from eleven to seventeen—clapped politely enough, but none of them looked particularly enthusiastic. That might have been because of the heat, however.

Johnny stood beside the podium with his arms folded and studied the witch behind the microphone. *Generous benefactors, huh? I wonder if anyone told her who this land belongs to. And the buildings. And the supplies.*

On the other side of Mr. Brownstone, Leira leaned forward to look past the hulking wall of muscle and met Johnny's gaze. "It has a nice ring to it, don't you think?"

He snorted and muttered through the dying applause, "Just 'cause she said your name first."

The witch at the podium—Glasket, he thought her name was —continued her drawn-out conclusion to the opening ceremony.

Brownstone's short laugh came out more like a grunt. "Are you worried about your reputation, Walker?"

The dwarf craned his neck to look at the other Level-Six bounty hunter and wrinkled his nose. "How many times have I gotta tell you how to say my name?"

"More than once, it would seem."

Leira darted them both a crooked smile and shook her head.

The man nodded and scanned the rows of students seated on the chairs on the lawn. "I think we did okay."

"The best part is that we get to leave after this and let the drill sergeants do their jobs," he responded brusquely.

"They're teachers, Johnny," Leira said.

The dwarf circled his finger in the air and glanced around the grounds. "Does this look like a regular school to you?"

"You said Quantico for magical kids." Brownstone shrugged. "I'd say that fits the bill."

"Trainers, then." He leaned sideways to look around the huge man beside him and jerked his chin at Leira. "Does that tickle your fancy the right way, darlin'?"

She raised her eyebrows in warning. "What was that?"

Johnny raised both hands. "Sorry. Force of habit, *Ms. Berens*."

The woman looked away from him to study the compound and its buildings that, while sparsely decorated, fitted their purpose perfectly. "Trainers works for me."

"Right." Johnny sniffed and scratched the side of his face under his wiry red beard. "Then we let the trainers do the trainin' And I can get back to my cabin."

"To do what?" Brownstone asked and glanced at the dwarf from the corner of his eye.

"To do…" He scoffed. "You been down here a month and you're tellin' me you ain't—"

"And with that," Ms. Glasket pronounced and clapped briskly, "you're all expected to meet in your assigned dorms in an hour for a more thorough orientation. Until then, help yourselves to refreshments. You'll find those in the tent beside the martial arts building. They include everything you'll come to know and enjoy about Southern cooking, I've been told." The witch grinned and spread her arms effusively. "Welcome to the Academy of Necessary Magic."

The full headcount of a hundred and seven students bounded from their chairs immediately. The trainers stayed to applaud Ms. Glasket's speech. Low conversation filled the lawn as the kids hurried toward the refreshments tent, which had been fitted with mist fans to help stave off the sweltering July heat.

Johnny thumped the back of his hand against Brownstone's arm beneath the leather duster. "And that's our cue. Nice knowin' ya both."

The giant man snorted and glanced at his arm before he looked up slowly to watch the dwarf walk away.

"I don't know about you," Leira said and gave him a cursory study, "but I need something cold. Aren't you hot in that?"

"Nope."

"Huh." She left it at that and strode across the lawn toward the refreshments tent. Brownstone remained where he was, content to simply enjoy their joint accomplishment for a few moments.

"Johnny! Hey." Doc Leahy walked briskly across the field toward the dwarf.

The bounty hunter turned and widened his eyes when he saw the usually reserved doc in a pair of Bermuda shorts, a Hawaiian t-shirt, and Berkinstock sandals approaching. The man's unruly gray mop of hair had been tied in a ponytail. Johnny's nose twitched as he scratched his face again and let the man catch up. "I didn't recognize ya, Doc."

"Oh." The man glanced at his outfit with a self-conscious smile. "Well...it's not my usual style, I'll admit. But when in Rome—"

"This ain't Rome. It's the Everglades."

The man held a laugh back. "Yes, I'm fully aware of that, Johnny."

"Do you see anyone else 'round here dressed like that?"

"No, but—"

"You look like a tourist." He folded his arms and snorted a laugh.

"Because I am." The doc swatted at a swarm of gnats buzzing past and chuckled. "I gave myself two days off and made the trip from LA to see for myself what the three of you managed to pull together. And yes, now that I've seen it, I'm heading to Miami for the night to be a tourist."

"Yeah, you'll fit in fine on the other side of the state. Does everything meet your expectations?"

"The academy? Very much so." The man turned to look over his shoulder at the now empty chairs and podium and the crowd of students and trainers who descended on the tent. "I suppose congratulations on your newest endeavor are in order, especially with such a fast turnaround. All this in a month."

"When you have the money and know the right folks, it's simple."

"Indeed. I wanted to thank you personally too, Johnny. For offering your land and funding the project."

The dwarf nodded toward Brownstone, who still stood motionlessly beside the podium with his arms folded. "I didn't do it all on my lonesome, that's for damn sure."

"No, I know. Leira and Mr. Brownstone bring their unique outlook to every…project."

"Huh. You don't say."

Doc smiled. "So what's next for you?"

"Me? I'm goin' home, Doc. Enjoy your trip." He nodded at the wizard and turned toward the dirt road leading away from the compound. *The academy, now. It's one of the weirder things I own but it's for a good cause. These kids will learn everything they need to know about breakin' the rules and gettin' paid for it.*

That thought made him chuckle before he stuck two fingers in his mouth for a loud, piercing whistle. "Rex! Luther! Time to get on, boys."

Splashing and panting rose from the thick, draped foliage hanging over the swamp beside the dirt road. His two black-and-tan coonhounds bounded through the reeds, dripping muddy water and covered in soggy leaves and pieces of grass. They raced toward him and skidded to a stop when he snapped his fingers.

"What's wrong, Johnny?" Luther's tail wagged furiously and flung water everywhere.

"Yeah, if we're goin' home, let's go home." Rex's head nodded up and down as he turned toward the field and sniffed. "But we shouldn't. I smell catfish."

"Oooh! Johnny, please—"

"We ain't stayin', boys. The work's done so we're goin' home."

"Then why are we—" Luther shook himself vigorously from head to toe and flung mud, water, and reeds all over the road and his brother.

Rex couldn't help but do the same, then both hounds flicked their tails and panted as they stared at their master.

"That." Johnny pointed at them. "That's why we stopped in the middle of the road."

"We can't help it, Johnny," Rex said and twisted his neck to nip at something in the fur along his back. "It's like all you two-legs with yawning. You see another hound do it, you simply—"

"Can't help yourself," Luther finished and mirrored his brother's turn to nibble at his rear hip.

The dwarf snorted and nodded down the road to where he'd parked Sheila. "And now it's over."

"Johnny!" Amanda waved her hands as she ran toward them across the lawn. "Wait!"

"Hey, look." Luther's tail thumped against his brother's rear end before Rex finally stepped away. "It's the pup."

"Hey, pup." Rex yipped at the girl as she slowed to a walk and caught her breath as she reached them. "Are you ready to go?"

The girl tossed her dark hair out of her eyes and stared at Johnny. "Are you leaving already?"

He sniffed. "I have no other reason to be here."

She looked over her shoulder and laughed. "You do know Darlene's in that tent handing out catfish left and right, don't you?"

"I knew it." Rex licked his muzzle. "Johnny…"

The dwarf snapped his fingers again and lifted an index finger without looking away from his ward. Both hounds sat instantly with short whines of disappointment. After a moment, he nodded. "I'm the one who asked her to feed everyone, kid."

"And you're passing up on her food." She folded her arms. "Are you feeling okay?"

"It's the atmosphere. Somethin' about eatin' in her trailer and not in a tent makes a whole world of appetizin' difference." *Plus, the trailer's not full of juvenile delinquents who only know how to fight and run.* "Go ahead and have one for me too, though, yeah?"

"Okay." Amanda's smile faded as they stood in the road. "So this is it then, huh?"

Johnny nodded and rubbed his mouth before he tugged on the ends of his scraggly red beard. "This ain't goodbye, kid. Only a see ya later. I reckon they'll let you out on leave a couple of times a year—"

"On leave?" The girl scrunched her face up with a chuckle. "What's that supposed to mean?"

"Break. I meant break." He cleared his throat. "You know, come on back to the cabin and stay a few nights. Only if…I mean only if you want to."

"Why wouldn't I wanna come home for break?"

Home. That one word put a hard lump in the bounty hunter's throat, and if he'd looked at his hounds in that moment, he would've seen their eyebrows moving up and down like his as he tried to yank his emotions under control. He grunted. "No reason. All I'm sayin' is you know how to make your own choices. So if you end up takin' a likin' to this place and don't wanna leave when you're able, I won't take it personally."

Amanda grinned. "I'll come home for break. I'm not sure exactly when that is, though…" She turned again to scan the compound. "I have a feeling this isn't exactly like normal schools that way either."

Johnny responded with a gruff chuckle. "What makes you say that?"

"Well, the buildings kinda make it look like a prison, and I heard some of the teachers talking about how all the other kids here were the 'magical rejects' of LA—"

"They said that out in the open for anyone to hear?" He glared at the trainers scattered in conversation on the lawn while the students raced here and there and shouted at each other as they simply let off steam on their first day of "school." "Who the fuck was it? That ain't part of the—"

"Johnny."

"—lesson plan. That Light Elf told me they were—"

"*Johnny.*" Amanda leaned toward him and raised her eyebrows, smiling broadly. "Shifter hearing. Remember?"

He glanced at her and narrowed his eyes.

"Whoops." Rex panted heavily beside his brother and glanced from his master to the girl who'd been with them in the swamps for the last two months. "It's a big thing to forget, Johnny."

"Yeah, the pup can hear almost as good as we can," Luther added.

"*Well*, bro." Rex snorted. "Almost as *well* as we can."

"Yeah, that's what I said."

The dwarf gritted his teeth and forced himself to breathe slowly and evenly to bring his unwarranted frustration under control. Fortunately, Amanda didn't encourage the hounds with a comment of her own.

"They're very nice, Johnny." She nodded. "The teachers, I mean. One of them helped me carry everything to my room and asked me all about what it was like living with you."

"Huh." He cocked his head. "What did you say?"

She shrugged. "That I love it. Come on. You let me take the airboat out whenever I want, you bought me a phone, and I get to run around with the two best coonhounds in the Everglades."

"And that's it?"

"Well…I maybe said a few things about how you taught me to clean guns and shoot and tie up wild pigs and fire a crossbow— oh, and that one time when you took me out to throw grenades—"

"Jesus." He rolled his eyes.

"But that's it, Johnny. I didn't say a thing about your work or anything. That's all secret stuff, right?"

The dwarf nodded slowly and pressed his lips together so hard that they almost disappeared beneath his wiry red mustache. "Well, it would be if the staff here had no idea who I was or what I do for a livin'."

"Oh. Okay, so it's no big deal."

"How 'bout you keep that kinda thing to yourself from here on out, huh? Focus on what they're teachin' you instead."

Amanda frowned. "Why?"

He shrugged. "I reckon it might make the other kids feel a little…behind."

She burst out laughing. "Johnny, those kids were living in LA. Underground."

"Not with a bounty hunter and two coonhounds. It ain't the same."

"Okay. Fine. I won't introduce myself and say, 'Hi, I'm Amanda, Johnny Walker's shifter kid. He taught me everything he knows.'"

Johnny Walker's kid. He wanted to storm away, climb into Sheila, and rip the goddamn Band-Aid off then and there.

Instead, he merely grunted. "If I taught you everythin' I know, kid, you wouldn't be here."

"Uh-huh." She laughed again and swatted absently at the insects flying around them now, although mostly around the swamp-infested hounds. "Fine. I'll make something up, then."

"Now, I didn't say you have to do that—"

"Well, my other story isn't anywhere near as cool." The girl scuffed the sole of her shoe against the dirt road and muttered. "It's more depressing."

Johnny stared at her but her gaze remained fixed on the ground. His throat constricted. "All right. Come on, now. You—"

Amanda looked quickly at him with wide eyes.

Damn, she's good. "You tell people whatever you want."

"Truly?"

"It's your life, kid, and it ain't my place to tell you how to live it. I wouldn't be doin' my job if I did."

She grinned, threw herself at him, and wrapped her arm around his stiff shoulders. "Thanks, Johnny."

He tilted his head away from her and endured the hug but he couldn't help raising a hand to pat her gently on the back. "But don't say nothin' 'bout my tech, ya hear? That Glasket lady already made a whole big deal outta me bein' a benefactor. If you tell anyone what I got inside my house, those kids will come lookin' for trouble where I ain't tryin' to have it."

"No, totally." Amanda stepped away from him and shook her head. "I won't tell anyone where you live."

Johnny pointed at her. "Or about the tech."

"Or the tech. Promise." She crossed her heart with a finger and grinned. "But it's gonna be so cool to show people what I know." After glancing over her shoulder again at the other magical kids who remained engrossed in their various activities on the lawn, she leaned toward the dwarf and muttered, "I heard one kid say the swamp around the academy is fed by the sewers. Like from Miami."

He snorted. "That's a perfect example of why kids need to stay in school. You'd better set him right."

"Come on." Grinning, she spread her arms. "I know more about the Everglades than anyone here. Except for you, obviously. And Darlene."

"Oh, yeah, thanks." Luther chuffed and sat back on his haunches. "Way to forget about the hounds you can hear."

Rex swung his head away from the girl and stared at the lawn. "We didn't even show you half of what we know."

His brother looked quickly at him. "We didn't?"

Laughing, she dropped to one knee and pulled Rex's head toward her to give it a thorough scratch. "You're included in that, boys. What will I do without you?"

Johnny folded his arms and watched her. *Make friends, have a life, and be normal. Relatively speakin'.*

Luther stood and butted into his brother's head-scratching session while his tail wagged in wild circles. "Hey, me too. Scratch me too. Oh, *yeah...* Man. We're gonna miss you, pup."

She laughed when the smaller hound's rear leg lifted and pumped at the air in enjoyment. "I'll miss you too. But it's not like I'm across the country." The girl stood and grinned at Johnny. "You guys can visit whenever you want. You do own the place."

The dwarf wrinkled his nose and scratched his red-haired cheek again. "Naw. It's best we don't. You have all kinds of other things to focus on without a dwarf and his hounds stickin' their noses where they don't belong."

"It wouldn't bother me at all."

But I'd have a hell of a hard time leavin' her again. "We'll see." They stared at each other for a long moment before he spoke again. "Look, kid, I know when I brought this whole idea up, you were right on board from the get-go. And I never asked because it seemed like it made sense. So, uh...I mean, if you don't wanna be here—"

"I do, Johnny. I truly do." Amanda swiped her long dark hair out of her eyes again and exhaled a quick, contented sigh. "I'm sure."

"Well, okay…"

"I'm at an academy learning to be a bounty hunter. This is the coolest thing I've ever done."

"It might not always be cool, kid. You know that, right?"

The girl's smile faded but she didn't look away from him. "I'm counting on it. After what happened to my family… Well, that's why I wanna be here. If I can track and apprehend scumbags like those who killed my parents and Claire and stop them before they do the same to anyone else, that's worth it. Even if things aren't always cool, you know?"

"Yeah." Johnny swallowed and nodded. "I know exactly what you mean, kid."

"I thought you would." Her small smile returned. "And when I graduate, maybe I'll even be better than you."

He snorted. "It's a lofty goal, kid."

"Not impossible."

"Well, we'll see. Do you have the service box?"

Amanda grinned. "Stashed in my dresser under all the new clothes you bought me. And thanks for those, by the way."

"You keep that hidden, understand? It's for emergencies only."

"Yep."

"All right. Be good."

"I aim to be the best, Johnny."

Chuckling, he turned away and wagged a finger at her. "That's the headspace. Come on, boys. It's time to get outta here before our window closes."

"See ya, pup." Rex barked as Amanda raced away again across the lawn toward the other kids her age.

"Don't do anything we wouldn't do," Luther called after her. "Not a whole lotta things, but they exist."

The girl tossed her hand up in a brief wave before she slowed in front of the crowd of students and joined the ranks of her new classmates.

"Let her go, boys." Johnny hooked his thumbs through the belt loops of his black jeans and strode across the dirt road toward Sheila. "We have shit to do."

The hounds trotted after him. "Hunting, Johnny?"

"Hey, or fishing. Lots of fish right now."

"Lots of warm water and 'gators."

"Oooh, yeah. Or we could stop at Darlene's for a—wait." Luther turned toward the field again and sniffed. "Darlene's here."

The dwarf opened the trunk of his red Jeep and nodded for the hounds to hop inside. Their claws scrabbled across the smooth, uncarpeted floor before he shut the door and moved to the driver's seat.

"So what's the plan, Johnny, huh?"

"Yeah, you always have a plan. Spill it."

Sheila's engine roared to life and he shifted into drive. "Whatever we want."

Both hounds lurched as their master accelerated sharply.

"Aw, man. That doesn't mean anything."

"Yeah, when he says it like that, *we* means Johnny."

CHAPTER TWO

When the bounty hunter stepped through the front door of his tidy cabin, he stopped in the hallway and glanced around. *Damn. It already feels empty.*

Rex and Luther trotted past him through the house and their claws clicked on the wood floors. "How about a snack, Johnny?"

"Yeah, you made us hang around while that weird lady talked for hours and we didn't even get to stay for the grub."

The hounds turned and stared at him. "Johnny?"

He sniffed and shoved the door closed behind him. "You ate before we left."

"I already said we were out there for hours." Luther backed away and stared after his master, who walked past them down the hallway and turned into the workshop. "What's wrong with you?"

"Nothin'." He took one of the older rifles from the shelf and retrieved his cleaning box. The lid pinged against the table when he threw it back and pulled out the bottle of solvent.

"Uh-oh." Rex lowered his head with a low whine and entered the workshop slowly. "You're angry-cleaning."

"No, no, no. It's a different smell when he's pissed." Luther pressed his snout against Johnny's pant leg and sniffed up and down before he stepped away and sat. "Johnny?"

"What's he doing?" Rex had moved under the worktable and now glanced from his brother to his master's legs.

"He's…uh, staring."

The dwarf placed the rifle on the table with a loud thunk and looked at Luther. "No, that's you. If you can't stop, get on outside, huh?"

"No way, Johnny." The hound's tail thumped the floor. "Something's wrong with you."

Rex stretched his neck out as far as he could from beneath the table and sniffed his master's other leg. "Is that… No."

"I think it is."

They looked at each other, then Rex left his place under the table and sat at his brother's side. He cocked his head and whined. "Are you…sad, Johnny?"

He sniffed. "No."

"Then why do you smell like soggy bread?"

"Oh, shit. He misses the pup." Luther's tail thumped twice. "Johnny."

"Hey, we miss her too. No reason to be sad."

"I ain't—" With a low growl of frustration, Johnny clutched the edge of the worktable with both hands and hung his head. "I'm…contemplatin'."

"Huh?"

Rex lowered his head to scratch behind his ear with a rear paw. "He can't shit."

"Aw, hell, Johnny. That's easy." Luther stood and backed away and his tail returned to its usual wild wagging. "There's this huge patch of grass out back that's real good for something like that. Come on. I'll show you."

"*Contemplatin'.*" Johnny snorted. "It means I'm thinkin'."

"Oh. Why is that making you sad?"

"He misses her already," Rex replied. "We miss her too, Johnny. Don't let it get you down, though."

"Yeah, that's a waste of time." Luther trotted into the hall and his words trailed after him. "Think of all the things you can do now that it's only us again. Hunt whenever you want. Bring over whatever ladies you want."

"Yeah, it's been a while for you, Johnny."

The dwarf stepped back, scowled at Rex, and pointed into the hall. "Git."

"I'm only sayin'—"

"You can eat whatever you want that's in the fridge," Luther added from the living room. "And she won't get mad 'cause she wanted it. And you won't get mad 'cause she ate it. Hey, Johnny. You're not gonna try to eat all the food in there by yourself, are you?"

Rex snuck around his master to head into the kitchen, not the hall. "Yeah, throwing out all that food's a big waste. If you don't want it to go bad, we could help—"

Luther barked and scrambled through the mudroom, taking the back way into the kitchen. "If that's your plan, Johnny, we're your hounds."

"For life."

"Nothin's goin' to waste, and y'all quit talkin' about it." Johnny returned to his worktable and rested his hands on the surface. "Better yet, quit talkin' altogether. I need a minute."

Both hounds backed slowly away from the kitchen's entrance into the workshop. "I think that means we should go outside," Rex muttered.

"If it doesn't, he'll stop us."

"Oh, *Johnny*… We're going *outside*…"

Five seconds of silence passed before they turned and raced to the dog door in the back. "Go, go, go! Before he changes his mind."

It clapped open and shut, followed by the thump of paws

down the back porch stairs. "Hey, Luther. Where was that patch of grass you were talking about?"

"Oh, yeah. Come on."

Johnny rubbed his mouth and exhaled a heavy sigh. On the other side of the worktable was the file Agent Nelson had brought him after they'd solved the Logree case. *It took him a week longer than he promised, but at least it's here.*

He hadn't touched the fifteen-year-old case file on his daughter's murder since his first attempt to look through it. Now, it seemed like the only thing he could focus on. *No more cases. No more school to build. No kid to put up with.*

The dwarf packed everything into the cleaning case again, locked it, and replaced the box and the rifle on the shelf. He walked slowly around the worktable and scowled at the file as if it were a cottonmouth coiled to strike. *Naw, that's a snake I know how to handle. I ain't too clear about this.*

When he reached the other side of the large surface, he sniffed and stared at the plain manila envelope that looked like it had been stored in the bottom of a box for fifteen years.

"Fuck it." He snatched it up and thrust it under one arm as he headed to the kitchen. It took only a moment to retrieve the bottle of Johnny Walker Black and a rocks glass recently unloaded from the dishwasher. He poured himself four fingers, inclined his head in thought, and added another two in case.

After a long sip, his grimace faded and he felt a little more prepared. Before he could find a reason to talk himself out of it, he took the folder and the whisky with him into the living room and got to work.

He allowed himself another sip and placed his glass on the table, then opened the envelope. The papers slid out easily enough but a few on top were stuck together. Prying them apart carefully, he found smudges of dark purple and a dusting of crumbs between them. *It looks like some fed likes his jelly doughnuts as much as the next asshole. I swear, if mice got into this shit before I did, Nelson will lose a finger.*

Fortunately, all the reports, written depositions, and interview transcripts were still intact. Then, he found the photos.

The second he recognized the first one for what it was, Johnny dropped the entire pile onto the coffee table and almost spilled his whisky when he brought it hastily to his mouth. *You knew these were in here, Johnny. It's nothin' you ain't seen before.*

Still, it took another long sip of whisky before he could focus on the stack of papers in front of him—all that remained as proof that Dawn's murder had been left unsolved for fifteen years. He reminded himself that the stack was a hell of a lot bigger now than when he'd gone through it fifteen years before. The quiet anger at the knowledge that information had been withheld from him gave him the impetus to continue.

He slid the photos beneath the large envelope, drew the rest of the file onto his lap, and began to read.

The first few case reports covered all the things he already knew. Her body had been found in the doorway of a shop on the Lower East Side of Manhattan. She'd been shot in the head and the shop owner had been apprehended in his home later that night but was eventually released and never charged. No eyewitnesses came forward and no other evidence was found. Everyone had scattered to flee the scene of the crime before anyone could determine what had happened.

"No gunshot residue on the owner. He didn't even own a weapon. Yeah, yeah. And nothin' says shit about the red boar or how fuckin' incompetent the feds are."

The Red Boar had been Johnny's discovery four days after the murder. He'd gone through the pictures on Dawn's digital camera, red-eyed and halfway through the bottle. The device was filled with pictures of his daughter and her friends on their school trip to NYC—chaperoned, of course. But kids knew how to have fun however they could.

One photo had a red boar silhouette graffitied on a brick wall behind the youngsters. Four pictures after that, he'd seen the same boar lit up in red neon above a bar that hadn't lasted longer than a year past her death. The next time he'd paid a visit to the department—in person—he'd caught Director Fitzgerald in the middle of studying a file on his desk. Quickly, the man had shut the file and shoved it into the top drawer of his desk before he addressed the grief-addled bounty hunter, but not before he caught a glimpse of the photo resting on top of the reports. He recalled it vividly—a little plastic baggy with the boar stamped across its surface in bright red ink, evidence from another case.

"Oh, only a college kid caught up in the wrong kinda fun on the wrong weekend," Fitzgerald had explained nonchalantly when Johnny asked about it. "The war on drugs is never-ending, unfortunately." That had been moments before the man refused for the third and final time to let him work on Dawn's murder.

But the bounty hunter had already made the connection to the baggie and the red boar in his daughter's photos, and he went off on his own to get justice for his daughter.

He snorted and took another long drink of whisky. "I tore that bar to pieces trying to nail the guy," he muttered. "Nothin' but a fake-ass name and a slap on the wrist."

And retirement. This asshole went underground for a long time before he grew the balls to start sellin' his shit again in New York.

Johnny worked through page after page as he sifted painstakingly through the information he'd seen in the original reports, all of it completely useless.

When he turned the last report marking the case *Unsolved*, he stopped.

The next sheet was blank but for the huge letters stamped across the top. *Deadroot: Classified.*

"What the fuck is Deadroot?" He put his glass down again and flipped to the next document with both hands. He certainly hadn't seen this before.

The first part of the report contained pictures of Ben Hamilton, his wife Kay, and their daughter Lucy—Dawn's best friend. It made sense that the family was mentioned in her murder file as both parents had been chaperones on the school trip, but this was Deadroot. It was something else entirely.

Johnny scanned the details with a deepening scowl. Most of it focused on Ben and he drank more whisky to help him curb his impatience. At the bottom of the report was an affirmation of Hamilton's involvement:

Subject 32 for Operation Deadroot will continue to be surveilled for the duration of an upcoming visit to New York City in October with his family. He is not to be engaged but depending on how deep his involvement extends into the hub of Deadroot's central dealings, he may be flagged for further consideration as a CI.

"Motherfuckers." The dwarf growled in disgust. "October. They knew the guy was dippin' his fingers in illegal fuckin' pies and didn't say shit."

What the hell would Dawn be doin' walkin' 'round Manhattan alone with Lucy's old man? Did he pull her into some dirtbag deal?

He didn't find anything very useful within the innumerable reports on Ben Hamilton and his money troubles with off-the-books gambling, a few loan-sharking mishaps, and a close call with a DUI after Dawn's death that was dismissed because the feds were still using him as an informant by that time.

Finally, he found the transcripts.

The first was of video surveillance from what had been a vape shop on Johnny's last visit to New York but had been something else fifteen years before. Of course, no one would tell him about it because they knew he'd investigate the establishment on his own—which he'd ended up doing anyway but fifteen years too late.

October 27th, 2015.

16:59:57 – Figures A (male; shifter; unidentifiable age; muscular build; 6'2") and B (male, human, Caucasian; 30-35, average build; 5'11") close the storefront and remain on the premises.

17:23:34 – Figure A moves to the back door located on the ground level.

17:24:54 – Figure C (male; human; Caucasian; 40-45; slight build; 5'10") enters the shop through the back door. All three stand in close proximity to the exit. Conversation escalates.

Beside each of the marked moments in the footage was a single frame from the video itself printed in grainy black-and-white. *That's as good as they could get?*

The dwarf studied the third frame and recognized Ben Hamilton's hunched shoulders before he saw the note made in faded pencil below the image—*Figure C – Deadroot Subject 32.*

"Aw, shit, Ben. What were you doing?"

He turned the page to keep reading.

17:37:48 – Figure A draws a firearm and aims it at Figure C. Figure C steps away but does not move to leave. No other weapons drawn.

17:39:22 – Figure B moves slowly to the back door, Figure A still aiming a weapon at Figure C.

17:40:04 – Figure B returns to the main room with his hand clenched around the arm of Figure D (female; dwarf; age 11-14; 4'11"). Figure A's weapon still aimed at Figure C.

"Jesus." Johnny drew in a shuddering breath. He stared at the grainy outline of his daughter struggling in some asshole's grip as he dragged her into the shop, caught forever in this frozen second. *Why the fuck didn't they show me this? I should have seen this.*

He took another sip of whisky, gritted his teeth, and turned to the next page.

17:41:01 – Figure B shoves Figure D forward to form a circle inside the premises.

17:42:25 – Figure C gestures to the front door. Conversation escalates.

17:43:09 – Figure D steps toward Figure A. Figure A swings his firearm toward her.

17:43:49 – First shot fired from Figure A's weapon. Bullet strikes the back wall of the shop.

17:43:50 – Figure C lunges toward Figure A. Figure D runs to the front door of the shop, avoiding Figure B's attempts to catch her.

17:43:53 – Figure D reaches the front door.

17:43:54 – Figure A aims his weapon at Figure D. Second shot fired. Mortal impact to the back of the head (See Internal Federal Report #157843M: D. Walker).

17:43:55 – Figure D falls to the floor.

17:43:59 – Figure C attempts to approach Figure D. Figure A aims his firearm at Figure C again.

17:44:31 – Figure C runs to the back door and leaves the premises.

17:46:52 – Figures A removes a cell phone from his pocket and makes a call.

17:47:11 – Figures A and B leave the premises through the back door.

Manhattan PD arrived at the scene at approximately 17:53.

CHAPTER THREE

Johnny could hardly read the last part through the tears that stung his eyes. He shoved the stack of papers away from him on the coffee table and downed the other half of his drink in one swallow.

I need another one. That was the only thought in his head as he stood and hurried to the kitchen. His shoulder caught against the doorframe and he managed to balance himself on the counter. In silence, he stood for a moment and stared at his bottle of Johnny Walker Black.

It wasn't the booze making him woozy. He could hold his liquor better than half the moonshine drunks in his neck of the woods. *They knew exactly what happened to her. This whole time, they knew. Why the fuck didn't they catch the bastard?*

By sheer force of will, he forced the tears back, snatched the whisky, and returned to the living room. He drank from the bottle before he reached his chair. His phone buzzed in his back pocket and he pulled it out to glance at it as he sat. It was Agent Breyer and he grimaced.

Sorry, darlin'. Today simply ain't the day.

He declined the call and set the phone aside on the coffee

table before he resumed reading. It took him longer than he expected to pull his gaze away from the final frame printed on the transcript—his daughter lying on the floor at the front of the shop in a crumpled heap.

Nestling the whisky bottle in the cushions of the couch beside him, he turned the page and found exactly what he'd tried to find fifteen years before.

Interview from Internal Federal Report #157843M: D. Walker.

Suspect: Creed Vilguard

Human male. Caucasian. Age 32. 5'11" and 232.5 pounds.

Charges: Accessory to murder. Possession of Schedule II Narcotics with Intent to Sell. Two counts of Extortion. Aggravated Assault.

Suspect was apprehended on October 29th, 2025 in response to an emergency call reporting shots fired.

Interrogating Agent: F. Cordon

Interviews starts at 00:02:18

Cordon: Please state your name for the record.

Vilguard: Creed Vilguard.

Cordon: Tell me about what happened at RedHero Comics two nights ago, October 27th.

Vilguard: Man, I can't remember what I ate for breakfast this morning. Had to be like any other day.

Cordon: Don't play dumb with me. We have video footage of you in the shop with Ben Hamilton, Dawn Walker, and your friend.

Vilguard: (chuckling) Who?

Cordon: The shifter who shot the dwarf girl in the back of the head. You're already in here, Creed. We have so much shit on you, you'll be lucky to get out of this with thirty years served. Tell me what happened.

Vilguard: Man, you ain't got shit.

Cordon: Huh. (creaking chair). Nice shoes. What are those? Custom-made?

Vilguard: Fuck you.

Cordon: Sure, but I promise you won't like it. Do you think you're protecting this shifter? You're not. Right now, we have a unit heading to his place on 130th. We gonna round him up and whoever else is with him. So do yourself a fucking favor and tell me what Ben Hamilton was doing in that store two nights ago.

Vilguard: (sighing heavily) Shit. A'right, look. The yuppie stopped by unannounced to say he wanted out.

Cordon: Hamilton?

Vilguard: Sure, whatever. I called him shitstain.

Cordon: Wanted out of what?

Vilguard: Man, the dude was itchy, you know? Said he thought he was being watched. Followed. And he wanted to turn back on a deal he'd made.

Cordon: With you?

Vilguard: I guess.

Cordon: What was the deal?

Vilguard: The guy found his way into dealin' for us. Small shit. I guess his conscience caught up to him and he wanted outta the game.

Cordon: Hamilton was dealing drugs for you?

Vilguard: (laughing) Man, how do you think this shit gets everywhere it does? Even the pawns got pawns, know what I'm sayin'?

Cordon: Are you saying you're a pawn?

Vilguard: Ain't we all?

Cordon: For whom?

Vilguard: (chair creaking) I don't know, man. Honest truth right there. None of us know the guys at the top of this chain, a'right?

Cordon: Then who do you answer to?

Vilguard: Prentiss, man.

Cordon: Prentiss Avalon? The shifter who was in the store with you that night?

Vilguard: Yeah, the fuckin' shifter.

Johnny's cell phone rang again on the coffee table. Without looking at it, he picked it up and tossed it distractedly against the far wall of the living room. It clattered on the floor and continued to ring until it finally stopped, but he'd already focused on the transcript.

Cordon: (pause) What was Dawn Walker doing in the store?

Vilguard: The dwarf? Shit, I don't know what that kid was thinkin'. Prentiss heard some shit out back. Shifter hearin' and all that. He told me to check it out, and there she was, tryin' to listen in on the whole thing.

Cordon: So you brought her inside.

Vilguard: Fuckin' right I did. Boss tells you to do something, you do it.

Cordon: You're referring to Prentiss again, right? (pause) I need a verbal confirmation of that, Creed.

Vilguard: (throat-clearing) Do you ask your old lady for verbal confirmation when you're railin' her?

Cordon: (drinking water) Why was the girl there?

Vilguard: Man, I don't know. She must have followed the bastard across town.

Cordon: Hamilton?

Vilguard: Yeah, fuckin' Hamilton. They knew each other. You could tell. The dude looked like he was about to have a heart attack when he saw her.

Cordon: Did they say anything to each other?

Vilguard: Nah. He was tryin' not to piss himself, and she did all the talkin' anyway. She said if we hurt him, we'd be sorry—tough kid but not a lotta brains. Obviously.

Cordon: That's when Prentiss shot her?

Vilguard: That's when he tried to scare her off, man. He told her to get lost and this had nothin' to do with her. And a little girl can't do shit. (heavy sigh) The kid shoulda listened to him. She had her chance but she wouldn't quit mouthin' off.

Cordon: About what?

Vilguard: She said if he hurt the yuppie or her, we wouldn't get away with it 'cause her old man was a bounty hunter. Then he got the go-ahead to— (throat-clearing)

Cordon: To shoot Dawn Walker?

Vilguard: That's what he did, ain't it?

Cordon: The go-ahead from whom? (pause) If you ask me, Creed, that little slip-up makes it sound a hell of a lot like someone else told Prentiss to shoot the girl. Who else was in that shop? (pause) (slamming) I'm not fucking around, Creed! A twelve-year-old girl was murdered. You're catching an accessory to murder charge with at least four other felonies. Do you want to add obstruction to that list too? Of a federal case?

Vilguard: You already know Prentiss shot her.

Cordon: Yeah, and our people are picking him up right now, so I don't give a shit about that shifter anymore. You said he 'got the go-ahead.' So who else was in the shop?

Vilguard: (soft chuckling) You're the one with the video footage, ain'tcha? You wanna see exactly who was in there that night, go ahead. Take another look. If you find anyone else in there, you should get your head checked.

Cordon: I want to hear it from you.

Vilguard: (pause) Man, I ain't sayin' nothin' else. This is bullshit.

Cordon: This is your only chance, Creed. I can't do anything about the possession charges or aggravated assault, but if you—(crosstalk)

Vilguard: Don't matter anyway. If you're so sure you got Prentiss in the bag, that's all you need. (chair creaking) That's all you sonsabitches are ever gonna get.

Cordon: (papers shuffling) (chair scooting) Then you're on your own. You wanna take the blame for whoever was calling the shots last night, that's on you.

Vilguard: We done with this shit?

Cordon: Yeah. We're done.

(End of Recording)

Johnny's hands shook as he held the last page of the interrogation printed in black and white. *These two-timing assholes kept all this from me. They knew exactly why she was murdered. Where, when, the whole fucking shebang. And she tried...* He swallowed thickly and sniffed. *She tried to get the man outta there by droppin' my name.*

He turned the last page of the interview and set it on the stack of upside-down ones on the table. The next was an arrest report dated November 3rd, 2015.

Prentiss Avalon. Male. Shifter. Unidentifiable age. 6'2". 284 pounds.

Apprehended in Brooklyn, NY, at President Street and Brooklyn Avenue and charged with Possession of a Schedule One Narcotic with Intent to Sell, Aggravated Assault, Racketeering, Public Endangerment, and Felony Murder in the First Degree for the death of Dawn Walker.

The suspect was apprehended after Brooklyn Police received a call of shots fired at the site of the crime. Avalon was found with 12 grams of Methamphetamine, 10.4 grams of Heroin, and 14.6 grams of an as yet unidentified substance on his person at the time of his arrest.

Also in his possession was the weapon assumed to be used for the murder of Dawn Walker on October 27th, 2015 (see Internal Federal Report #157843M: D. Walker). Narcotics sent to forensics for confirmation. The firearm, a Ruger LCP 380 Auto, Model #3701, as submitted to ballistics for confirmation as the murder weapon.

Reporting Agent: F. Cordon

At the end of the arrest report, two photographs had been stapled to the page—one of Prentiss' firearm and the other of the entire collection of drugs he'd had on him during his arrest, all of the tiny plastic baggies stamped with the red boar.

The next page held an additional report of Prentiss Avalon's case hearing. His weapon had been confirmed as the murder weapon in Dawn's case, and that together with the interrogation of Creed Vilguard was enough to find him guilty of First-Degree Felony Murder among the other slew of charges. The shifter had been found guilty on every count and received a life sentence.

"They fucking got him!" Johnny pounded his fist on the stack of papers and grasped the whisky bottle with the other for another long swallow. *The motherfuckers put him behind bars a month after he killed her and didn't say shit 'cause they knew he was simply the trigger finger. They knew the fucker who killed her wasn't calling the shots, and they couldn't even have the decency to tell me that.*

The dwarf grunted and glared at the open file in front of him.

I should stop right here but it can't get much more fucked-up than this, right?

His hand was no longer shaking when he flipped the arrest report and continued. What followed were more reports of Prentiss' sentence hearing, a transfer to the max-security prison most of Johnny's bounties ended up spending a minimum of five years in, and another report of having closed Dawn's case at the state level—but not federal. The feds had left Internal Federal Report #157843M: D. Walker open for investigation, and the last stapled collection of papers told Johnny exactly why.

The top page was a memo sent to the Deadroot team from Agent Frank Cordon and dated February 27, 2026.

Ongoing work with CI Ben Hamilton has led to valuable insight into where Deadroot plans to strike next. According to Hamilton, he has arranged an in-person meeting with one Harold Nolgan. If you don't recognize the name, look it up (reference Operation Shadow). We believe we have every reason to give credence to Hamilton's claim. His information has pointed us to their next rendezvous point in The Bronx on March 18th, 2026 (see attached location details). This is our chance to strike and apprehend both parties if we time this right.

I want to reiterate the importance of keeping all aspects of this operation under wraps, especially when it comes to the Bounty Hunter Division. This includes Agent Tommy Nelson and any contracted bounty hunters he currently handles. We'll only have one attempt at this, and that will be in less than three weeks.

Strategy meeting this Thursday at 8:00 a.m. Let's bag these assholes.

With a snarl, he turned the page and poured through what scattered reports remained of Operation Deadroot and all the details of every meeting held by the team assigned to the operation up to three days before the sting. They'd dotted all their i's and crossed all their t's, and then...nothing.

He flipped back through the stapled reports in case he'd missed something, but that was it. Nothing else in the file mentioned the final maneuver that would have tied up Operation Deadroot in a neat, back-stabbing bow.

"What the fuck happened?" The dwarf growled and took another long swig from the bottle.

He already knew, however. The sting op had failed—gone south, somehow. *And no one had bothered to write anything up about it 'cause they're all too chickenshit to admit they fucked up. That they pushed me out and fed me crumbs and still couldn't bring the bastard in.*

And that bastard, Johnny knew, was the same bastard running around New York two months earlier calling himself Lemonhead. He'd let the slippery fuck escape so he and Lisa could rescue Amanda from the penthouse. Now, Lemonhead or Deadroot or whoever he chose to call himself was still out there and back in action.

"Fuck!" He thumped both fists on the coffee table and breathed heavily through his rage and the decent alcohol haze he'd built up in the last hour.

Outside, the coonhounds bayed together and their voices drew steadily closer.

"Incoming, Johnny!"

"Someone's rolling up. Two someone's."

"Two cars, Johnny."

Their barking and howling passed the side of the house and continued at the front of the property. He grunted, gulped another shot of whisky, and ignored everything but the files in front of him. *I'm gonna get him this time. No fuckin' doubt about it.*

CHAPTER FOUR

"No! Back up, you—" Tommy Nelson's whine of frustration cut off seconds before the door to the screened-in porch slammed shut.

"Johnny!" Rex howled. "That salty asshole's back."

"Yeah, let us in!"

Both hounds bayed and barked outside the front porch until the front door opened.

"Back door, Luther."

"Yeah, yeah. We'll tear his arms off!"

They raced to the back again, barking nonstop. Tommy stepped into Johnny's entry hall, followed immediately by Lisa Breyer. "Johnny? What the hell are you doing in here?"

Lisa tapped her colleague on the shoulder and nodded down the hall toward the living room. All they could see was Johnny's bent knees at the edge of the couch, his boots, and a pile of papers on the coffee table.

Tommy grimaced in frustration. "Whatever happened to a—"

"Hold on," she muttered and stepped in front of him to hurry down the hall.

He shook his head and gave her a few seconds' head-start. *There'd better be a reason for this cocky dwarf not answering my calls.*

The dog door clapped open and shut, and both hounds raced through the kitchen and into the hall. They skidded to a stop beside Tommy, crouched with their hackles raised, and snarled like they'd trapped wild game on a hunt.

"How many times do you have to get your ass beaten before you get the picture?" Rex snarled.

"Ass *bitten*, you mean." Luther snapped his jaws at the agent. "You tell us when, Johnny. We're all over this."

The agent stared at them with wide eyes, adjusted his tie, then bolted toward the living room. He stamped deliberately on the hardwood floor as loudly as he could.

Without any instruction from their master, Rex and Luther turned and stalked slowly after him, ready to pounce if they had to.

Lisa reached the entrance to the living room first and stopped. She didn't need to read any of the documents strewn in a messy heap on the coffee table to recognize what the bounty hunter was doing. The second she saw the edge of the photos peeking out from beneath the envelope, she knew. "Johnny—"

"What the hell are you trying to pull, huh?" Tommy stopped beside her, and she darted him a scathing glance before he recognized the contents of the huge file he had brought for the dwarf. He cleared his throat. "Oh. You're finally taking a look, huh?"

Johnny leaned forward slowly on the couch, the half-empty bottle of whisky dangling loosely from one hand.

"Are you okay?" Lisa asked softly.

The bottle thumped onto the table.

"I ain't got the time or the patience for stupid questions." He stood from the couch, turned to face them, and glared at Nelson. "So I'm gonna cut to the important ones right here and now, understand?"

"Shit," Tommy whispered. "I'm guessing you found somethi—"

"Oh, I found somethin', all right." He stalked toward them, his footsteps heavier than usual despite the straight line he maintained as he approached relentlessly. "A whole lotta bullshit, Nelson. A whole lotta coverup for a goddamn op that up and disappeared like a fart on the wind. Do you have any idea why the hell that happened?"

"Hey, I didn't take the liberty of going through that file first, Johnny." The agent raised both hands in surrender. "That's yours. It's not my place to—"

"Not your *place*?" The bounty hunter seized him by the lapels of his black suit jacket, shoved him back, and turned to thrust him against the wall.

"Johnny!" Lisa shouted.

"You mean it's not your place to tell me what the fuck was going on?"

"What are you doing?" Tommy muttered and squeezed his eyes shut when he was thumped against the wall again.

"Uh-oh…" Rex and Luther uttered low whines and crouched even lower where they stood four feet down the hall.

"I'm the one askin' the questions, Nelson." Johnny growled in the man's face and even though he didn't quite reach Tommy's chin, he was no less menacing because of it. "You knew they bagged the motherfucker who shot her!"

"What?"

Johnny pushed him against the wall again. "You knew about Ben Hamilton, didn't you? That she got sucked into his fuck-up trying to help the guy."

The man spread his arms in a helpless gesture. "Johnny, I swear, I had no—"

"The whole damn FBI kept it from me, Nelson!"

"Johnny, stop." Lisa stepped toward them but paused when her colleague looked quickly at her and shook his head.

"Listen to me," Tommy said.

"No, you listen, asshole." The bounty hunter released his

jacket with one hand and shoved a finger in the man's face. "This whole time, I thought the trail simply went cold. I thought I'd failed. It turns out your people swept the trail right off the map when they couldn't get the job done and didn't say a fuckin' thing. What did you know?"

Spit flew from his mouth and tangled in his beard and his eyes were wild and glazed-over. The agent cleared his throat and endured the abuse without trying to free himself. "You've been drinking."

"Wrong answer!"

"Johnny, let go of me."

"*What did you know?*"

They stared at each other, and Nelson raised his hands slowly to try to pry the dwarf's hand free from his jacket. It didn't work. "I didn't know anything."

"But they made you promise not to tell me, didn't they? Whatever you found out. Did you sign an agreement for that? Huh? That you wouldn't—"

"Do you honestly think I would have risked my neck to pull that file out of the damn basement for you if I'd signed something like that?" Tommy yelled. "Really? *Think* about it, man. I'm the only one helping you right now."

"You're fuckin' lyin' right to my face, Nelson."

"No." He gave up trying to get the bounty hunter's hands off him and leaned against the wall instead. "How much have you had to drink?"

Johnny growled.

"Don't go down that road again, Johnny. Come on." The man frowned and tilted his head. "I was here to pick you up off the floor fifteen years ago. Do you think I did that 'cause I wanted to keep you in the dark? Wake up. Whatever you found in that file, it's not worth sliding into that hole again. Do you hear me? I swear on my mother's grave, Johnny, I knew as much as you did back then and right now, you know a hell of a lot more than I do."

The dwarf narrowed his eyes and leaned closer to stare into his face. "On your mother?"

"Do you want me to say it again?"

With a grunt, Johnny shoved the man against the wall again but finally released him and stepped back. Tommy rolled his shoulders and jerked to straighten his lapels before he unbuttoned the garment. "If I find out you're full of shit—"

"If you do, I give you full permission to rip me apart, okay? But you won't."

"Fine." He fixed the agent with a warning glare, his upper lip curled in a snarl.

"What about now, Johnny?" Luther asked softly and growled at the visitor. "You want us to pin him now?"

"Just say it, Johnny."

The dwarf snapped his fingers without looking away from Agent Nelson, and both hounds sat instantly. "I want everything there is on Deadroot."

Tommy's eyes widened and he glanced at the coffee table in the living room. "Johnny, Dawn's file was in the box for Deadroot. Everything that exists is right here in your living room."

He sniffed and ran a hand through his thick auburn hair. "Then why the fuck are you here?"

With a sigh, Nelson glanced at Lisa and shrugged sheepishly.

"We have another case, Johnny," she said and watched the bounty hunter warily.

"Bad fuckin' timin', Nelson." He shook a finger at the agent and turned toward the couch.

"Honestly, I think it's the perfect time." Tommy stepped into the living room. "Why don't you put the bottle down and—" A helpless sigh escaped him when Johnny lifted the bottle to his lips and took two gulps.

The dwarf jammed the lid on, thumped the bottle on the table again, and spread his arms mockingly. "And what?"

"And take a look at this case." The man nodded toward Lisa,

who pulled the file out from under her arm. "It'll give you a chance to clear your head. Something else to focus on for a—"

"I don't *need* nothin' else to focus on," he retorted. "And I ain't interested."

"It's not the usual," she added and moved forward to stand beside Tommy. "It might take a little more work on our part, but that shouldn't be a problem. We've had eight reports from Portland—"

"Portland?" He scoffed and waved dismissively. "No way in hell am I truckin' out to *Portland.* There's nothin' but hipsters and beer out that way, and I ain't fixin' to run around in all that. Forget it."

"The case is in Portland too." Lisa set the file on the side table next to the couch's armrest. "That's what's there. Tommy and I think it's—"

"Tommy and you, huh?" The dwarf glanced from one to the other and his eyes narrowed in suspicion before he lowered himself onto the couch. "Are you two goin' over all your plans together? Teamin' up ahead of time so y'all can come bustin' into my house and show a united front or some shit?"

The agents shared a knowing glance. "We tried to bring you into the briefing an hour ago," she said, "but you didn't answer your phone."

"Yeah, for a reason. I still ain't interested."

"Johnny, this is—"

"I ain't changin' my mind so don't even try."

The living room fell into a heavy silence as he leaned back against the couch and closed his eyes. *If they don't leave in the next thirty seconds, I'll throw 'em out.*

Tommy turned to scan the hallway and ignored the hounds as he tried to peer into the kitchen through the workshop doorway. "Where's the kid?"

"School." He grunted. "Now get out. Both of y'all."

"Won't you—"

He snapped his fingers and pointed at Tommy as he muttered, "If y'all were waitin' for the word, boys, this is it."

Rex and Luther snarled at Agent Nelson. "You heard the dwarf."

"Better get a move on, asshole."

"Johnny." The man stared at them and sidled down the hall along the wall. "Come on, man. These dogs are nuts."

"Might eat some nuts if you don't start moving," Rex growled.

"Yeah. Yours!" Luther barked sharply, and Tommy jumped before he raced down the hall toward the front door.

"Johnny, I'm serious! Get these dogs—ah!" He managed to leap away from Luther's snapping jaws before they came down on his finally healed ass cheek, then threw the door open and bolted out.

Rex yelped when the door shut firmly. "Aw, shit. Asshole nearly took my nose off." He pawed at his snout and snorted.

"Is that a real thing?" Luther growled at the closed front door. "Can it come off?"

Rex shook himself from head to toe, snorted again, and padded slowly down the hall toward the living room.

"Hey, wait. Johnny said to get him."

"Johnny wanted him out."

"I said both of them," Johnny muttered.

Lisa frowned and turned to look at the dwarf. "Who?"

"You. Both of y'all." He leaned forward on the couch and stared at the hounds. "You missed somethin', boys."

"Come on, Johnny…" Lisa folded her arms.

"You want us to chase the lady out too?" Luther asked and he panted and wagged his tail as he and his brother entered the living room.

"Not *her*." Rex sniffed Agent Breyer's pant leg and leaned against her. "She's one of the good ones, Johnny."

"Yeah, probably the best."

Lisa patted Rex's back and stood her ground against fifty-five pounds of coonhound leaning up against her.

Luther tried to get in on the petting action, but his brother shifted to block him out. "Not cool. How come you get all the attention?"

"I'm smarter." Rex's reply rose as a groan of enjoyment in Johnny's head. "Everyone knows that but—*oh*, yeah. Johnny, she scratches better than a tree trunk."

As she removed her hand from the hound's back, Lisa stared at the dwarf sulking on the couch. "Look at the case, okay? I know you don't want to—"

"Damn straight."

"But I think it's something worth looking into. These people in Portland need our help. And you need a distraction, especially after the last month you spent building that school."

He slumped forward and rubbed his face with both hands as he sighed heavily. "I don't need a distraction, darlin'. Everythin' else has been a distraction—from this."

After a glance at the coffee table, he shut his eyes again quickly.

Lisa tilted her head, hoping he'd look at her. "Remember what I said when you first brought her file up?"

"Yep."

"I meant it, Johnny. Whenever you're ready to put whatever's in that file to use, I'm here."

"I'm ready right fuckin' now." The dwarf glowered at the floor. *But I have no fuckin' clue where to start.*

"If that were true, you'd already be gone." Lisa pointed at her case file on the side table. "Take a look. Call me after that with whatever you decide."

The only reply she got was another grunt.

Without another word, she turned slowly and walked down the hall, giving the bounty hunter plenty of time to say something before she left if he felt the need to.

He didn't.

Johnny waited until the sound of tires crunching across gravel faded away before he snatched the bottle of whisky off the table and stood. All he wanted was to down it all and leave the rest to chance. Instead, he marched across the room and set the bottle firmly in its place on the kitchen counter.

I need to get out of the house and clear my head, and it ain't gonna be with a case in fuckin' Portland.

CHAPTER FIVE

Half an hour later, Johnny stood in front of the giant propeller on his flat-bottomed airboat and cruised through the swamp at less than half the speed he usually preferred. Rex and Luther sat in the bow and their tails wagged while their tongues lolled from their mouths.

"What are we going after this time, Johnny?"

"Hey, I smelled raccoons back there. What about raccoons?"

Rex lowered his head toward the water breaking in front of the boat and sniffed at the floating vegetation. "What would he do with a raccoon?"

"I don't know. Let us eat it?"

"That bigass 'gator's still out there, Johnny."

Luther yipped and spun in two tight circles before he stopped to face his master. "We'll get him. We'll sniff him down, then flush him out, and you can blow him to smithereens!"

The dwarf glanced at the smaller hound, then returned his attention to as far downriver as he could see. "No huntin' today, boys."

"What?"

"Seriously?"

"Johnny, what's the point of being out here if we're not hunting something?"

He rubbed his mustache and scanned the swamp. "It clears my head just fine." *But does the opposite for a couple of hyped-up hounds, I guess.*

"Aw, man. Is he serious?"

Rex turned to look over his shoulder at their master. "Looks serious to me."

Luther slumped to his belly on the deck. "This sucks. I thought we were hunting game."

The only game I aim to bring down now is the Red Boar. The whole damn network.

For two minutes, a calm, blissful silence reigned as the craft cruised downstream. Only the buzzing drone of insects and frogs in the early July heat rose above the trickle of the tide along the banks and the low, steady whir of the fan. No talking dogs and no talking shifter kid intruded. Johnny swallowed. *I gotta quit thinkin' 'bout the kid.*

"Hey, Johnny." Luther's tail thumped on the deck. "Hey, what's that?"

"We know that guy." Rex's ears perked up as he stared downriver at the small fishing boat and the man seated in it. "Don't we?"

Johnny adjusted the throttle to the lowest speed and changed direction slightly to approach the portside bank where the second boat was moored. As soon as they were close, he cut the throttle completely and let them drift.

The man straightened and cupped a hand over his eyes to look upriver. "Well, I'll be. What's good, Johnny boy?"

"Ronnie." He raised a hand in greeting before the airboat thumped gently against the bank.

"Where's your kid at, huh? E'rytime I see that boat, I see that young'un sittin' up there with them hounds. She ain't feelin' good or what?"

As he hopped off the boat into the squelching mud and water-logged reeds, the dwarf sniffed and turned to catch the docking rope. "I sent her off to school."

"School?" The wizened Wood Elf tittered and shook his head as he returned his attention to drawing the trap lines out of the water. "Done figured you'd be schoolin' her yerself, nah. What with all that girlie's lived. Reckon that school's got all them basics? Readin' 'n writin' 'n 'rith-o-matics?"

Luther cocked his head and stared at the dripping lines Ronnie pulled hand-over-hand from the water. "What the hell did he say?"

Johnny hopped onto the airboat and moved to the bow. "The school's got everythin' she needs. Math included. The girl already knows how to read and write anyway."

"Oh, sure. Sure. She's way ahead o' the game, then. It ain't that public school out in—"

"Naw, it's private. There's a slightly different process than other schools, but she'll make her way through."

The Wood Elf nodded and hauled up a crab trap, the bars laden with weeds and soaked fronds and mud from the bottom of the swamp. "Hey, lookie here!"

The square cage thumped onto the seat of his fishing boat and splashed water everywhere. Five large crabs crawled over each other, jerked their hard-shelled legs, and snapped their claws angrily. The Wood Elf snatched his wide-brimmed hat off his head and smacked it against his thigh. "Hoo-ee. I tell you what, Johnny Boy. I been out here crabbin' since you was a little-un runnin' 'round with yer old man, and I ain't never seen no one set them traps like you. How do you get them to pull every time, huh?"

He fished in the water on the starboard side of the airboat and caught one of the trap lines before he pulled it up slowly. "It's practice."

"Practice! Ha. No sirree, boy. If I ain't known better, I'd

reckon you been usin' some kinda magic on them traps."

The dwarf smirked. "If I were, you'd be in serious trouble, wouldn't ya?"

With his hat returned, Ronnie stretched over the side of his boat for another line connected to the floating buoy marking its place and chuckled. "Reckon I would. Sure. Wrinkled ol' Elf with all the time in the world to brush up on rusty magickin' oughtta know by now how to cast a crabbin' spell. But somehow, I ain't —whoa!"

The Wood Elf lurched forward toward the boat's side rail when a spray of water erupted from the river.

"Johnny." Luther whipped his head to look from one craft to the other. "Johnny, can we get it?"

"Well, I ain't *never*." Ronnie grunted and leaned far back and as he hauled on the rope. "By everythin' on this good green planet, what the hell?"

"Holy crab!" Rex barked at the trap that had half-emerged from the swamp and now thumped against the side of the Wood Elf's fishing boat.

"Johnny, let me at it!" Luther's feet clicked across the deck as he paced in excitement. "That old guy's gonna lose it."

"It's in a cage, dummy."

The dwarf's eyes widened at the massive single Florida stone crab in Ronnie's trap. He snapped his fingers and both hounds sat. "That's a hell of a catch you got, Ronnie. Do you want a hand?"

"Naw. Naw, I—" The old Elf groaned with the effort of pulling his prize fully out of the water. He finally rolled the cage over the side of the boat and kicked it away from him across the deck. "Hot damn! Would ya lookit that monster? Ha!"

The massive crab was almost wide enough from one side of its body to the other to fill the entire cage. Legs and claws extended through the holes in the gridded bars and they flailed and snapped wildly with sharp clicks.

"Hoo-ee." Ronnie swiped his wrinkled brow. "What'dya reckon this feller is, eh? Two feet across?"

"Might be." Johnny hauled another trap over the side of the airboat and tossed it onto the dock. Six crabs clacked and scrambled inside.

Rex backed away from it and barked again. "How 'bout a little warning next time, huh, Johnny?"

"Aw, come on." Luther stepped toward it and sniffed. "I wanted the big one, Johnny. These little guys can't do—ow!" He yelped and scrambled across the airboat as he pawed at his nose. "It bit me! Johnny, it bit me. That's worse than a door, man. That's…that's…"

"A claw," Rex added dully. "Not a mouth."

"Huh?"

Johnny ignored them and reached for another trap line.

Ronnie chuckled. "You never brought them hounds out to pull lines before?"

"No, I have. It seems only one of 'em remembers."

"Hounds'll do that. The trick is to get 'em out doin' one thing e'ryday and them brains o' theirs will pick up on what's what. But you already know how them hounds work, Johnny. I ain't here to tell ya nothin'."

The dwarf smirked and helped his friend pull the traps like he'd done so many times before. The hounds kept their distance and sniffed the side of the boat and the bank instead before they finally leapt off to go exploring.

When all the traps were retrieved, he lifted the first to haul it onto Ronnie's boat. "You gonna sell these down at Earl's?"

"Oh, sure. 'Cept that big bastard over there." The Wood Elf took the trap the dwarf dragged closer and tossed it up against the monstrous crab. "Him, I aim to boil up and eat all by my lonesome. Say, if ye're lookin' for some comp'ny now that yer kid's gone off to learn her some knowledge, come on by. I'll share him with ya. S'yer traps, after all."

45

He heaved another trap closer. "Do I look like some lonesome charity case you gotta invite to dinner for the first time now?"

"Hell, you know ye're always welcome to stop on by. Even when I ain't steppin' out to fill a few fidgety bastards full o' buckshot." They both chuckled, and the Wood Elf focused on stacking all the crates before he pried the lid off the metal bin bolted to the side of the boat to start emptying his haul into it. "All's I'm sayin' is, you been used to havin' that young'un 'round. Don't get me wrong, Johnny boy. School's a good choice. They need all that, ya understand? Friends, playin' 'round, a buncha hooligan's runnin' all over gettin' into trouble."

"Hooligans." He snorted.

"I reckon both y'all find yerselves better for it in the end." Now, Ronnie was merely rambling as he tipped the traps and shook the crabs free into the metal bin. "Nah, I ain't got little'uns myself, mind, but my sister'n her get live in Tampa. Sure, they come down e'ry twenty years or so to say hi and remind me how far I let my cabin go to hell."

Johnny chuckled and shook his head.

"But I tell you what. E'rytime they roll in, that niece o' mine... Man, she sure does have no end of things to say and tellin' stories 'bout all the times she and her friends got into some real trouble down here in the Glades. Even when her mama took them all up north, she still got stories. One time, she even brought that ol' girlfriend o' hers down to see me. First time they'd seen each other in decades, by my count. And they was rollin' 'round laughin' like they was sisters." Ronnie shook his head with a fond, nostalgic smile. "Reckon they was laughin' at an old Elf livin' in a shack, but don't matter none to me. You won't mind it neither, understand? Yer girl, whatever young'un she makes her friend at that special school, mark my words. At least one o' them's gonna be her friend for life. Yessir."

"Which is exactly what she needs." Johnny tossed the ends of the trap lines off the edge of his boat and paused. *Friends for life.*

There's a lotta history between best friends. And a lotta time to muddle it up over fifteen years too. But maybe that's where I need to start.

"You good, Johnny boy?" Ronnie looked at him with a wide, gap-toothed grin, his eyes squinted against the sun. "Lookin' a little flushed there."

"Just because I don't mind the heat don't mean the heat's stopped mindin' me."

The Wood Elf threw his head back so far when he cackled that he almost toppled onto his empty traps. The giant crab snapped at him with an enormous claw. He scrambled away from his catch and chuckled. "Shit. Ya got the best damn traps, Johnny, but if I lose a finger or five to this bastard, I'm blamin' you and yer jokes."

"Who said I was jokin'?" Wiping the sweat off his forehead with the back of his arm, he turned toward the bank and uttered a piercing whistle. "Time's up, boys! Let's go!"

A sharp yip came from the thick foliage of the swamp, followed by heavy splashes and a low growl. Rex darted to the edge of the bank and leapt onto the airboat and his claws clicked and scraped across the deck as he skidded to a stop. Luther stumbled out of the trees and tried to gain traction but slipped in the mud and splashed around.

"Somethin' wrong with that one," Ronnie muttered and narrowed his eyes at the dog.

"I'm startin' to think the same." Johnny glanced at Rex, who looked at his master with wide, expectant eyes.

"What? Hey, it's not my fault he's a dumbass."

"Who you callin' dumbass, huh?"

"Any hound who tries to eat a prickly pear, dumbass."

Luther limped to the edge of the bank, then leapt toward the side of the airboat. His rear paws missed the deck by a foot, and his front paws scrabbled for purchase before his weight dragged him down into the swamp with a splash.

Ronnie cackled again, thumped a boot on the deck of his boat, and slapped his thigh.

With a snort, Johnny leaned over to grab Luther by the scruff of the neck and hauled the hound onto the airboat. "Come on, you big sack with fur."

"That's *Mr.* Sack, Johnny. How about a little—" Luther thumped onto all fours, slipped, and slid before his front paws gave out and he crashed head- and chest-first onto the deck. After a moment, he scrambled to his feet again and sat perfectly straight to stare downriver. He licked his muzzle. "I'm hungry."

Shaking his head, Johnny hopped off to untie the docking rope, then returned to his place at the control throttle. "Good seein' ya, Ronnie."

"Hoo, boy. Got yer work cut out fer ya with them two." The Wood Elf chuckled. "Thanks for the catch, Johnny boy."

"Naw, you hauled that one up all on your own. Lemme know how he tastes."

"Will do. Sweet as a pie, I reckon." Ronnie tittered and slammed the lid of his metal crab bin down before he started the engine of his small fishing boat.

The dwarf cranked the throttle and the airboat's fan whirred to life as he made a sharp turn along the river to take them home.

"What are we doin' now, Johnny?"

"Yeah. How 'bout that hunt?"

"I have a few phone calls to make." He glanced briefly at his hounds and saw Luther lying on the deck, his lower half sideways and his front paws propping him up in an oddly twisted position. The smaller hound panted and whipped his head, oblivious to the odd looks both his master and his brother settled on. "Maybe one of them to the vet."

Rex's ears flattened against his head.

Luther's ears flopped around as he snapped at the flies buzzing around him. "They have treats there, right?"

CHAPTER SIX

"Man, we never get to do anything fun anymore." Luther slunk through the dog door, followed closely by Rex. "First the pup goes off to some stupid school, and that's one down from the pack. Now, we can't even hunt."

"How long has she been gone again? It's been like a year, right?" Rex moved quickly away from the back door as Johnny opened it to step inside.

"At least. Probably won't even recognize her." Luther cast a pitiful glance over his shoulder at his master. "She probably won't even know how to hunt anymore. We'll get fat and lazy and die of boredom."

The dwarf closed the back door and grunted. "She ain't been gone a full day. Hush up."

Luther padded onto the thick area rug in the living room, spun in three tight circles, and curled beside the empty fireplace with a heavy sigh. "I probably won't ever get up after this."

Rex trotted after Johnny and sat at his master's feet when the dwarf slumped into the couch. "What's wrong, Johnny?"

"Nothin'."

"First you were pissed, then you were laughing with that old

Elf, now you're making your planning face." Rex scratched behind his ear. "You losing your mind or something."

Johnny pulled his phone out and scrolled through his contacts. "Go on, now."

"Was it the crabs?"

"Out."

Rex lowered his head and shuffled morosely toward his brother before he settled beside him. "I don't get it."

"We're gonna die of boredom," Luther muttered.

"He's going crazy. Smells kinda crazy too. You know what it smells like?"

"Boredom."

Rex's furry eyebrows lifted as he glanced at Johnny. "Lemons."

"Huh?"

"Hush." Johnny snapped his fingers and pointed at the hounds as he lifted his phone to his ear with the other hand. "I can't have a talk when y'all are yammerin' away."

"Boring…" Luther dropped his head onto his forepaws and uttered a low whine.

The bounty hunter propped his boots on the coffee table—ignoring the stack of fifteen-year-old reports beneath them—leaned back on the couch, and waited for the call to be answered.

"Who's this?" a gruff voice demanded.

"It sounds like your manners ain't changed that much."

"Johnny?" The wizard hacked and coughed and cleared his throat. "Is that you?"

"Come on, Harry. Do you think I'd let some asshole get away with tryin' to be me?"

"Ha! No one says it like you do." Harry paused for another round of hacking coughs and his voice was significantly scratchier when he continued to speak. "It's been a long time, Johnny. And I guess this isn't exactly a social call, is it?"

"It didn't start that way but now, I'm wondering how you are."

"Oh, don't even." The sound of slurping through a straw came over the line. "It's only me catching something. I think they call it old fucking age."

Johnny snorted. "You should get yourself outta the freezer up there and come here where it's warm. I hear that's a decent balm for what ails ya."

"And do what? Join a retirement home in Venice? No thanks."

They both chuckled until Harry was seized by another coughing fit.

Damn. That ain't old age, no sir.

"So what—" The wizard paused for a long, wheezing breath. "What's the special occasion for the unexpected hello?"

"I was hopin' you could find someone for me."

"Ha! Still behind the times, huh? Do you even know how a cell phone works?"

The dwarf rolled his eyes. "Yeah, Harry. I'm callin' you on one. But I ain't—"

"Yeah, yeah. You don't have time for learning technology unless it's yours. Same old spiel as back in the day, huh?" Harry chuckled, followed by the sound of compressed air being released, probably an inhaler. "I remember when you had no clue how a floppy disk worked."

"Harry."

"Yeah."

"Are you still in business?"

"Me? No, not me. I don't have to fiddle with other people's personal squabbles anymore. But the business is still in business. I let my son take over...oh, about seven years ago. He's good, Johnny, and might even be better than me. What's the name?"

Johnny grunted. "Hamilton family. Ben and Kay and their daughter Lucy. They lived in Georgia when I did. I'm not sure how long they were there before, but—"

"All right, stop with all that extra BS." Harry slurped through his straw again. "All I need is a name and you know that."

"What does your son need?"

"Hell, probably only the initials." The wizard coughed again and sighed heavily. "I gotta let you go, Johnny. My energy lasts about as long as my bladder. I'll send this to Davie and he'll get back to you. How's that?"

The dwarf stared at the boar's head mounted above his fireplace. "It sounds fine."

"All right. Good to hear from you. I would've been pissed if it turned out you kicked the bucket first."

"Consider Florida. The heat and humidity will clear that plague right outta ya."

"You're barking up the wrong tree, Johnny. My roots have grown deeper in this world than they ever were back home. Same as you. Watch for Davie's call."

"Thanks."

The line went dead and he stared at the background of his home screen—a picture he'd taken of Sheila when he'd first restored her and fitted her with all the extras. *That damn wizard ain't gonna make it through another winter soundin' like that. But it ain't none of my business, no matter how much I want it to be.*

His stomach growled fiercely and made both hounds whip their heads up to stare at him.

"That you, Johnny?"

The dwarf patted his stomach and stood. "I guess I skipped a few meals."

Rex and Luther glanced at each other and scrambled to their feet. "Yeah, we did too."

"We missed a lost count of how many meals. Catfish in a tent. Leftovers. Could've had that crab, but no. *Someone* said we couldn't—"

"Y'all ain't missed nothin.'" Johnny strode into the kitchen, cast a speculative glance at the bottle of whisky on the counter, and turned toward the fridge instead.

"But what about an extra snack, huh, Johnny?" Luther skidded out of the way when the fridge door opened, then padded around his master to look inside.

"Yeah, the pup always gave us—"

"She gave you what, now?" He looked at Rex and raised an eyebrow.

The larger hound glanced all around the kitchen and turned his head slowly away from his master. "Very good...belly rubs?"

Luther panted and stared at the contents of the fridge. "But she was way better than you at dropping scraps on the floor. Like big, hulking, juicy piles of—"

Rex snapped at his brother. "What's wrong with you?"

"*Hey.*"

Johnny pulled out the makings of a sandwich and kicked the door closed as he went to the counter with an armful of ingredients.

"Rex, Rex, Rex."

"What? Oh." Rex lunged toward the closing fridge door and snorted when it closed against his snout.

"Yeah. Yeah. Yeah." Luther's tail thunked against the floor as he glanced at his brother, then at Johnny, then back again. "Don't screw it up."

"How about you shut up," Rex retorted.

The bounty hunter took a plate from the overhead cabinet and a knife out of the silverware drawer.

"Hurry! No, no, no—"

A jar of pickled okra fell from the shelf beneath Rex's fridge-exploring head. Johnny spun and stared at the hounds with wide eyes.

"Shit."

"You *ruined* it."

He raised an eyebrow. "Are you boys up to somethin'?"

"Yes."

"No."

Luther's tail hit the kitchen floor once before he yelped and spun. Rex knocked him off balance as the larger hound raced to the dog door.

"Hey, hey! Wait for me!"

"No way. I only have to be faster than you."

The hounds' sharp barks continued as they barreled across the soggy back lawn and disappeared under two loud splashes in the swamp, one right after the other.

Johnny sniffed and turned to face his unmade sandwich. He looked at the knife still clenched in his fist, smirked, then shrugged and made his lunch.

CHAPTER SEVEN

Despite the promising plan of finding the Hamilton family through Harry Malkenshire and his half-wizard son, Johnny didn't feel any better about his prospects the next day. He spent the first hour wishing Lisa had shown up with a cup of coffee, the second hour sweeping the floors of every room in the house, and the third hour fiddling with the reinforced—by steel and magic—armor around one of his spy-bug gadgets.

"Yeesh. What is that *smell*?" Rex sniffed the perimeter of the kitchen and stopped once to scratch the baseboard and listen for critters in the walls. After a moment, he snorted and continued into the workshop. "Luther, you smell that?"

"Like something died in here? Oh, yeah." His brother came from the opposite side of the house and circled the living room before he sniffed down the hall. "Huh. Johnny, you got any dead rats in your workshop?"

The dwarf grunted. "No."

"What about a vole, huh? Kinda smells like vole."

"No way. Johnny, this smells like a skunk's been rubbing its butt all over the—" Luther's nose bumped into his master's ankle, and he sniffed farther up the dwarf's leg before he sat back on his haunches and licked his muzzle. "Johnny."

"I'm busy."

"Johnny, you wrestle any skunks lately?"

Rex sniggered.

"Now why the hell would I—" Johnny stopped, raised one arm, and turned his head slightly to sniff. "Dammit."

His tools and the spy-bug landed on the worktable with a clatter and he stepped around Luther into the hall.

"I *knew* it! You've been wrestling skunks!" The smaller dog trotted after him, panting. "How does that work, exactly? You know, without getting your skin melted off by that spray. That shit's nasty, Johnny."

Rex chuffed and curled to nip at the base of his tail. "It's *him*, bro."

"Johnny can spray like a skunk?"

"Y'all need somethin' else to focus on." Johnny nodded toward the back of the house. "Outside."

"Don't have to tell *us* twice." Luther spun and headed to the dog door. "Hey, Rex. Maybe we'll find a skunk."

Rex licked his muzzle and trotted slowly after his brother. "Yeah, and you can wrestle it. If you get your skin melted off, you can tag me in."

The dwarf shut the bathroom door behind him and took the moment of privacy to double-check his pits. *Damn. It's only been two days. I think.*

He hopped into the shower and took his sweet time. A familiar tune made its way to his mind, and he started humming. *Let's see that kid try to pin the tail on this song—*

The humming stopped immediately, and Johnny chucked his loofa against the wall of the shower. *She ain't here, numbskull, and can't hear you fallin' apart at the seams because you had to go diggin' through the past.*

With a scowl, he cranked the water to its highest heat and forced himself to finish the shower before it boiled him alive.

When he stepped out with a towel wrapped around his waist and walked to his room, habit made him glance through the open door of what was now Amanda's bedroom. She'd kept what was there when she'd first come to stay with him—the purple camo blanket, the bedspread, and the star-shaped light dangling from the ceiling. The things he'd bought her and she hadn't chosen to take with her to the academy were scattered everywhere. Socks hung from the desk chair. Hair ties littered the floor and the dresser. A book propped open upside down on the desk was titled *Crossbows for Beginners*.

A thick knot of emotion caught in his throat, and he grasped the handle to yank the bedroom door shut with a bang. *I need to get outta here. It's my cabin and my home and now, I got the ghosts of two girls livin' in it with me.*

Thirty minutes later, he pulled Sheila to a stop in the parking lot in front of Darlene's trailer with a roar and spray of gravel. Tripp Bolton poked his head above the open door of his pickup and looked at where the gravel had peppered the side of the cab. "Oh, ho, ho. Gotcha now, Johnny."

The dwarf jumped out of his Jeep and shut the door. "Yeah, Tripp. You got me. Merely another guy needin' a fix of somethin' homecooked and—"

"You're the one been throwin' rocks at my truck!" The man grinned and shook a finger at him. "I been wonderin' what the hell that was for years. I thought it was them damn kids down at the Sallerville place chuckin' shit when I ain't lookin'. It's you."

The bounty hunter glanced at the small, almost invisible dents in the side of the black pickup and nodded. "Sorry."

"Shit, Johnny. You solved the mystery of a lifetime." Tripp laughed easily. "I guess that's what you do, ain't it?"

"Uh-huh. Bill me if you want." The dwarf strode to the stairs to the raised trailer.

Tripp slipped into his vehicle, still laughing, and shook his head. "Johnny and *Sheila*. Hot damn."

Darlene's wasn't nearly as busy as it had been over the last two months, and only four locals sat alone at individual tables while Fred leaned half passed-out on the bar. Johnny closed the door softly, hooked his thumbs through his belt loops, and chose the closest barstool.

"Heya, Johnny."

"Helluva hot one today, ain't it?"

He grunted in reply and climbed onto the seat. *The last thing I'm fixin' for is a friendly chat.*

The door at the back of the bar swung open, and Darlene emerged with two paper-lined plastic baskets in hand. She gave Johnny a warm smile. "Be right there, Johnny."

"Yep."

"All right, Fred. I fixed you up somethin' nice." She set one basket in front of the drunk and patted the bar.

The man blinked wearily and stared at the basket. "I didn't order this."

"No, but you been here for four hours. If that won't soak up at least some of the booze in your gut, I don't know what will."

"You're a…shweetheart, Darlene. But I ain't—"

"One meal for every four hours of straight drinkin', Fred. Those are the rules."

"Well…if they are…"

"Of course they are." Darlene nodded and stepped around the end of the bar. "But don't you think for a second that I'm not chargin' you."

The other patrons chuckled.

"I can get that." Bobby Harland started to stand from his table and got a glowering stare from Darlene in return.

"What do you think this is? You sit yourself down right now, Bobby. I'm not runnin' a serve-yourself." The woman scoffed and dropped the basket on his table while the other hand went to her hip. "And I can walk six feet much easier than you can. How's the knee?"

He grinned at her and took the napkin-wrapped silverware on the other side of the table. "Better now that you're here."

"Huh." She studied him with a smirk. "How long has it been since you used that line?"

"Since the last woman who turned him down!" Harry shouted from the far end of the trailer. The other locals laughed and ate their meals at their one-person tables.

"Well, now the clock's reset, honey. Eat your crab cakes." Laughing with them, Darlene returned to the bar and snatched the rag off her shoulder to wipe at the permanently embedded sticky patches in the wood's rough grain. "Now, Johnny. What can I getcha?"

He looked up at her with a self-deprecating grimace. "Got anythin' for vengeance?"

She stared at him. The other patrons in her trailer-diner stopped their low murmuring between tables and the space fell completely silent. Even the crunch of the baskets' paper lining and the slow, meticulous chewing had stopped.

The dwarf sniffed. *I reckon I came on too strong with that one.*

"Who was it, Johnny?" Rick called from his table. "We'll set him straight for ya."

"Yeah." Pete nodded and thumped a fist on the table. When Darlene darted him a warning glare, the man hunched his shoulders and removed his fist. "Young'uns can be right assholes, Johnny. She ain't been two days at that school, but it don't surprise me she already got her heart broken."

Johnny turned slowly on the barstool and frowned at the man. "'Preciate it, Pete, but that ain't it."

Harry chuckled and popped a handful of fried oysters into his mouth. "Pete ain't got it through his thick head yet. Amanda ain't no pinin' kiddie gon' let her heart get broken in two days."

"Naw, that kid's got more'n that flowin' through her. She can take care of herself, yessir. How's she doin' at that new school anyhow, huh, Johnny?" Bobby asked and wiped a thick smear of tartar sauce off his beard.

"As far as I know, just fine." Johnny turned away and slumped his forearms onto the bar. *Everywhere I go, it's Amanda. Of course she told the whole damn town where she was headed.*

"Then what's the problem?" Harry asked.

"No problem." The bounty hunter clenched his fists and stared at the bar's worn, stained wood.

"You look like you lost a trophy catch," Rick added.

Bobby crammed a forkful of crab cake into his mouth and said around his food, "I thought that was his normal state —ain't it?"

The dwarf pounded a fist onto the counter and stared straight ahead with wide eyes. "I thought y'all came here to eat!"

Fred jolted in his seat at the opposite end of the bar, saved himself from falling onto the floor, and snatched a French fry and crammed it into his mouth. The other locals ignored him, as usual, and stared at Johnny. Darlene cocked her head and studied the bounty hunter curiously.

"Hell of a way to work up an appetite," Pete muttered before he took a huge bite of his Po' Boy.

"Sure, Johnny," Darlene said gently and flopped the rag onto the bar. "I got just the thing for what ails ya."

She retrieved his staple bottle of Johnny Walker Black from the well, but he shook his head. "Thanks, darlin', but I ain't drinkin' today."

One of the locals gasped and immediately tried to cover it with a fake cough. The others turned their attention to their baskets of food and no one said a word.

The proprietor returned the whisky bottle slowly. "Well, that was merely the appetizer, honey. Now you sit tight and let me handle the rest."

He nodded at her before she turned toward the back of the

bar and the door leading into her homemade kitchen. She glared at the locals who continued to shoot Johnny wary, confused glances before she disappeared behind the door.

Maybe this was a bad idea. He took a few deep breaths and finally straightened his hunched shoulders. *But if anyone can make a dwarf forget about lying federal bastards and the murdering sonofabitch they let slip away, it's Darlene and her cookin'.*

The front door of the trailer opened with a creak, and Arthur walked in, a broad smile stretching below his white handlebar mustache. "Heya, fellas."

The other locals murmured hellos but kept their attention on their baskets.

"Huh. You know, I heard'a the mid-week slump, but it ain't like y'all got nothin' to complain about." Arthur saw the dwarf at the bar and grinned. "Johnny. It's the first time you've beat me here in a hot minute."

When the bounty hunter didn't reply, he glanced around the trailer and frowned when the other locals shook their heads at him in warning.

"Now what the hell's goin' on in here, huh? Y'all look like the bogeyman rolled in and took all yer toys."

"Or he never left," Bobby muttered without looking away from his crab cakes.

"Hush up, you ol' git," Harry whispered harshly.

Bobby spun in his chair to glare at the man. "Ain't no one talkin' to you, Harry."

"Ain't no one talkin' at all," Rick muttered and glared at the large man with the injured knee. "We came here to eat, remember?"

The old-timers grumbled at their tables and returned to their meals with scowls instead of their usual easygoing smiles.

Arthur scratched the side of his face, then brushed the stray hairs of his handlebar mustache that tickled his upper lip and strolled toward the bar. Johnny sat rigidly at the counter. He stared directly ahead and didn't move when Arthur took the stool directly beside him. "How ya doin', Johnny?"

"I'm doin'."

The old-timer nodded. "Uh-huh. That's clear as a bell, all right. But I reckon there ain't a 'just fine' attached to that."

He grunted.

"Is the kid doin' all right at that school o' yours?"

"Ain't everythin' about the kid, Arthur." *At least not that kid.* The dwarf rubbed his mouth and his wiry red beard before he thumped his hand onto the bar.

Arthur shifted on the stool, leaned toward his friend, and lowered his head as he muttered, "You know as well as I do that ain't the truth. It might be true for the rest of these good-for-nothin's sittin' around starin'."

The man turned to glare at the other locals over his shoulder. Caught in the act, the old-timers shifted and grunted and got the hint. One of them ripped a nervous fart and no one said a thing.

"Once a kid's in the picture," Arthur continued and turned to face the bar again, "ain't nothin' not about them. Amanda doin' all right?"

"It ain't Amanda." Johnny cleared his throat. "Mostly. I ain't worried 'bout her, at least."

"Sure." The man nodded sagely. "But it is a kid on your mind."

The dwarf's head tilted from side to side. *That's what I get for knowin' folks who know my whole life.* "Might be."

He didn't have to say any more than that. Of all the locals out there who knew what he could do with traps and guns and tech and the occasional breaking up of a fight, Arthur was the only one who knew about Dawn.

The rest of it on folks' lips is only hearsay and rumors, and I ain't fixin' to feed 'em one way or the other.

His old friend leaned over the bar, studied the rows of beer bottles lined up where liquor bottles normally were at any other legit bar with a license, and sniffed. "The past has a way of catchin' up with us. I tell you what, Johnny. Learnin' how to not let my old mistakes rip me apart was one helluva thing. Life's funny that way, and I ain't sayin' that 'cause I'm closer to the end o' mine than when I made those mistakes. Understand?"

Johnny snorted and looked slowly at the man beside him. "You forget I still got seniority on you, old-timer?"

"Not when you bring it up every chance you get." Arthur chuckled. "It don't mean I ain't lived a life worth livin', just the same."

"Uh-huh."

The door behind the bar popped open, and Darlene emerged. Instead of a paper-lined basket, she carried an actual plate loaded with the type of Southern feast that didn't fully exist on any menu, even if she'd had one.

"Hot damn," Bobby muttered and sniffed the air. "That is the best smell in the whole damn state."

The woman set the plate in front of Johnny, took a set of wrapped silverware from the pocket of her apron, and nodded in satisfaction. "Just like I told ya, Johnny. That'll set ya right."

He stared at the meal. Blackened catfish filled the center of the plate, surrounded by heaped piles of sweet-potato mash, mac 'n cheese, collards, cooked okra stewed in tomatoes, two slices of fried green tomatoes, coleslaw, and baked beans. Two ramekins of tartar sauce and a lemon wedge balanced precariously at the edge of the plate. "It looks fine, Darlene."

"'Course it does. That there okra's a family recipe, Johnny. Mind you eat all of it or my great-grandmama Alice is sure to turn in her grave. Maybe she'll even leave it to pay you a midnight visit."

"What's all this, Darlene?" Rick called from his table. "You been holdin' out on us this whole time?"

"And how come we never get plates?" Pete added.

"Y'all mind your own." She pointed at them. "And if I gave y'all plates, I'd be pickin' the pieces up off the floor with the rest of the mess you old goats leave behind. Especially you, Pete. Yeah, I'm takin' stock."

Pete scowled and returned to his meal as the other locals chuckled.

Darlene wiped her hands on her apron and nodded at Johnny. "Don't let it get cold, now. Want a Coke?"

"Water's fine, darlin'. Thank you."

She turned briskly to take a paper cup and fill it at the small bar sink. "How you doin', Arthur?"

"I've seen worse days."

"Better days too," Harry called as he wiped his mouth and tossed the crumpled napkin into his empty basket.

"Better'n yours?" Arthur turned to grin at the man over his shoulder. "You bet."

Darlene set two cups of water on the bar and stuck her hands on her hips. "You fixin' to eat somethin' too?"

Arthur glanced at the steaming plate in front of Johnny. "I don't suppose you got any more of that sittin' around back there."

"Not for you."

He rolled his eyes playfully. "All right. How 'bout one of them oyster baskets? And throw some o' that slaw in there on the side."

"That I can do for ya." She nodded at the dwarf and gave him a warm smile. "Whatever it is, Johnny, you know you got friends 'round here."

"Always have."

"Ain't that the truth." The woman put her hands on her hips and waited.

Johnny looked at her, then nodded and unwrapped his utensils to dig into the okra and tomatoes first. "Yep," he said around a mouthful. "Great-grandmama Alice will be sleepin' like a baby tonight."

"Mm-hmm. That's what I thought." With a final glance around the trailer, Darlene disappeared through the kitchen door again to prepare his companion's meal.

Arthur leaned toward the bounty hunter and staring long-ingly at the mountain of food on the plate. "You know, friends are known to—"

"Not this friend. Get your own." He shoved another forkful into his mouth and chuckled through his nose when the man leaned away again quickly.

"Every damn time. I swear, Johnny, if I didn't know you as well as I do, I'd say that woman's sweeter on you than the rest of us."

"That ain't sayin' much, though, is it?"

The old-timers burst out laughing at their tables. Harry stood and dropped his usual seven dollars on the table for his meal as he tried to hold back his smile. "Y'all got some nerve over there, I tell you what."

"Ain't nothin' you never heard before, Harry," Pete said.

"That's Johnny payin' us a compliment," Bobby added.

"Uh-huh. Y'all can eat 'em up much as you like. But don't wring any necks in here, huh, Johnny? Least not until I'm gone."

"Better run, boy," Pete shouted to another round of gleeful old-timer laughter.

Harry swatted his hand through the air and hobbled out of the trailer. The door clicked shut behind him, and the others continued to laugh until his crooked steps down the wooden stairs were muted by the gravel parking lot.

The bounty hunter shook his head and dug into Darlene's specially prepared meal with renewed vigor. *Cures what ails me, huh? The woman's a genius.*

Halfway through his meal, his phone buzzed in his back pocket. The call was from an unknown number, and he frowned at the screen.

Arthur wiped one ramekin of tartar sauce clean with the last of his fried oysters and nodded. "You gonna answer that?"

"You keepin' tabs on my calls now too?"

The man chuckled and shook his head.

Johnny grinned and answered the call. "Who's this?"

"Johnny?"

"Yeah."

"It's Davie Malkenshire. Harry's son—"

The dwarf straightened on the barstool. "Sure. He said you'd be callin'."

"Good. I found those names you wanted. Is now a good time?"

"Now's fine."

The clack of typing came across the line. "All right. The first name was a bust. Ben Hamilton passed away July of 2037 from a combination stroke and heart attack."

He grimaced and dropped his fork onto the plate. "Okay."

"His wife Kay left the US for Denmark in 2038. She shipped off to play house with a new man, Kyle Jensen."

No way am I headin' to Denmark to chat to that woman. She's been through enough as it is. "And the daughter?"

"Lucy Hamilton…yeah." Davie cleared his throat. "She's still in the US. She left Wisconsin six months after her mom moved and made her way across the country. Now, she owns some kind of… spiritual gift shop in Portland. It's a successful business, it seems. I hear they're big on that out there."

Johnny wrinkled his nose. "Thanks, Davie. Send me the address."

"Sure thing. Do you want me to look into the mother's new boyfriend too? He'll be easy enough to find."

"Naw, you gave me everythin' I need."

"No problem. Hey, hold onto my number. It made Dad's day to hear from you, but he got way too excited for his own good. It's not your fault, of course. You didn't know. Just for the future. Does that work for you?"

"That's fine. Tell him I said to get his ass to Florida. It'll knock out that cough."

Davie chuckled. "That's what I've tried to tell him. The man's as stubborn as a bull."

"Might be we'll have to team up. Thanks for the call."

"Anytime, Johnny." The man hung up and he shoved his phone into his pocket. "Fucking Portland."

"What's that now?" Arthur chewed his mouthful of coleslaw and looked at the dwarf with wide eyes.

"I'd say things are lookin' up, but it's more like movin' forward." He retrieved his wallet to flip through the bills inside.

"Don't you dare." Darlene scowled at him. "Unless you want to insult me today too."

He smirked at her, took a twenty from his wallet, and dropped it on the bar in front of Arthur. "Make sure you tip extra well today. Those oysters looked good."

The man chuckled and snatched the bill off the bar before Darlene could get her hands on it. "Don't I always? Hey, do you mind if I—"

"I ain't gonna stop ya." He slid off his stool, shoved the front door open, and headed down the stairs.

Grinning, Arthur pulled the dwarf's half-eaten meal down the bar and looked at Darlene. "Got an extra fork lyin' around?"

She scowled at him.

"Oh, come on. We wouldn't want Great-grandmama Alice to come after both of us, would we?"

CHAPTER EIGHT

"I can't believe this." Johnny chose a few changes of clothes from his closet and packed them into his black duffel bag with the silver skull and crossbones embroidered on the side. *No means no. It ought'a stay that way. That girl simply had to end up in Portland, huh?*

Rex sat in the open doorway of the bedroom and watched his master move between the closet and the bed. "Whatcha doin'?"

"Blowin' off steam with somethin' productive."

"Like hunting, Johnny?" Luther trotted down the hall toward them. "'Cause I saw this giant squirrel earlier—"

"Fox," Rex interrupted. "That was a fox."

"No, it was a squirrel. Didn't you see its tail?"

Rex stared at his master and licked his muzzle.

Luther cocked his head. "Must've been something wrong with it, though. Squirrels don't usually chase rabbits. So how 'bout it, Johnny? Hunt for the giant squirrel?"

"We're goin' huntin' all right. Merely a different kind of animal." The dwarf hauled his mostly empty duffel bag off the bed and strode through the doorway. Both hounds moved quickly out of the way and followed him into the workshop.

"Yes!" Luther yipped excitedly. "I knew you'd be into that."

"He's not talking about the giant squirrel, dummy. It's probably something like that talking octopus."

"The swimming flamethrower?"

Johnny shook his head and dropped the duffel bag onto the table before he packed his regular stash of modified weapons.

Rex sniffed his master's footsteps along the floor. "Hey, Johnny. Did you go out for food and not tell us?"

"I told you exactly where I was goin'."

"So you brought us treats, right?" Luther sat beside the worktable and wagged his tail. "Frog legs? Pulled pork? Mashed potatoes?"

"I bet he put some of those in his pockets for later," Rex muttered.

"Yeah, yeah. Best place to keep 'em."

After fitting his utility belt with a full supply of black disks, the bounty hunter glanced around his workshop and searched for whatever else he thought he might need.

"So where is it, huh?" Luther asked.

"Hush." He took his phone out and made a call to Agent Breyer. She answered after the second ring.

"I gotta say, this is much sooner than I expected."

"I'll do it."

"What?"

Johnny retrieved the square black canvas case holding his portable rifle pieces and added it to the duffel bag. "The case. I'll take it."

Lisa paused. "Have you been drinking again?"

"Ain't got nothin' to do with it."

"Johnny…"

He stopped packing to glare across the workshop and grunted. "No. I'm as dry as a bone."

"Okay, then. What made you change your mind?"

"Call it a feelin'."

"That's good enough for me. I'll be there first thing in the morning."

"We gotta wait until tomorrow?"

"Yep. That's what it says on the tickets."

The dwarf scowled. *You're gettin' a little too comfortable, Nelson.* "Fine." Before she could hang up, he added, "Lisa."

"Johnny."

"Did you mean it when you said you'd stick around and help with the Red Boar when I'm ready?"

She paused. "I don't make promises on a whim."

"I didn't think so. Tell Nelson we're going to Portland." He hung up and dropped his phone on the table to finish loading his highly explosive gear into the duffel bag.

Rex and Luther glanced at each other. "When he says *we…*"

"He has to be talking about all of us. Right, Johnny?"

"Johnny, you're not gonna leave us here, are you?"

"I've always wanted to go to Portland."

The dwarf stopped and looked at Luther. "What's wrong with you?"

"What?"

Rex nipped playfully at his brother's face. "You even know where Portland is?"

"Yeah. Somewhere in the middle."

After a soft snort, the other hound padded out of the workshop without another word.

"So we're comin' too—right, Johnny?"

Johnny zipped the bag quickly, turned to face the smaller hound, and frowned. "'Course you are. I reckon I'll need someone to keep all the hipsters at bay."

"Got it. You can count on us, Johnny. We'll chase 'em all down. Maybe catch a few for fun." Luther followed his master into the living room. "Wait—what's a hipster?"

"That's how they say 'hamster' out there," Rex muttered from where he'd curled in a tight ball on the rug. "Rodents."

The dwarf sat on the couch and snorted. "It's close enough."

They caught the first flight to Portland International the next morning. The hounds had curled in their assigned first-class seats in front of Johnny and Lisa. Rex's snores filled the cabin, accompanied by Luther's short, soft yips and the jerk of his rear paws in his sleep.

Johnny sniffed. *He's probably dreamin' about chasin' down hamsters. It's fine with me.*

He adjusted himself in his seat and turned to one side, then the other. Still unable to settle, he flipped the armrests up, then down, and tried to stretch his feet out.

Lisa darted him a sidelong glance and cleared her throat. "Are you okay?"

"This damn seat feels like a saggy mattress." He grimaced and shifted again. "For how much you pay for first-class, you'd think they'd put more work into checkin' the seats."

"The Bureau paid for the tickets."

"Yeah, and I wanna get their money's worth." He grunted and finally slumped back and folded his arms. *I wish this flight would hurry the hell up.*

She smirked and returned to the book she was reading on her tablet. "So. What did Amanda think of the new school?"

"Oh, you too, huh?"

"What?" She smiled at him in confusion.

"Everyone and their damn mama wants to know 'bout the kid and her new school."

"Well, it's kind of important, right? I mean, she is—"

"Yeah, yeah. I know." *She might as well be mine.* "She's fine and didn't seem too upset to be livin' on a base with a horde of kids her age."

Lisa squinted at him. "You mean a campus?"

"No, I mean a base. That place ain't teachin' 'em American History or music class for the off-pitch teenager or...that common crap that passes for math these days."

"It's still a school."

"Uh-huh." He folded his arms and stared at the back of the seat in front of him, which jiggled as Luther's hamster-chasing dream continued. "The kid reckons she'll come out of it better'n me."

Lisa laughed and covered her mouth quickly.

The dwarf tried not to smile, but it didn't quite work. "Do you believe that?"

"If it was anyone else but Amanda, I wouldn't. It sounds like you both made the right decision."

"Yeah, it looks that way."

"And now you can focus on this next case. Nelson thought it was a good one to get you back into—"

"Nelson said, huh?" Johnny shook his head. "That balding sack of walking dogfood still thinks he can keep up. Like he knows what will get me anythin' after fifteen years of actin' like I fell off the face of the Earth."

"Johnny, that's essentially what you did."

"Huh." He sniffed and glanced at her tablet. "Why did he come to you first with this case, huh? That's what I wanna know."

Lisa tried to hide her smile as the bounty hunter scowled at her. "I didn't think you cared about who saw the new cases first."

"I don't." He shifted in his seat again. "But it don't make sense. Unless the two of y'all have been stayin' at the same hotel for the last month, I don't see the reasonin' behind it."

With a slow sigh to gather her patience, she skimmed the faces of the other first-class passengers across the aisle. "Well, to start, I'm the one who works with the Bounty Hunter Division."

"Uh-huh. And he's my liaison." Johnny sniffed. "He has been since he took over from that dipshit McMayard thirty years ago. Nelson ain't much better, but improvement's still improvement. So that's thirty years he and I been workin' together with many other agents in the Division tryin' to check in on me. You're the only one who gets to see this shit before I do. What gives?"

"Johnny, I'm your partner."

He rolled his eyes and stared at the back of Luther's seat again. "We ain't decided on that, darlin'."

"No, it's decided. You merely haven't said it out loud yet."

'Cause sayin' a thing out loud means I can't take it back. He turned slowly to meet her gaze. "Why did he come to you first?"

Lisa shrugged. "I think he wanted my opinion on whether or not you'd take this case."

"You said he thought it would be good for me."

"Yeah. And he wanted my take."

"Look, darlin'. We both know you're runnin' yourself 'round in circles and ain't throwin' all the cards on the table. Quit holdin' back."

They stared at each other for a moment before she finally sighed and leaned back in her seat. "Okay, fine. Tommy was told to bring the case to me first and ask if I thought it was something you'd want."

"So the Department's tryin' to keep their eyes on me."

"Well, yeah. Johnny, you made some serious waves at the Monsters Ball in New York. After what we had to do to get Amanda out of there and after what we saw… That's part of the reason I haven't been reassigned out of Florida and why I'm here with you, so we can keep working together. I think the Department wants to keep closer tabs on your wellbeing."

"My wellbeing." He scoffed. "What is that shit? They think a few heavy-hitters in organized crime are gonna screw up my whole view of the world? Trust me, darlin'. I already been there and my view can't get any more skewed against the system than it already is."

Lisa closed her eyes. "I meant because of why you agreed to take that case. And who you found in that penthouse."

The armrest creaked when his hold tightened around it. "They know 'bout that?"

"They know why you were more likely to pick up a case that

involved a twelve-year-old girl losing her entire family and being kidnapped all in the same night."

"And the other thing?" *If those fuckers know I found the Red Boar, they'll have to kill me to stop me.*

She shook her head. "Not as far as I know. And if they are aware, they didn't hear it from me."

"So they sent you out to pull the kid out of that shit situation and...what? Now they want you makin' reports on me?"

"No..."

The hesitation in her voice made Johnny straighten instinctively. "Goddammit."

"Johnny, the only reports I make are the ones the Bureau wants to see. They have their doubts but they don't want those doubts confirmed or they lose one of their best bounty hunters. Again."

"And now you're reportin' that ol' Johnny's merely a big puddle o' sunshine and rainbows and puppies, huh?"

Lisa glanced at him in exasperation. "I'm good at my job—especially when it comes to knowing what information to share, what to hold back, and what to not make look like a joke."

To avoid answering immediately, he ran his tongue along his upper teeth. "I ain't sayin' you don't know how to do your job."

"Then stop implying it."

"Fine." He studied the wobbling back of Luther's chair and felt Agent Breyer's unmoving gaze on him. *I'm diggin' a hole for myself on this one.* "Sorry."

Her eyes widened briefly before she returned her attention to her tablet. "Thank you."

"Why did they wanna know if you thought I'd take the case?"

Lisa shrugged. "They thought you'd laugh at them and refuse to be sent on a ghost-hunting party."

"What the fuck?" It burst out of his mouth without any volume filter whatsoever.

Luther snorted and whipped his head up. "I got it. I got it!

Hamster won't get away from…me…" The hound's head settled wearily on the seat and he went back to sleep.

Johnny glared at Agent Breyer. "Are you tellin' me we're flyin' across the country for a goddamn ghost?"

"Keep your voice down, huh?" She glanced at the other first-class passengers who darted them dirty looks and gave them an apologetic, it's-under-control smile. "You don't want to start something on a plane while we're halfway to Portland."

"Who cares? I'll buy the damn plane. What ghost?"

She frowned at him, studied his face in silence for a moment, then sighed. "You didn't read the file, did you?"

He returned her stare.

"Oh, come on." Lisa slumped in her seat. "If you didn't even look at it, why did you say yes?"

"I'll tell you when we get there."

The woman shook her head, returned her attention to her tablet, and closed her book before she swiped through to find something else. "Here."

She handed him the tablet, and after he'd stared at her for a long moment with a dubious frown, he took it. "What's this?"

"That's the case, Johnny."

"If you had this case on your fancy…whatever-pad, why the hell did you and Nelson come all the way to my place to drop a file off?"

Lisa shrugged and stared at the tablet. "It's not exactly a secret that you don't do mainstream tech so we make you hard copies."

"Uh-huh. To be clear, that's 'cause I don't trust anythin' I ain't made myself."

"No, I know." She pressed her lips together to fight back a laugh. "Fancy whatever-pads still have numerous bugs to work out."

"Are you tryin' to start somethin', Agent Breyer?"

"Read the damn file." She pointed at the tablet and covered her smirk with a hand.

Johnny grumbled and studied the frame of the device with a frown. "It doesn't have any buttons."

"Because it's a touch screen. Look, you simply—"

He glanced scathingly at her and she pulled her hand away.

"You...do your thing because you seem to already know how it works."

With a sniff, he forced himself to stare at the tablet's screen instead of Lisa's failed attempt to stop smiling. He poked the screen, and the backlight glowed again to show him the scanned documents of their next case.

After five minutes of reading and relatively successful attempts to swipe to the next page, Johnny handed the tablet to her and shook his head. "It's the stupidest thing I ever seen."

"That's our case."

"Folks in Portland have lost their minds and are kickin' up a storm, ramblin' about seein' a demon. I don't do demons."

"They're getting much more attention lately, Johnny, and—"

"I thought you woulda known by now I don't do attention either."

Lisa stared at him until she was sure he'd finished talking. "I get it. It looks stupid. The Department thought you'd say that. But here's the thing. All eight of these people who 'lost their minds,' as you put it, were perfectly normal people with perfectly normal lives. They had no belief in ghosts or the supernatural— beyond Oricerans, obviously. None of them has any history of mental illness, either personally or in their families. Tox screens all came back negative for prescription drugs, illicit substances, hallucinogens, poison, you name it. There's nothing there."

"And sometimes, folks simply spill their marbles all over the floor and can't pick 'em up."

"And sometimes, you need all the facts before calling it." She frowned at him. "So if you don't mind—"

"Yeah, fine. Keep goin'." He leaned back and folded his arms.

"This has all happened in the last month," Lisa continued.

"Yes, they talk about seeing demons. They're also completely terrified, endangering themselves and others and freaking their families out. Doctors haven't been able to do anything about what presents as hallucinations, and they have no clue what this is."

"I never trusted doctors anyway."

"Okay, well, that's not the point. All eight victims have the same mark on them. On some, it's the forearm. Most of them have it on the side or the back of their neck. One man has it on his calf. Eight strangers with no previous connection to each other anyone else can find, all show the same...symptoms and talk about the same demon."

The dwarf shrugged. "Maybe it's a cult."

"Johnny..." Lisa rolled her eyes and dropped the tablet in her lap.

"Hey, don't rule it out. There are cults everywhere, and Portland's the kinda place likely to have a helluva lot."

"Because..."

"Because I don't like cults and I don't like Portland." He sniffed.

She shook her head and swiped through the pages on her tablet. "You should have gone through that file before we left."

"It's a good thing for you I didn't, darlin', or I woulda sent it back to them with a big hell no."

"Look." She held the tablet over his lap so he could see. "Proof at the very least that it's not a cult."

He glanced at the image of one of the marks left on these victims—an oval about two inches long with two stripes cutting it diagonally into thirds. The lines of the mark were faded, thin enough to pass as scratch indents from sleeping on a pillow the wrong way if no one looked too closely. "Is it the same on all of 'em?"

"Exactly the same. These marks were left by magic—dark

magic, if I had to guess. And old too, based on how crude the symbol is. And all eight victims are human."

"Huh." Johnny tilted his head, and Lisa pulled the tablet into her lap. "So we're lookin' for a magical cult recruitin' humans and brainwashin' them into thinkin' they're workin' for demons?"

"Very funny, Johnny." She closed the case file and pulled her book again up. "This is the case. For whatever reason you took it, we're on it now. And it's not a cult."

"Yeah, we'll see." He rubbed his mouth and studied the back of the seat in front of him again, which had finally stopped wiggling. *Magical marks on people. It sounds like somethin' that can wait until I'm done with my business in that stupid city.*

CHAPTER NINE

Their Black SUV rental was ready and waiting for them at Portland International when they landed, courtesy of the Department's Johnny Walker budget. Almost everyone they passed in the airport gave Johnny dirty looks when they saw him with two unleashed hounds despite how close Rex and Luther stayed at their master's side.

It don't matter how well you train 'em, someone's always got a bone to pick.

Lisa checked them in with the rental agency and didn't even try to argue with him about who got the keys. When they loaded the hounds and their small amount of luggage into the SUV, Johnny accelerated away from the airport and followed the signs for downtown Portland.

"Okay, you need to make a left up here on 5th Avenue."

"Not right now."

"Johnny, that's where the hotel is. Here. Left right here—Come on!"

"Sorry, darlin'." He glanced in the rearview mirror to where both hounds peered over the back seat from the cargo area, their tongues lolling as they scanned the city streets that raced past them. "I have one stop to make before we settle into ghost-huntin' mode."

She sighed and stared at his profile. "I thought you said you've never been to Portland."

"I haven't but it don't mean I can't read maps." He grinned and pressed the accelerator to make the next yellow light. "Or memorize 'em."

They pulled up in Goose Hollow alongside the curb outside a brightly painted house with a sign over the front porch written in swirling lime-green letters—*Divine Seed*. The steeply angled street was mostly a residential neighborhood that included houses here and there that doubled as shops like this one. Grumbling, Johnny jerked the emergency brake up and turned the engine off. "Damn hills. If you gonna build a city, why not knock the whole thing down?"

"Because that's the way cities were built." Lisa unbuckled her seatbelt and shook off the odd comment as she stepped out of the SUV.

Johnny went to the back and opened the rear door for the hounds.

"Yes!" Luther leapt from the back of the vehicle and sat the second his master snapped his fingers. Rex stayed where he was.

"Come on, Rex."

"That's…" The bigger hound whined and stared down the steep hill that stretched in front of him. "That's a long way down, Johnny."

"Three feet to the ground."

"I mean all the way down there."

He glanced over his shoulder and scowled. "I don't care for 'em either, but it's only a hill. You'll be fine."

The hound glanced at his brother, then at Lisa, and stepped forward timidly to the edge of the SUV.

The bounty hunter cleared his throat. "The door's closin' one way or the other, Rex. You choose where you end up."

The dwarf pulled it shut and Rex bounded out of the car through the narrowing space. "You sure as shit aren't gonna leave me in a car, Johnny. What's wrong with you? I'd cook in there."

With a smirk, he waved his hounds forward and stepped onto the sidewalk. "Naw. I knew you'd jump."

Luther sniffed his brother as they followed their master down the walkway to the two-story house turned storefront. "What's the matter, Rex? Leave your balls at home?"

Rex sat on the walkway and lowered his head to sniff between his legs. "Nope."

Lisa stared after the dwarf and his hounds and whispered, "I swear he thinks they can understand him."

"Johnny!" Luther spun and yipped at a woman on a bicycle who strained up the hill with her Australian Shepherd leashed and tied to the handlebars. "Hey, hey. They have dogs here!"

"It don't make it any better," Johnny grumbled and walked up the front porch steps.

Rex tilted his head and panted as the Australian Shepherd trotted past with her cycling owner. "Lookin' good, bitch!"

The dwarf snorted and spun quickly, then realized who his hound was talking to. *Canine pickup lines. Kill me now.*

The shepherd responded with a low growl and studied the two hounds warily. She even twisted to keep staring at them over her shoulder.

"You're only jealous because you have to get walked by a bike," Rex shouted.

"Yeah, and your two-legs stinks!" Luther yipped at the shepherd, spun enthusiastically, and trotted toward Johnny. "Rude."

"Tell me about it. I was only trying to be friendly."

"You totally were."

Lisa joined the dwarf on the porch and scanned the front windows. "I can stay out here with the dogs if you want."

He scoffed. "I took those hounds on the New York subway with me, darlin'. I ain't gonna let a...happy-slappy cottage stop us.

Besides, if there ain't a sign on the door says no dogs, we're all good."

"And if there is?"

The bounty hunter grasped the handle and pushed the door to step inside. "Then I ain't seen it."

The hounds trotted after him but separated to skirt Lisa as they looked at her. "No such thing as a no dogs sign, lady."

"Yeah, ever heard of the *Humane Society*? Means we're basically humans."

Of course, Agent Breyer didn't hear a word they'd said, but she frowned after them and stepped slowly into the shop and let the door close quietly behind her. The wind chimes hanging beside the door tinkled when the edge brushed against them.

Johnny stopped before the first rack of clothing beneath a sign that read, *Wear your free-flowing spirit*. He snorted. *Call 'em shirts and be done with it.*

"Oh, man, Johnny." Luther sneezed violently and shook his head. "It smells like that one time I stuck my head in that five-gallon bucket you keep in the shed. What was in there again?"

"Bleach," Rex muttered with a snigger. "Doesn't smell anything like that, dummy."

"Yeah, I know. But kinda. Plus…" Luther sniffed the air and sneezed again. "Shriveled old two-legs and dead flowers."

Johnny scowled and gazed around the shop. "I hate patchouli."

"Yeah, me too, Johnny. What's that?"

Rex sniffed at the clothes rack and buried his head in the hanging linens before he whipped it out again and moved on to the next rack. "You think they have any snacks in here, Johnny? I'm finding pockets but zero snacks."

Luther sneezed again. "This place sucks."

Lisa stopped beside the bounty hunter with a smirk and folded her arms. "Do you think this has what you're lookin' for?"

"I ain't here to shop." He scowled at shelves stacked with books on astrology, personal mantras, vibrational healing, and something called tantric illumination and snorted. *If I stay here too long, I'm gonna step out wearing flowers and moaning like a damn hippie.* Finally, he caught a glimpse of the checkout counter in the back along the right-hand wall. "I shouldn't be a minute."

"Where are you going?"

"To talk to the owner."

She sighed and glanced around the shop while her eyes watered from the intense mixture of incense and burning candles. Her gaze settled on a hanging tapestry with the outline of a human body and seven colored dots filling the silhouette. "Balance your chakras, huh?" she muttered. "If he's here to buy something, I'll quit my job."

Johnny wove through the disorganized display tables of energy crystals, spiritual talismans, and garden goddess essentials. Of course, if they hadn't been clearly labeled, he'd have had no idea what they were. He glanced at a small statue of a naked woman with her arms spread wide and the words, *Embrace Your Inner Goddess* painted from one arm, across her body, and to the next. *More like get the hell off my lawn.*

A short, mousy woman wearing at least four different draped, sheer robes one on top of the other stood in front of the counter. She giggled and took her wallet from her purse. "I'm so excited about this. You have no idea. I've waited for six months."

"I know." The woman behind the counter gave the customer a sympathetic smile. "Our local supplier was buried in backorders. I don't think they expected this much interest."

"Oh, believe me. There's interest." The robed woman giggled again. "And I'll tell all the members of my women's circle that you have first pick of the whole collection."

Johnny raised an eyebrow and glanced around the shop. *What the hell did I walk into?*

"How much was that again?"

The attendant—tall with light-auburn hair and hazel eyes—double-checked her register. "Forty-two, twenty-six all together."

"Wow. That's so reasonable."

"I know. They're trying to keep this sustainable for everyone."

"All part of the rising vibration, right?" The customer placed her bills on the counter, then lifted her huge, sagging cloth purse beside them.

"Oh, I love that bag," the employee said.

"Thank you! There's a new local vendor at the Farmer's Market. They make all their merchandise from recycled clothing and they were having a sale on hobo bags, so I—"

Johnny snorted.

The service attendant looked at him with wide eyes and her customer turned with a wide grin. "Have you seen some of the new tents at the market this summer?"

He frowned, turned to make sure she wasn't talking to someone else, and shook his head. "No, but I seen actual hobos with bags lookin' less worn out than that one."

"Oh, I know. We should come up with a new name for them. It's such a harmful stereotype against homeless people."

The dwarf pressed his lips together and held back the urge to shake some sense into the woman. *Fucking Portland.*

When he didn't reply, the eccentric customer turned to the counter and pulled a huge rock closer to her. She wiggled it into her purse before she slid the strap carefully over her shoulder. "It's heavier than I expected."

The employee nodded although she continued to stare at Johnny with wide eyes as she chuckled self-consciously. "That's a good sign, right?"

"Oh, certainly. The light ones are either fakes or they've already been picked clean."

He couldn't help himself. "You mean the rock?"

The woman turned and smiled at him. "I'm sorry?"

"You paid forty-five bucks for a rock and it's the weight that surprises you?"

"Well, it's not merely a rock—"

"Does it fly or mow the lawn or…I dunno. Cook eggs and bacon?"

She frowned but it disappeared quickly beneath another giggle. "Well, no. It's a geode. The quartz is on the inside. They're hard to find."

Johnny sniffed and made no effort to hide his disdain. "In all that rock? Sure. I bet they are."

"I meant this specific size." With a self-conscious chuckle, she smiled at the woman behind the counter. "You might have a new student on your hands. If he's willing to open his aura to the healing power of—"

"I ain't." Johnny hooked his thumbs through his belt loops and stared at her. Lisa snorted where she browsed through the racks of strangely designed clothing.

"Oh. Well, your journey is your own." The customer's smile wasn't nearly as warm and inviting this time. "Have a blessed day."

"Yeah, enjoy your rock."

She closed her eyes and took a deep breath before she hurried to the front door of the shop.

Johnny took two solid steps toward the counter and studied the auburn-haired woman who continued to stare at him. *Dammit. I knew I spilled somethin' at the food court.* He glanced at his black button-down shirt but it was completely clean. Then he noticed the large black utility knife strapped to his belt and cleared his throat. "It's only a tool, darlin'. I ain't gonna pull it on ya, if that's what you're worried about. I'm lookin' for Lucy Hamilton."

The woman's eyes widened even further, and she drew a sharp breath. "Johnny?"

He glanced around the shop again and sniffed. *It's like walkin' into the damn Twilight Zone.* "Yeah."

With a small shake of her head, the woman chuckled in disbelief and studied him intently. "I don't even know what to say. You look exactly the same."

With a frown, he stepped closer to the counter and pointed at her. "Listen here, darlin'. I ain't fallin' for all this mystical woo-woo mumbo jumbo. Say you saw my face in a crystal ball or some shit. Now I ain't never hit a lady didn't hit me first, and hard, so I'm only gonna ask you once. Who sent you to follow me out here?"

"What?" The woman's grin widened.

"You heard me. You got a lotta work to do on your poker face, but as long as you're straight with me, I won't—"

"Johnny, it's me."

"And?"

"Lucy Hamilton." She put her hands on her hips and grinned at him. "You were looking for me and you found me."

The bounty hunter squinted, leaned forward to scrutinize her from to toe, then lowered his hand slowly. "Are you pullin' one over on me?"

"No, sir."

"Well, I'll be." He slapped the counter and took a step back. "You never did quit callin' me sir even when I threatened to kick you outta the house for it."

Lucy smiled in amazement and shook her head. "You remember that?"

"I remember more than I should about way too many things, darlin'. Look at you. All grown up and… Shit, last time I saw you, you were this big." He raised a hand level with his shoulder.

"You didn't come in here looking for a twelve-year-old girl, did you?"

"What? No." He scoffed and gazed around the shop. "I simply didn't expect to see you without all the baby fat tacked on."

"Oh, jeez." The woman rolled her eyes.

"Naw, it's a compliment, darlin'. You were a cute kid." He studied her again. "And now…you're—"

"I'm gonna stop you right there and save us both from what's bound to make this an even more awkward conversation."

He raised an eyebrow. "This your definition of awkward?"

"Well now." Lucy tucked her hair behind one ear and continued to regard him with a somewhat bemused expression. "You're a little brusque sometimes. You know, with no filter whatsoever. At least you were."

"Shit, I ain't changed that much in fifteen years."

"Yeah, I know." The wind chimes hanging above the front door tinkled again when a new customer stepped inside, and Lucy looked up briefly to nod a greeting at the newcomer. "I have a hard time picturing you wanting to buy anything in here. Although you did seem interested in that geode."

"That was a rock." He pointed at her and sniffed. "And I ain't here to buy. I was…hopin' you might have a few minutes for a chat."

"Right now?"

"Mm-hmm."

She hesitated and looked around her shop. "Yeah. Jolene should be finished with her lunch break soon. I'll put her behind the counter and we can go sit in the lounge."

"You have a lounge here?"

With a smirk, she moved down the counter as her new customer approached. "Not the kind you're thinking of." She looked at the woman and smiled broadly to welcome her. "How can I help you?"

"Yeah, hi. I'm looking for astral projection."

Johnny sniggered and his gaze traveled over her, taking in her baggy pants—or was it a skirt?—all the bangles that clinked and jingled on her wrists, multiple rings on every finger, and her glassy, reddened eyes. *She should be lookin' for a reality check instead.*

"Oh, it's across there on the bookshelf marked *Beyond the Self*. If you need any help with something specific, let me know."

"Thank you." The customer spun away briskly and seemed to almost float as she walked across the shop. Her jewelry jingled with every step, which brought Rex and Luther racing toward her from the back of the shop, yipping excitedly.

"What is that?"

"Johnny, something's coming."

"Whoa. Look at that two-leg. Hey, Rex. Think I could push her over on the first try?"

"Bet you could stare at her and she'd fall. That lady needs help."

Luther wagged his tail furiously as the over-accessorized woman passed them and ignored both hounds completely. "Yeah, I'm gonna try."

Johnny snapped his fingers and they whipped their heads toward him. "To me, boys."

"Johnny, what's that lady doing walking like that?"

"She must've sat on a cactus or something. Ooh, or a porcupine."

"Y'all stay close, ya hear? I can't have you sniffin' 'round underfoot and trippin' up these…folks."

Lucy leaned over the counter. "Aw, you brought your dogs?"

"Is that a problem?"

"Are you kidding? We love dogs here." She stepped around the counter and dropped to one knee. The hounds forgot all about Johnny's order and padded toward her while their tails wagged wildly. They practically threw themselves at her to get a good petting. "And you can tell, can't you? Yes, you *can*. Look at you, you sweet little doggie—"

"All right, they ain't babies, now. Don't talk to 'em like that."

"Johnny, we love it!"

"Yeah, we'll be babies for this lady any day."

Lucy finished petting them, stood, and brushed her hands off. "They're sweet."

He glanced at the dogs, who gazed adoringly at the shop owner. "Only when I want 'em to be."

"Very funny." She gave him a playfully disapproving glance that faded when the door behind the counter opened. "Oh, Jolene. Would you mind watching the counter for me?"

The incredibly pale Jolene scratched her head, exposed a fully unshaved armpit, and studied Johnny with a coy smile. "No problem."

"Thank you. We'll be in the back."

"Uh-huh." She stepped slowly behind the counter and her gaze remained fixed on the bounty hunter.

"Right this way." Lucy gestured toward the back and moved through the clothes racks and the oddly arranged tables of merchandise.

I can't believe folks pay for this stuff.

He found Lisa at the *Do It Yourself Witchcraft* station and cleared his throat. When she looked at him, he nodded toward the back and ignored the uncomfortable sensation as Jolene's intense gaze practically crawled all over him.

A quick chat. Yeah. It had better be.

CHAPTER TEN

Johnny squirmed in the rattan chair at the back of the shop. Lucy and Lisa both watched him silently as he grunted and tried to find a comfortable position, but the chair's curved padding kept sliding away from him in all the wrong places. "Who the hell in their right mind thinks this is a decent way to kick back and take a load off?"

Lucy raised her eyebrows. "You're welcome to choose another seat."

"Yep." Johnny sprang from the chair, which wobbled on its base and almost toppled before he caught it. "The damn thing's a liability."

"How about the pouf?"

"Say what now?" He stared at her with wide eyes.

Lisa cleared her throat with a small smile and patted the huge round cushion beside the stack of pillows she'd chosen. "Otherwise known as an ottoman."

"I know what a damn ottoman is." He slumped heavily on the cushion and grunted as a painful jolt raced up his spine. "I thought it'd be softer."

"Well, that one's so firm because it helps the energetic alignment…" Lucy paused with her mouth hanging open and shut it abruptly. "And you have absolutely no interest in that. Which is fine."

"And you do?" The bounty hunter watched her warily as she lifted the lid of the teapot on the low table beside her and leaned closer to sniff the steam.

"I've found something I can align my beliefs with, yeah. Don't worry, Johnny. I'm not about to preach personal enlightenment to you." She chuckled and opened a small leather pouch, the contents of which she sprinkled in a circle around the teapot and three small cups on the table.

"What are you doing?"

"This? It's a little cleansing ritual I like to perform."

"Hey, Johnny." Luther approached his master and sniggered as his tail thumped against the abandoned rattan chair. "Betcha that'll clear your constipation right up."

Lying on the floor at Lucy's feet, Rex laughed. "Cleansing. Good one."

He lowered his fist at his side, and Luther lay obediently at his feet. "What's that for, huh?"

"Johnny." Lisa wrinkled her nose and shook her head a fraction of an inch.

He sniffed and stared at the sprinkled whatever it was. "'Cause I ain't fixin' to get poisoned. Not again. Not today."

Lucy muttered something under her breath, her eyes closed as she spread her hands over the tea-table. When she was finished, she turned toward him with a warm smile. "Sorry. What was that?"

"Nothin'." The dwarf shifted uncomfortably on the hard ottoman, crossed one leg over the other, and tried to lean back, then gave up when he remembered there was nothing to support him. "I didn't realize you were one of them humans tryin' to cast their own spells."

"It's only a ritual, Johnny." Lucy poured them each a cup of tea. "Magic doesn't have to be actual spells and illusions and… flying creatures for it to exist. Although that's one of its forms."

"Huh. It's the only form I know."

"And that's simply the way you choose to look at it." She offered him the first cup of tea but he shook his head and jerked his thumb toward Lisa. "Go ahead and let her take the first one."

The agent scoffed. "Will you let me take the first sip too to see whether I live or die?"

He smirked, but his expression remained a little wary. "Maybe."

She took the cup from Lucy and laughed. "You're being paranoid."

"No, I ain't. I reckon you never been poisoned before, darlin'. Lemme tell ya, that'll make anyone think twice 'bout acceptin' weird ritual…whatever from strangers."

"Not anyone," Rex muttered and stared lovingly at the shop owner. "Luther's too stupid to keep eating those mushrooms down the road."

"No, I'm not. They're delicious."

Lisa made a big show of slurping her tea and sighed contently afterward. "Ah. That's good. I can't even taste the poison."

Lucy choked back a laugh, and the women shared an amused glance.

"That ain't funny."

His partner lifted the teacup to her lips again and grinned. "No, it truly is."

When Lucy offered him another cup, he took it hesitantly, sniffed the steam rising from it, and placed it on the floor beside him. "I'll get 'round to it."

"Okay. Oh, I'm sorry." Lucy gestured toward Agent Breyer. "We haven't officially been introduced, right?"

"Huh." Johnny sniffed and waved a hand in Lisa's general direction. "Lisa Breyer. She's my—"

"I'm his partner." She grinned. "Still fairly new."

Goddammit, we need to find a better word.

"Well, it's nice to meet you." Lucy leaned in her chair that looked like a regular armchair but with the legs sawed off. She glanced at each of her guests as her smile widened. "That's great, Johnny. I mean yes, it's a wonderful surprise to see you after...so long. But it's especially good to see you so happy. You know, that you were able to move on and find someone to share your life with again."

"What?" He gaped at her and from the corner of his eye, he saw Lisa turn away to sip more of her tea. "Not that kinda partner, darlin'. Sorry to burst your peace-and-love bubble."

"Oh." Lucy set her teacup down and frowned. "But she said—"

"I'm on a case."

A laugh of realization escaped her, and she shook her head. "I'm sorry. I merely assumed—"

"Trust me," Lisa interjected. "It's hard enough to crack him open when it comes to working together."

"Well, don't give up hope, Johnny." The young woman nodded. "There's enough love out there for everyone. You merely have to open yourself up to receive it."

Johnny shifted again on the ottoman and cleared his throat. "I ain't here for love advice or to drink tea potions or get my future spouted at me from a deck of playin' cards. Got it?"

Lucy nodded and winked at him. "Got it."

Not a cult, my ass. We're sittin' in one.

"You said you're on a case?" their hostess asked after a short silence.

"Yep."

Lucy took a small sip of her tea and held the cup at chest level with both hands. "I thought you were retired."

Johnny sniffed. "Now how'd you hear 'bout that?"

"Well, after...everything happened, the investigation seemed to simply stop without warning. When we didn't hear from you at all, we assumed you'd withdrawn—which is completely normal and valid, by the way, and I'm not here to pass judgment on your personal choices."

Lisa tilted her head to stare at him. "What investigation?"

"I'm not goin' there." He stared at Lucy. *I'm only workin' on a case from the past. I don't need the whole damn thing catchin' up with me.* "Listen, Lucy. We're here for an active case, sure. But I came to talk to you about Dawn."

The woman's eyelids fluttered and she set her teacup down again. "Oh."

"Now, I reckon you weren't expectin' that but I'd appreciate anythin' you might have to tell me."

"Um...sure." She looked shell-shocked as she leaned back in the leg-less armchair. "But it's been a long time, Johnny. I suppose it doesn't matter anymore, right? After fifteen years? Dad passed about four years ago, and Mom flew off to start over in a different country. So it's only me and I'm free to say whatever I want."

He tilted his chin and studied her curiously. "What do you mean it don't matter anymore?"

"Oh, only that... You know. We never talked about what happened. Not much, anyway. As a family."

"Well, sure. I get that." He rubbed his mouth and beard and took a deep breath. "Do you remember anythin' about the statement you gave to the police that night? What you said, what questions they asked, any of that?"

"Yeah..." Lucy rubbed her forehead. "I told them everything I knew. That we were on our school trip. We'd had a great day in Central Park and went back to the hotel. Dawn and I were sharing a room. A group of the other kids went into someone else's room to watch this stupid show together after dinner. She said she was tired and wanted to go to bed early, and I...well, I assumed that was where she was going."

"And that's it?" He leaned over his lap and tried not to frown too deeply. "Do you remember anythin' else? Anyone actin' off or followin' y'all, maybe?"

"No, nothing like that. The police got everything I knew." Lucy glanced at her hands clasped in her lap and a slow flush rose in her cheeks. "That night."

The dwarf nodded slowly. "I have a hunch you ain't said much of what happened after that night."

She shook her head slowly.

"If there was ever a time to start talkin' 'bout it, darlin', that'd be now."

"I know." She sighed heavily. "It was a few months after that. My dad had started to go downhill. He wasn't ever the bravest guy or the type to stand up for himself and carry the family with his confidence, you know?"

"Sure. That was more your mama's part."

"Right. But after—" Lucy stopped and chuckled when Luther butted his nose against her calf. "Hey, buddy."

"Johnny, you think *she* has any snacks?"

The dwarf snapped his fingers. "Not now, boys."

"I can't even tell," Rex added as he sniffed the perimeter of the "lounge" while his tail wagged furiously. "I think this place burned my nose out. All I smell is…too much of everything and nothing."

"It's on her too." Luther stuck his muzzle into the crook of Lucy's bent knee, and the woman chuckled.

"I know what you want." The woman leaned over the side of her armchair to open a small silver box shaped like a treasure chest. When she turned again, she held out both fists. "Do you guys know how to sit?"

"Do we know *how*?" Luther sat immediately and gazed at her.

"Lady, you're looking at two hounds who were *born* to sit." Rex trotted toward her and sat beside his brother. "It depends on what we get out of it."

"What are you doin'?" Johnny grumbled.

Lucy smiled at him. "You have two exceptionally good dogs, Johnny."

"I know that. What are you doin'?"

"Is it okay if I give them a treat?"

The dwarf scowled and shook his head. "No, it ain't. Absolutely not. No one feeds my hounds." He snapped his fingers, opened his hand, and stood from the ottoman as he reached toward her. "Gimme that."

"Oh. Okay." She dropped the treats into his hand and shrugged. Both hounds craned their necks to watch the exchange and stared hopefully at the tidbits they couldn't even see. "Most people don't mind."

"Well, I ain't most people."

"Aw, come on, Johnny." Rex licked his muzzle.

"Yeah, what gives?" Luther uttered a high-pitched whine. "The lady with hound treats can't give the hounds the actual treats? Something's wrong with you."

"We've been good, Johnny."

"We'll be better."

"Come on, come on, come on."

Johnny sniffed what looked like two Milk-Bone treats, leaned away, and looked slowly at the hounds' huge, pleading eyes. "Catch."

He tossed both treats, which were caught by two slobbering, eager mouths without hesitation.

"Yes! Johnny, you just redeemed yourself."

"They don't make 'em better than you, Johnny." Rex and Luther sniffed the floor, looking for more, and he shook his head.

"Tasty, right?" Lucy laughed as the hounds returned to her and sniffed vigorously for more. "I think you're good with only one. Don't worry, Johnny. They're made with organic, local, sustainably-sourced ingredients. Free-range too, as far as the meat goes."

"Meat?" Luther whipped his head up to look at him.

Rex immediately did the same. "Where?"

"What?" Johnny asked.

"The dog treats." Lucy grinned at him. "There's a local company who sells these at the Farmer's Market too and they—"

"All right, all right. Dog treats. I don't need to know where every speck of it came from." The dwarf gestured impatiently. *We won't get outta here if I let her gush 'bout organic dog-treat farms. Jesus.* "You were talkin' 'bout your old man."

Her smile faded, and she glanced briefly at Lisa.

"It's okay," the agent said gently. "Anything you can remember is helpful."

The bounty hunter raised an eyebrow at her but she ignored him and nodded encouragingly at the shop owner.

"Right." With a deep breath, Lucy leaned back in her chair. "Dad wasn't himself for months afterward. I think it was almost a year, or maybe a little more. Mom and I started to worry. Honestly, we thought he was sick—you know, like some kind of illness—until he sat us down together and told us way more than we already knew. He said he had to get it off his chest or it would kill him."

With a grunt, Johnny gestured for her to continue.

"In a nutshell, he said he'd been in considerable trouble," Lucy continued. "Things like illegal gambling and owing tons of money, and that he'd ended up selling drugs on the side to maintain his gambling habit. He'd been investigated by the FBI, and they'd contacted him about his involvement in everything. It was the weirdest conversation. He completely fell apart and two weeks later, we packed up and moved from Georgia to Wisconsin, of all places. He said it was to get away from all the trouble he'd landed in—that he didn't want to keep reliving all the awful things he'd done by staying in Atlanta. And he didn't want to endanger Mom and me anymore so we went with him, and he completely turned his life around. I think before he passed…

Johnny, I think he'd finally managed to move on and be happy. So I'm grateful for that, at least."

He shook his head vigorously and rubbed his mouth to curb his instinctive outburst. "Why didn't anyone tell me?" he asked after a moment.

The woman's eyes widened. "We couldn't."

"Y'all knew how to reach me."

"No, I mean we couldn't legally. The agents working with my dad—if that what's it called when someone has become an informant for the FBI—came to him a few days after that and told him not to tell anyone about that night or what he was involved in and the gang or whatever he'd gotten tangled up in. I guess they wanted to catch the top people running the whole thing."

"They were usin' him as a CI to feed them information about that gang, if we're callin' it that." Johnny grimaced and held back the outburst that still threatened to break through and ruin this relatively peaceful chat. *It ain't her fault her daddy got all caught up in this shit.* "Do you remember when you moved to Wisconsin? When Ben said he wanted to get y'all away from the danger?"

Lucy's eyes widened. "Yes, I do. It was right after Easter— impossible to forget, honestly. Mom was pissed that we had to cancel all our holiday plans and trying to move from the south to Wisconsin is one of the worst memories I have from that time. Not the worst but that time was brutal on all three of us."

"I reckon it was." *Right after Easter. The feds cut Ben Hamilton loose after fuckin' up the sting they never mentioned to the one magical who could have secured them a huge win.*

"It was right after the FBI released him as an informant," Lucy added, "so I guess Dad was free to do whatever he wanted after that. I think they might have even helped with the move, but I don't honestly know. All that is probably in whatever file you have, right?"

Johnny's hands clenched into tight fists. "The file was missin' a few key pieces, darlin'," he muttered through clenched teeth. "You handed me most of 'em."

She shrugged and picked her tea up again for a slow sip. "At least some of it was useful. I haven't gone back through it in a very long time."

"You did fine."

The makeshift lounge fell into an expectant silence. Lucy tried to give the dwarf a sympathetic smile. "So are they reopening the case, then?"

"No. I'm reopenin' it." He pressed his lips together and they all but disappeared beneath his thick mustache. "I appreciate your time, Lucy. It ain't easy to dig all that up, especially when you got a business to run and…customers to tend to."

"The perks of owning a business, right? And having employees."

"Sure." He glanced at Lisa, who looked expectantly at him. "Sorry to hear 'bout your old man too. All this aside, he was a good man."

"Thanks, Johnny. So are you."

The dwarf's breath caught in his throat and he cleared it forcefully. "We'll see. I reckon I still got a ways to go before I can claim anythin' like that."

"Don't even." Lisa frowned playfully, then turned to Lucy. "Johnny's taken on a fair amount recently. I think some of his best cases are in the future. You know, the ones that'll bring him the most."

He grunted. "Like a kid."

"A what?" Lucy grinned at him. "You have another kid?"

"A ward." He sniffed and shifted on the ottoman again. *And there I go openin' my big mouth. Dammit.* "I just sent her off to school."

"Johnny and I rescued Amanda from a situation no one should ever have to go through," the agent added. "He did so much good for that little girl—and vice versa."

Lucy's eyes shimmered with tears but she grinned at her best friend's dad. "I stand by what I said, Johnny. You've always been someone to look up to. For me, anyway. And for Dawn."

"Aw, hell..." He stood and stared at the brightly colored rug with overlapping geometric shapes beneath them. "I reckon we're done here."

"Oh, before you go. Can you wait for one more minute?"

"Uh-huh."

"Great." Lucy stood, glanced at his untouched cup of tea, and hurried toward the counter again with a chuckle.

Lisa folded her arms. "You could've told me why we were stopping here first. I get it."

"And listen to you ask me the whole way if I thought it was a good idea?" He shook his head. "I already knew it was."

"Did you get what you wanted?"

"For the most part, although I still ain't done with this search."

"Okay."

Lucy returned to them with two strips of paper and a pen. "Here, Johnny. This is my number—my cell. I want you to have it, just in case."

"Uh...all right." He took the small paper, folded it in half, and slid it into his pocket. "Thanks."

She held the blank strip and the pen toward him. "Would you like to give me yours?"

"Not really..." He glanced at Lisa, who gave him a disapproving frown, and he sighed. "But I'll do it for you, darlin'. I ain't partial to handin' my info out."

"I know. So thank you."

Johnny scribbled his number down and handed her the paper and pen brusquely. "You take care, now."

"You too, Johnny." Lucy grinned at him as he and Lisa hurried across the shop to the front door. "And give me a call the next time you're Portland."

"Not fuckin' likely," he muttered under his breath and raised a hand in farewell.

Rex and Luther sniffed around Lucy's feet, bumped into each other, and wagged their tails furiously. "Got any more of those treats, lady?"

"Yeah. If you hurry, Johnny will never know."

The dwarf snapped his fingers. "We're leavin', boys. Get on."

"Fine..."

"She give you anything? I saw you put something in your pockets."

Johnny pulled the door open and held it for Lisa as the hounds trotted out with her. *Only a number I'll forget is there and probably shouldn't.*

CHAPTER ELEVEN

They stepped out of Divine Seed to a blaze of red and blue lights from a police car pulled over on the opposite side of the road. Pedestrians on that side stepped into the street to avoid the officer's confrontation with a Portland local and simply continued to walk.

"Aw, come on, man." The guy in his twenties with messy hair, who wore faded skinny jeans and a black t-shirt that hugged his torso as tightly, spread his arms and scowled at the officer. "It's a bike. I didn't do anything wrong."

"Except for the way you're riding that fixed-gear," the officer muttered as he ripped off the top sheet of his citation pad and handed it over. "That's an illegal bicycle."

"There's nothing wrong with my—"

"The law says differently, doesn't it? 'A bicycle must be equipped with a brake that enables the operator of the bicycle to stop it within fifteen feet from a speed of ten miles per hour on dry, level, clean surface.' That's a direct quote from the law."

"That was fifteen years ago!" The cyclist rolled his eyes and snatched the ticket from the officer's hand. "All that craziness died a natural death, and you're the only cop still running around trying to ticket people for this. Don't you have anything better to do? Like stop actual crimes."

"I'm doing my job. Unless you want another ticket or an arrest, I suggest you close your mouth right now so I can keep doing my job. Have a nice day." The officer turned and stormed to his car, scanned the street, and stared at Johnny and the hounds a little longer than the bounty hunter liked.

As soon as the car door shut, the civilian in skin-tight everything scowled at his ticket. "Fuck! This is bullshit. No one gives a shit about this anymore except for this yahoo."

Johnny turned toward Lisa. "Folks can't bike in the city?"

"No, they can...I think." She frowned a little as she watched the cyclist clamber onto his bike. "I have no idea what that was about."

The dwarf sniffed and stepped off the sidewalk toward the trunk of their rental SUV. "It's time to go."

The hounds leapt into the back. "What's wrong with that guy, Johnny?"

"It looks like he's wearin' lady clothes."

"It's weird."

"That's a hipster." He shut the trunk, and when he climbed behind the wheel again, Lisa was already in the passenger seat and buckling up.

"Now can we go check into the hotel?"

"Uh-huh." He started the engine and struggled to disengage the emergency brake before he made a sharp U-turn on the street.

A glint of steel flashed in the brief moment that sunlight cut through the clouds, followed by a screech of skidding tires and a thump on the hood of the SUV.

"What the—" Lisa braced herself against the doorframe as the cyclist they had almost hit turned sharply on his bike and skidded to a stop.

He removed his hand from the hood of the SUV and glared at

Johnny. "Come on, man. Look where you're going! I don't need my day to get any worse." He hopped the bike to face it down the steep hill again and raced away.

Johnny stared at the guy's receding shape and shook his head. "It's a hell of a way to stop with no brakes. I don't get the draw."

Lisa shrugged and shot him a sheepish smile. "Portland?"

"Sure. The city can take the blame." He accelerated down the hill again and scrutinized every street they passed to make sure there weren't any other weird bikes and weirder cyclists headed toward them out of nowhere.

The farther they drove through the city toward their hotel—with Lisa acting as the navigator—the more he knew he hated it.

"This was a big mistake," he muttered and ducked a little to peer as high as he could through the windshield at the tall buildings in front of them. "What the hell is that, anyway?"

"That would be a mural, Johnny." She gazed at the colorful public art that covered the brick walls the artists had made their canvas. "I think they're great."

"Are you kiddin' me? Look at that one. It's a fuckin' giant banana. Ain't no one in their right mind gonna call that great. Hell, I could throw a banana at a wall and do better than that."

"And then you'd let us eat it, right, Johnny?" Luther panted in the back of the SUV and sniffed the window despite it being tightly closed.

"We'll make wall art too," Rex added and crossed the width of the trunk to look out the opposite window as his brother. "Sniff around a little. Lift a leg. Bam. Instant success."

The dwarf snorted. "That's about right."

"What?" Lisa frowned at him.

He cleared his throat and stopped behind the tiny electric-powered car in front of them at the red light. "Are you still surprised to hear me talkin' to myself?"

"When I only get one side of the conversation? A little, yeah."

"Tell her, Johnny," Luther said.

"Yeah, you have to now. Tell her you can hear your hounds talking to you. What's the worst that can happen?"

Luther sniggered. "She'll either stay and think you're super-cool, or she'll jump out of the car and run away screaming. Win-win, Johnny."

Rex's ears flopped against his head when he turned quickly to look at his brother. "No, it's not."

"All right. We're here." Johnny stopped in front of the hotel called The Portland Spot and parked the SUV. The engine idled as they sat there and he leaned forward to get a better look at the front of the hotel. "Where's the valet?"

Lisa tapped at her phone. "Huh."

"Huh what?"

"They don't have one."

"Are you tellin' me Nelson booked us a hotel with no damn valet?"

"It looks like it. The website says they're going for an 'immersive community experience.'"

He scowled at her. "What the hell does that mean?"

"Well, right now, it means we park our own car."

"Fuck this city." He smacked a hand on the steering wheel, shifted into drive, and lurched toward the entrance to the parking garage behind the hotel.

After they'd checked in and he had a thing or two more to say about the hotel looking like a run-down shoe factory with art on the walls, he and Lisa parted ways to settle into their separate rooms. The bounty hunter thumped his duffel bag on the floor inside the closet—which had a curtain instead of a door—and pulled out the first thing on top of his packed belongings. Dawn's case file still made his stomach clench when he looked at it.

Or the Red Boar's file with hers shoved somewhere in the middle like a damn afterthought.

As he moved toward the bed, a brisk knock sounded at the door. "It's Lisa."

Grumbling, he strode across the room and opened it. "What?"

"Yes, I'd love to come in so we can go over our next steps for the case. Thanks for the invitation."

"Right." He sniffed and stepped aside to let her in.

"Great rooms, right?" She walked past him and gazed into every nook and cranny before she tapped her tablet. "I was reading up on this place. They use a number of recycled materials and grow all their produce in-house."

"Good for them." After he'd shut the door briskly, Johnny marched to the bed and sat.

She took a seat in the bright-green armchair—which looked more like a massive circular ottoman with an adolescent attempt at a back and armrests—and flipped through her tablet.

"So I think we should focus on—" The rustling of paper and a quick whump when Johnny pulled stacks out of his file and dropped them onto the bed interrupted her. "What's that?"

"Dawn's file."

"Oh, so you brought that with you but you didn't bother to read the actual file for the case we came here to work?"

"What's the big deal, darlin'? You have the whole thing in your fancy laptop."

Lisa stared at him, her expression unamused. "It's a tablet."

"Same thing." He sniffed and flipped through Prentiss Avalon's arrest records and the report of the shifter's sentence hearing. *There's gotta be somethin' in here I ain't lookin' at the right way. That Vilguard asshole almost let his lips fly too much. There had to be someone else in the shop that night.*

She cleared her throat. "Johnny."

He didn't hear her as he pored over the reports for at least the fourth time. He'd lost count of how many.

"Hello? Johnny Walker?"

Rex barked. "Hey, Johnny!"

"Anyone in there?" Luther leapt up and thumped his front

paws on the bedspread. "Johnny, if you can hear us, bark once. I mean..."

The bounty hunter slapped the files on his lap and shouted, "*What?*"

Luther immediately hopped off the bed and panted. "See? That worked."

Lisa gazed patiently at him until he finally met her gaze. "I'm tryin' to think."

"I can tell." She nodded and lowered her tablet into her lap. "Will you tell me why you took this case?"

"I think you already know the answer to that."

"I have a hunch but I think it's better for both of us if I hear your version."

He sighed heavily and pushed himself farther back onto the mattress. "Lucy."

She scoffed with a small, knowing smile. "A one-word answer's not gonna cut it."

"I'm workin' on it." He scowled at the bedspread with its clashing stripes of deep purple and a puke-like brown-green. "That girl—woman, now—was Dawn's best friend when they were growin' up. Back then, I had the cabin in the Glades and a place in Atlanta. That's where we spent most of our time and where I took the cases. I got to know Lucy Hamilton and her folks real well as the girls went to school together. They were in New York when she was murdered."

"On the school trip. I know."

"That ain't the half of it, though." He rubbed his mouth and frowned. "If I had a mind to, I could put a helluva lotta blame on Lucy's old man for what happened."

"What?" Lisa drew her legs onto the armchair and crossed them beneath her. "He cooperated with the officers who took his statement. It wasn't hard to glean that from your conversation with Lucy. He was obviously way more involved than we thought. I had no idea he was a CI but it makes sense."

"No, it don't." The dwarf looked slowly at her. "He wasn't the night Dawn was murdered but he was there—with her. I might even go so far as to say the man's mistakes are what got her killed." *And me. Raisin' a kid on my own and lettin' her know as much as she did 'bout what I do.*

Agent Breyer slowly shook her head. "I don't get it."

"Here." Johnny tossed her the transcript of RedHero Comics's security footage and nodded. "Real illuminatin' shit right there."

"Johnny, I don't need to go through this—"

"Sure you do. Go on."

She looked at the stapled pages, and as she read through the transcripts, he glared at the painting of four hands sprouting from the same wrist that hung above the dresser. After five minutes of complete silence broken only by the hounds' panting and the rustle of paper as she flipped the pages, she stopped and exhaled slowly. "This is what they kept from you."

"That's only the start. The bastard who pulled the trigger was cuffed and brought in a couple of days later."

Her eyes widened. "And they let you—"

"Believe for the last fifteen damn years that he was still out there? Yeah."

"Jesus." Lisa ran a hand through her hair and stared at the transcript. "Then why are you still pursuing this? The guy's been in prison the whole time."

"It ain't the shifter I aim to bring down."

"The Red Boar." She shook her head. "Johnny, simply because Lemonhead or whatever he calls himself is still out there doesn't mean he's responsible for what happened to your daughter."

"He damn well is. New York two months ago wasn't the first time I saw that red stamp. I reckon it won't be the last, not until I find that fucker and put him behind bars."

"That might be stretching it a little. After fifteen years out of the game, he came back in one city with only one known location where those thugs we dealt with above the vape shop were working on their little distribution baggies. That doesn't make for—"

"It's all I need to make my case, darlin'. That ain't all of it, either. If the Red Boar wasn't in that shop the night my kid was murdered, I'm outta the game again. For good. And I know I'm right, so tryin' to pull me out of it ain't gonna do no good."

"Okay." Lisa set the stapled transcripts onto the table beside the armchair and nodded.

"So now you know." Johnny scratched the side of his head. "And if you ain't still willin' to stick around when the times comes, I won't—"

"What do I have to do? Say it three times to make it real?" Lisa chuckled. "I told you I'm in whenever you're ready and have the pieces together. So stop asking."

"Right." He cleared his throat and stared at the hounds stretched across the floor at the foot of the bed.

"So for now..." Lisa picked her tablet up with both hands. "Why don't we take a break from the Red Boar and focus on this case for a while. We might as well while we're here, right?"

The bounty hunter rolled his eyes and gestured for her to continue. "We might as well."

CHAPTER TWELVE

"Eight human victims," Lisa said as she flipped through her tablet. "I think we should start with finding the best one to pay a visit to and ask a few questions."

"The best one?" Johnny scoffed. "Ain't no best one when they all lost their minds."

"I mean given the circumstances. So I'll simply go through them and you tell me which one sounds best. Fair?"

"I'm all ears."

"Okay. Victim one was...oh. Transferred to a psychiatric hospital four weeks ago."

He lay back on the bed and folded his arms behind his head. "Dud."

"Well, yes. Number two was also admitted to a psychiatric health facility. Nope."

"You mean the looney bin."

"I mean exactly what I said." She glanced at him but he stared fixedly at the ceiling. "Three went home to California so aren't accessible here. All right...victim number four is a ten-year-old boy."

"Shit." Johnny grimaced. "I ain't fixin' to go question a kid about his nightmares."

"Yeah, that sounds like something we can put on the back burner as a last resort."

"And the rest of 'em?"

"Victim five is a week into time served for reckless endangerment of a minor. It looks like the guy freaked out and —Jesus."

Johnny raised his head off the mattress and looked at her. "What?"

"He tried to get his kid to jump off the Morrison Bridge with him to 'get rid of the voices and save them both.'"

"Shit."

"The boy's with his mom still, though. At least there's that. It looks like the dad was one of the first victims of whatever this is." Lisa flipped to the next page. "Six, seven, and eight, as far as we know, are still in the area. They have no charges and no hospitalizations or psychiatric holds and any one of them would do fine, I think."

"The first one."

"Christopher Folsum. He lives about seven miles from this hotel and works for himself as an independent contractor."

"Doin' what?"

"Carpentry."

"Huh."

"He's single with no kids and lives alone."

The dwarf shrugged and shifted a little on the bed. "He sounds good to me. We can head out for a house call first thing tomorrow."

Lisa looked up from the tablet. "It's only six o'clock."

"Yep. Which makes it suppertime in my neck o' the woods, and I ain't fixin' to sneak up on a crazy man's house in the dark and make him lose whatever's left of his mind."

"Okay, yes. That's a fair point."

He pushed up and sat on the edge of the bed. "Did they put a mini bar in these rooms, or do I gotta fill it myself too?"

With a snort, she nodded at the large cabinet door centered in the bottom of the dresser. "Right under the TV, I think. At least mine was."

The dwarf slipped off the bed and hurried to the large cabinet door that looked like another drawer until he pulled it open sideways and peered inside. "All right. At least the fridge ain't powered by community experience."

He rifled through the bottles in the fridge and grew increasingly frustrated. Finally, he sat back on his heels and thrust his entire head into it. "You gotta be fuckin' kiddin' me."

"What's wrong?" Lisa watched him and tried not to laugh as the dwarf shifted to fit his head and an arm inside. Bottles clinked together and toppled over.

"Nelson *knows* what to stock in the goddamn fridge!" Johnny jerked away from the open door and pounded a fist on his thigh. "He booked the rooms." *Got your message loud 'n clear, asshole. But I ain't your charity case.*

"No whisky?"

"Not even the kind I don't touch. Only tiny water bottles and this shit." He studied one of the bottle labels and grunted in disgust. "Whatever the hell Pillowfist hazy IPA is."

"I think that's a beer from one of the breweries up on—"

"It doesn't matter where it's from, darlin'. It ain't my drink."

A bottle of water fell out of the fridge as he pushed to his feet. Luther trotted toward it and sniffed madly. "We'll take whatever you don't want, Johnny."

Rex lifted his head from where he lay and thumped his tail on the carpet. "Pillowfist sounds good to me. Think it has any of the same stuff as the smelly lady's treats?"

Johnny kicked the mini-fridge closed before the smaller hound could stick his nose in it and stormed across the room.

"Where are you going?" Lisa asked.

"To get a drink. Y'all better hop to if you're comin' with."

"Duh." Luther trotted after him.

Rex uttered a canine groan and stood. "We could use a drink too, Johnny. Hey, isn't bacon-flavored stuff a thing?"

The agent stood quickly and tossed her tablet onto the pile of scattered papers from the Operation Deadroot file as she hurried to catch up.

The hotel lobby was much busier now than when they'd first checked in. Johnny scowled at the full tables around him and the people seated to eat their meals. Some of them talked and laughed, but most were in their late twenties and early thirties and spent their meals with their smartphones in one hand and a fork in the other. Or a brightly colored drink.

He shook his head and marched toward the bar. *Real-life people sittin' there right in front of them, and all they do is take pictures of their damn food. I think the whole city is losin' their minds, magical mark or not.*

"Whoa, Johnny, check it out." Luther stopped as his master kept walking, and Rex yipped sharply.

"He meant watch out!"

The dwarf stopped barely in time to avoid a collision with a woman with dreadlocks who streaked across the hotel lobby on rollerblades. "What the fuck? Hey. Those are for outside."

She made a neat one-eighty and grinned at him before she glanced at the hounds. "And your dogs should be on a leash."

With a shrug, she spun and raced away.

"Bite me," he grumbled and wove through the people with weird-colored hair and even weirder choices in wardrobe. *There's always somethin'. Either the clothes are too tight or it looks like they tore a curtain down and wrapped it on. Are there any goddamn normal folk in this city?*

Most of the locals who milled around the wide curved bar held a drink and sipped casually as they held their conversations with serious expressions and slow nods. He finally reached the counter and rapped his knuckles on the counter.

The bartender—wearing a scarlet vest that looked like it had been cut from an 1850's smoking jacket and a bright teal bowtie —nodded at him. "I'll be with you in a second."

He shook a stainless-steel drink mixer and held it a foot above an ice-filled glass to pour, then lifted it even higher as the booze drained.

"All right," Johnny said. "Now how 'bout—"

"One moment, sir." The bartender nodded and picked through a silver tray of garnishes. He sprinkled some herbs on top of the drink and smiled at the conversations happening around the bar. With a small frown of concentration, he took an orange from a plastic tub, tossed it over his shoulder from back to front, and delicately shaved the peel over the drink.

Lisa finally caught up to her partner and leaned against the bar. "Do they have what you're looking for?"

"Look at this." Johnny stared in disbelief at the bartender, who seemed determined to extend the orange shavings ritual as long as possible. When the fruit was returned to the bin, the dwarf tapped the bar again. "Right. So all I want is—are you kiddin' me? What kind of a drink needs a damn blowtorch?"

"It's all part of the process," the man muttered as he glanced at him, although his smile had faded a little.

"For the love of liquor, man. Pour the damn thing and move on!"

The handheld torch clicked on and the bartender lowered the flame steadily toward the surface of the drink. It burst into flame with a whoosh, followed by a round of oohs and ahs by the locals standing nearby.

A woman on the other side of Lisa leaned back to look at Johnny and gave him a crooked smile. "You shouldn't try to rush him. What he's doing is an art form."

"Naw, that's blasphemy is what that is. And a waste of every-one's time."

"Johnny, we can try somewhere else," Lisa suggested.

"I've been standin' here for a damn lifetime, darlin'. I'm stayin' to get my drink."

The woman beside Agent Breyer—who'd opted to wear a black-and-white checkered pantsuit and a top hat with feathers sprouting from the brim—chuckled and studied him curiously. "Where are you from?"

The bounty hunter scowled as the bartender slid the finished drink toward his customer and ran the man's card. "Somewhere I'm wishin' I never left."

Wiping his hands on his apron, the man headed toward Johnny and tried far too hard to look inviting and personable. "Thanks for your patience. What can I create for you?"

The dwarf snorted. "All right, bartender—"

"Mixologist."

"Say what?"

The man's smile tightened as he leaned forward. "I'm not a bartender. See, there are certain tiers, if you will. Schools for mixology, which I attended. I got to study under—"

"Yeah, okay." He rubbed his mouth. "Give me a Johnny Walker Black. Neat."

"Oh…" The mixologist nodded. "We don't carry that."

"What the hell kinda bartender are you?"

The conversation around them lowered dramatically in volume as people nearby turned to look at the dwarf who seemed ready to cause a scene.

"Sir, I'm a mixologist."

"You said that." He pressed his knuckles against the bar.

"We cater to a little more refined palate, if you will." The man snatched a piece of thick card stock from behind the bar and slid it in front of her. "Here's a list of our signature craft cocktails. If you're looking specifically for whisky or bourbon, we have that right—"

"It ain't an either-or kinda thing."

When the bartender looked at Lisa, all she could do was raise her eyebrows at him with her lips pressed tightly together.

Scowling, Johnny studied the list and wrinkled his nose. "Starry-eyed Mistress. Lava Drape. What is this shit?"

Someone gasped, and the conversation at the bar all but ground to a halt.

"Sir, most of these cocktails have won numerous awards in the—"

"Stop. Please, stop. Go make your frilly damn whatever-the-hells. This is ridiculous."

"Have a good night, sir." The bartender nodded and stepped away to take care of his other customers with more refined palates.

"Goddamn." Johnny turned away from the bar and scanned the lobby. "And now the whole damn place is bein' overrun by 'em."

"By what?" Lisa asked and tried to ignore the dirty glances and muted whispers directed at them.

"You mean the hamsters, Johnny?" Luther stood at his master's feet and scanned the lobby. "Just tell me where."

"You want us to flush 'em out?" Rex added.

Johnny turned toward the checker-suited woman and jerked his chin at her. She grinned. "Are you stayin' at this hotel?"

She laughed and bit her lip. "No. I only come here for the craft cocktails." She studied him speculatively again and added, "And the company, depending on the night."

Lisa widened her eyes.

"Uh-huh." The bounty hunter gestured at the crowded tables in the lobby and the large groups of mingling Portlanders. "And what about all these other...them?"

"Most people here in the evenings are locals. This merely happens to be one of the best new venues and a hotel."

"Yep." He cleared his throat, then fixed her with a curious expression before he pointed at the feathers in her top hat. "Did you get in a fight with a peacock?"

"What?"

He snapped his fingers before he pushed through the standing crowd. The hounds trotted obediently after him and sniffed the ground and the locals they passed.

Lisa glanced at the other woman's hat and gave her a thin smile. "Don't take it personally." She followed the path Johnny had already cleared through the lobby when everyone offended on the mixologist's behalf stepped away from him to let him pass.

The bounty hunter thumped both hands against the front door and shoved it open.

"Johnny."

"Lisa."

"Where are you going?"

He looked up and down the street, scowled furiously, and turned left up the sidewalk. "I aim to get myself a drink. I assume at least one liquor store in this damn city has what I'm lookin' for."

"You know what? I bet a different bar that isn't so…uh…"

"Hipstery?"

"Where?" Luther turned in a tight circle to scan the street and the sidewalk. Rex trotted after their master with his nose pressed against the concrete.

"I intended to say upscale, but sure." She jogged until she caught up with him. "Another bar might be the best idea."

"How's that?"

"I don't know. Maybe it's the fact that you look like you're about to explode if you don't blow off a little steam."

He stopped abruptly and turned toward her with a raised eyebrow. "Are you askin' me out to a bar, darlin'?"

"I'm saying let's explore the city and if we happen to find a bar, it's probably not the worst place we might find ourselves if you don't take it easy."

He glowered at her for a moment, then shrugged. "Yeah, I'll take you up on that."

Lisa chuckled with exasperation. "Great."

He pointed at her. "But it ain't a date."

"I never said it was."

"Uh-huh. And I'm sayin' it again." Johnny shoved his thumbs through his belt loops and glanced around the street. "Do you know any bars?"

"Nope. And that's the fun of it."

CHAPTER THIRTEEN

"Haven't we already been down this street?" Johnny turned in a slow circle on the sidewalk in Old Town.

"Are you serious?"

"'Course I am. Everything here looks the same—old, fallin' apart, and tryin' to be somethin' it ain't."

"Or this city is exactly what it's trying to be." Lisa grinned and kept moving up 3rd Avenue. "We'll find you something."

"We shoulda gone with the liquor store idea."

The streets were busier now beneath the long summer days and Portland's nightlife had only begun to stir. The hounds remained dutifully at their master's side, although they sniffed the sidewalk and jerked their heads up to greet every person who passed them.

"Hey, lady. Nice clown shoes."

"What is that guy wearing? Is that spandex everywhere?"

"Where does he keep his snacks? Ooh, this one smells like that shop with the treats lady. Hey, Rex. Look at *him*."

"Whoa." Rex chuckled. "Think he's got enough plants?"

"Hey, hey! A food truck!"

"Johnny! Can we—"

"No." Johnny snapped his fingers, and the hounds fell into line again.

"Oh, *wow*. Luther, someone painted a flying hound on that building."

"Well, it's not Balto, but I guess we can go pay tribute. How 'bout it, Johnny?"

"No." A tall man wearing platform combat boots and a long-sleeved fishnet shirt knocked against the dwarf's shoulder. "Hey, come on!" Johnny protested. "Do you see all this space? Pick a side, bud."

The stranger cast them a disdainful glance over his shoulder and strutted down the sidewalk with his hands thrust into the pockets of his way too tight jeans.

"Look at this. Complete chaos."

Lisa smirked at him. "Compared to what?"

"Everywhere else."

She laughed. "You think Portland is more chaotic than New York?"

"Without a doubt. Do you see that guy? Folks in New York learn to avoid each other in crowds. We have all the space in the world here and that asshole had to walk into me. I'm the only other guy on the sidewalk."

"But he didn't acknowledge you when you challenged him."

"That's my point!" He threw his hands in the air with a frustrated grunt. "New Yorkers are dependable. You shout one insult and they retaliate. It's called synergy, darlin'."

"I see."

"Then there's the... Aw, what the fuck?" Johnny stopped on the sidewalk and folded his arms to watch the latest display of Portland's weirdness.

A woman on a unicycle pedaled down the middle of the street, juggling bowling pins. She wore striped knee socks in bright colors, and a purple cape flowed behind her as she rolled down 3rd Avenue. Stuck under one arm was either a burning stick or an actual blowtorch, which pumped gusts of flame into the air behind her in rhythm to some hip-hop song that blasted from the Bluetooth speaker dangling at her hip.

"And what the hell is that supposed to be, huh?"

Lisa tilted her head and watched the unicyclist disappear behind the cars parked along the street. "It looked like a woman on a unicycle juggling and spraying flames. Don't tell me that's weirder than anything you've seen in NYC."

"It ain't the things. It's the folks. No one in New York would give two shits about somethin' like that. But here? Look at this. Everyone stops on the street to smile and cheer and film the damn thing with their stupid little camera phones. Jesus Christ, it's like they're all tourists in their own damn city."

"And there you've nailed the issue right on the head." Lisa fought back a laugh. "You don't like it when people notice things."

"What? Naw, you've got it all wrong, darlin'. I don't like tourists."

They kept walking through the crowded streets until they reached the hub of Portland's bar scene. Outside one establishment, a woman with long purple hair had set up her solo gig on the bar's outdoor patio and finished playing one of her songs on a ukulele. Those watching her clapped politely, punctuated by a few whistles.

"Thank you. Thank you. It means so much to be here, sharing this space with you all. I want to take this opportunity to remind you why I'm doing this. If you enjoy my art and what I have to create and offer, please think of the kittens."

"Huh?" Johnny turned to look over his shoulder as they passed the entrance to the bar.

"Don't play into the capitalist scheme. Don't let yourself be brainwashed. I don't want you to buy a CD from me, although you'll find them at all major retailers. I want you to adopt a kitten and I have four right here who came to the show with me, hoping for someone with a big heart and a love for felines to take them to their new, loving home. After the show, come say hi. Now, this next song is something I wrote while I was on a spiritual journey…"

"I don't fuckin' get it." Johnny shook his head and strode down the sidewalk.

"No one said Portland didn't have its unique character, Johnny."

"Why d'ya care so much what I think of this wackjob city, huh?"

Lisa bit her lip through a smile and studied the mural in the alley of a half-naked old woman feeding herself grapes. "Honestly? Because you're turning into an even bigger asshole than usual. All that negativity can get heavy very fast."

"Aw, not you too." The dwarf clenched his eyes shut. "What do ya want me to say, huh?"

"Maybe nothing." She grinned at him and despite his very real frustrations, the bounty hunter laughed gruffly.

"Johnny. Hey, Johnny." Luther stopped in front of a restaurant with its doors wide open and sniffed the air. "Tacos."

"No way. Johnny, *please*."

"Move along, boys." He snapped his fingers. "This ain't the place."

"Sir." A man in a full brown velvet suit who stood outside the next bar with a prohibition-era theme nodded at the dwarf. "I have to ask you to put your dogs on a leash while walking through downtown."

"Are you the leash police?"

The man laughed. "No, but we do have certain—"

"I'm not interested." He brushed past him, and the velvet-suited guardian stared after them in disbelief.

"If you're trying to avoid people paying attention to you, Johnny, you're accomplishing the exact opposite."

"We're fine. All I want is a drink. How hard is that?"

Lisa paused to study the signs pointing into an alley, where another neon sign blazed in the dark space between buildings. "Greeley's Dive. Hey, I think I found your kinda bar."

The bounty hunter stopped, took two steps back, and peered into the shadowed space. *Alley, neon sign, grungy brick wall, and stairs to a bar underground.* He sniffed. "Yeah, all right."

"One point for Agent Breyer." She stepped into the thoroughfare and waved him forward.

"Well, you don't have to make it a contest or nothin'."

"I think I do at this point. Finding a place that doesn't make you look like you're going to have a heart attack is a challenge I'm completely willing to take on."

"Uh-huh. I ain't decided nothin' yet, mind."

She stopped at the iron railing around the top of the staircase and gestured with a flourish. "After you."

Johnny whistled and looked at the hounds. "What're y'all doin' back there?"

Luther scrambled away from a puddle of thick, oily liquid on the ground and looked at the high walls rising around them. "Enjoying the view, Johnny."

Rex swallowed and stared at their master. "Isn't it—" A cellophane wrapper popped out of his mouth.

"Get on before I have to come drag you down." Johnny pointed down the stairs, and the hounds trotted obediently toward him.

"Told you he was paying attention."

"When did dwarves start growing eyes in the back of their heads?"

Luther gasped. "He can *do* that?"

"Y'all stay close, understand? I reckon these folks'll try to set y'all free out in the woods somewhere if they find you unleashed on your own in a bar."

"Oh, *that's* what free-range means."

Johnny snorted and pushed the door open into Greeley's

Dive. Lisa waited for the hounds to enter before she stepped inside.

The bar was filled to capacity. Posters in black, yellow, and red boasting band names Johnny could hardly read were plastered over the walls. Leather chairs had been moved to either side to allow for more standing space, and everyone crowded into the long, narrow room wore all black. They clapped and whistled at the musician at the far end.

All right. Now we're talkin'.

The bounty hunter moved toward the narrow horseshoe bar in the center of the room as the woman seated at the microphone with her guitar hooked up to an amp started her next song. The guitar part was okay—a little on the dark ballad side—but when the woman opened her mouth and started to sing, he shuddered.

"What is this?" He frowned at Lisa and thrust a hand toward the guitarist.

"Music." Agent Breyer didn't look too convinced by her statement either.

"It sounds like she's dyin' or some—"

"Shh!" A man with black makeup on his eyes and an eight-inch mohawk pressed a finger to his lips and scowled at them before he whispered, "We're here to listen."

"Uh…" With a snort, the bounty hunter continued toward the bar and had to climb onto one of the high stools to get his head above the edge. "You got Johnny Walker Black, don'tcha?"

The bartender turned his head slowly away from the musician to glance at him. "Yep. But keep it down, huh?"

"Sure, pal." He wrinkled his nose at all the grungy Portlanders who nodded their heads to the music and glared at him at the same time. *And they like this? It's nothin' but a new spin on death metal and it ain't gonna last. It sucks.*

"Anything for you?" the bartender whispered to Lisa.

"Gin and tonic. Thanks."

The man got to work on their drinks, and Johnny turned on the stool. "Someone needs to break it to her."

She grimaced. "Yep. I'm with you there. And I didn't think this place would be...like this."

"Surprise, surprise." He rested his forearms on the bar, and the bartender glanced impatiently at him before he placed both drinks on coasters.

"That'll be twelve dollars."

"Yep." He couldn't get to his wallet fast enough and dropped a ten and a five on the counter. "Keep the change."

"Thanks."

"Yeah, and while you're at it, go ahead and pour another one and keep 'em comin'—"

"Shh!" This time, more than one punk-dressed hipster turned toward the bounty hunter to shut him up.

"It's a *bar*!" Johnny shouted at them. "I thought at least you folks would understand how a bar's supposed to work."

He snatched his whisky on the rocks up and gulped half of it.

Beside the high bar stool, Luther uttered a high-pitched whine and pawed at his ears. "Johnny, make it stop."

"Yeah, my head's about to explode."

"Even the rabbits don't squeal this much when we wring their necks, Johnny."

Lisa faced the musician and sipped her drink with a grimace.

A woman with her head completely shaved joined the bartender inside the horseshoe to whisper something in his ear. The man approached Johnny and leaned over the bar to see Luther still pawing at his ears and Rex trying to bury his face against his brother's coat.

"I'm sorry, sir," he whispered. "You can't have your dogs in here."

The dwarf glared at him. "I must have missed the sign."

"We don't have a sign. It's merely implied."

"How the hell is that implied?"

"Shh!"

"Damnit!" He slapped the bar. "My hounds ain't leavin' until I do. And I ain't leavin' until I finish my drink."

The bartender and over-sensitive patrons glowered at him. He slurped the second half of his whisky noisily and stared in return.

"Okay, Johnny. You got your drink. Maybe we should—"

"Naw, this is fun, ain't it?"

"We're trying to *listen*," a woman with rainbow stripes painted on her face protested in a whisper-shout. "You're being *so* disrespectful right now."

"Better yet." Johnny yanked another fifty dollars out and slapped them on the bar. "Go on. Pour me another."

"Then you'll leave?"

"Sure."

The bartender gritted his teeth, did as he was asked quickly, and slid the second drink toward the bounty hunter. He picked up the fifty dollars and shook his head. "You gave me too much."

"Nope. That'll cover the rest of the bottle. I'm takin' it with me." He gestured for the guy to hurry, and the whisky bottle thunked onto the counter. Once he'd thrown the second drink back, he slammed the glass onto the wood, hopped off the stool with a loud thud, and snatched the bottle to take it with him. "Come on, boys. We got what we came for."

"Shh!"

The hounds cut through the crowd toward the door. "Time to go."

"Let us out, Johnny."

"Out, out, out, out!"

The musician sang one last high, warbling note. Johnny threw his head back and howled. The hounds followed suit without question as he shoved the door open and trudged onto the staircase landing.

Lisa reached the door as the musician said meekly into the

microphone, "Thank you so much for…being here. That's…uh, that's the end of my set."

The applause was minimal, to say the least, mostly because the crowd inside Greeley's Dive was busy glowering at Lisa and Johnny as they let the door swing shut behind them.

"Happy now?" she asked and hurried up the stairs with the help of the iron railing.

"You bet. At least in Brooklyn, they woulda thrown shit and chased us out."

"And that's supposed to be better how?"

Johnny reached the top of the stairs, turned to face her, and spread his arms in a dramatic gesture. "It's more fun."

CHAPTER FOURTEEN

"So we'll go to the hotel with your bottle?" Lisa studied a rack of handmade postcards outside a lingerie shop, then hurried forward to keep pace with the bounty hunter.

"That's all I wanted, darlin'. If Nelson fucks up like that again, I ain't gonna be so easy to persuade onto another case."

"Yes, it was so easy." She shook her head. "Please tell me you'll eat something with your whisky dinner."

"This is for the whole stay." He lifted the bottle and wiggled his eyebrows. "Don't you worry yourself now. What you saw the other day was a dwarf reevaluatin' his take on a decade and a half. Now, it's done."

"All right. I can give you the benefit of the doubt on that one. I merely don't wanna find you passed out in your hotel room in the morning unable to walk straight."

Johnny snorted. "Come on. That ain't happened to me in… shit. It's been fifteen years." *And it's not what I need to be thinkin' 'bout now anyway.*

"Okay. So what time do you—"

A shriek rose from up the street. "No!" a woman shouted. "Give it back, it's *mine*—hey! Mikey, you're *hurting* me!"

Something banged against hollow metal, and Johnny growled. "Hell no. Hold my bottle."

"What?"

"Take it!"

Lisa snatched the bottle from him and saved it from slipping out of her hands before she raced after him. The dwarf drew his utility knife and flipped it open as the screams rose again from two alleys down.

"Right behind you, Johnny!" Rex called with a sharp bark.

"Those damn hamsters won't get away with it," Luther added.

He skidded to a stop at the alley entrance and saw exactly what he expected—a dirty, skinny man in soiled clothes pinned a woman up against the dumsper along the brick wall. He fumbled at something in the woman's hands and tried to pry it from her grasp as he hurled her back against the dumpster again with a hollow clang.

"I said get *off*!" the woman screamed and slapped his face with far more force than her tiny frame seemed capable of.

"You heard her, Mikey," Johnny muttered.

The assailant lurched away from her and stared at the dwarf with his knife out and two snarling hounds at his side. "Mind your own business, man."

The woman leapt at him and delivered another surprisingly strong slap. He grunted and stumbled back across the alley and into the opposite wall.

It gave Johnny enough time to see that the woman was as dirty and skinny as the man was. Her hair was matted in an unbrushed mess around the dirt smears on her cheeks and her baggy sweatshirt hung past her wrists, even in the summer heat. *Damn. It's not a mugging. At least not the kind either of them didn't get themselves into.*

"You little bitch," Mikey snapped. "If you weren't already in the gutter, I'd throw you there myself."

"Screw you!"

"Hand it over, Janice. You know that's all there is right now."

"No!"

Mikey lunged toward her and tried to pin her against the dumpster again. He barely succeeded and only with the full weight of his body behind it, which wasn't much.

"All right, cut it out." Johnny flipped his knife shut and returned it to his belt as he stalked down the alley. "I said stop."

"Give it!" Mikey shook Janice by both wrists, but she clenched her hands shut, shook her head vigorously, and groaned.

"No. No. I can't. I need it more."

"You already *had*—"

"Y'all need to quit it." Johnny caught the man by the back of his dirty jacket—which felt more like oilcloth but he assumed it was originally ordinary denim—and hauled Mikey away. The man's grip broke around her wrists. He stumbled, lost his balance, and landed on his ass with a grunt. "Janice—"

"How do you know my name?" The woman stared at Johnny, clutched both fists to her chest, and turned away from him. "I don't know you. I never seen you before."

"I'm the guy keepin' your friend from bustin' your head open against that dumpster. He's not much of a friend anyway, if you ask me, but we're all workin' with what we got, right?"

"What do you want?"

He opened his hand and raised an eyebrow.

"No. Uh-uh. It's *mine!*"

"Yeah, you said that. Come on, darlin'. In my hand."

"Johnny?" Lisa asked at the mouth of the alley, her right hand crossed over her body to rest cautiously on the grip of her service weapon in its shoulder holster. "What's going on?"

"I'll tell y'all what's goin' on." He held the wide-eyed woman's gaze and nodded slowly. "You see them hounds behind me? If you run, darlin', you'll be at the wrong end of a couple of coonhounds trained to bring down their mark, you understand?"

"Johnny, what's wrong with her?" Luther padded slowly

forward behind his master. "She one of the crazies seeing demons?"

"That goes for you too, Mikey." Johnny snapped his fingers and pointed at the man grimacing on the ground. Rex immediately headed toward the guy, who scrambled away until he was stopped by the alley wall.

"You can't," Janice whispered.

"You drop it there or I'll take it from you." He wiggled his open hand. "And I ain't as easy to slap around as *he* is."

"You… What are you?" She looked warily at him. "You a cop or something?"

"FBI," Lisa said. "And I wouldn't test your luck with him if I were you."

"Fuck." It wasn't clear whether Mikey said it because he thought they'd been caught or because Rex was inching slowly closer.

Janice scrunched her face up, uttered an indecisive moan, and slapped her hand onto Johnny's open palm.

The dwarf caught her wrist to make sure she emptied everything into his hand before he released her. "Good choice."

"Man, you can't take it." She wrapped her arms around herself and bounced up and down in her hole-ridden sneakers. "We need it."

"No, you don't." Johnny looked at the small plastic baggie filled with a thin spread of brown powder. When he flipped it, a sharp hiss escaped him and he scowled at the Red Boar stamp he'd seen on the drug baggies in Manhattan. *Is this fuckin' shit all the way out here now too?*

"Come on, man." Mikey sniffed and ran a soiled sleeve under his nose before he scratched the back of his neck. "You have no idea what you're—"

"Where'd you get this?" The bounty hunter shook the baggie at him. Both addicts stared at the brown powder in the clear plastic. "You're clear-headed enough to fight each other. I know y'all understand the question."

"If...if we tell you, will you give it back?" The man's eye twitched as he glanced at Janice.

"Sure. Tell me exactly where."

"Back up that way." The woman leaned toward the head of the alley and pointed left. "Toward 11th Avenue."

"I said exactly, darlin'."

"W-wait. Wait!" Mikey clenched his eyes shut and muttered to himself. "We got it from our regular guy but he moved. Now he's up on...shit. He's up on Park and Salmon."

"Yeah!" Janice nodded vigorously. "That's where he is. Every day. Big guy in a—"

"Shut up." The man glared at Johnny. "That's what you wanted, right?"

"Exactly what I wanted." The dwarf sniffed. "Much appreciated."

"So you'll give it back now?" The woman stepped tentatively toward him and jolted when Luther growled softly. "Our stuff?"

"I lied." With a grimace, he pocketed the baggie.

"Hey, you can't do that, man."

"Watch me." He started to turn, then stopped and pointed at each of them in turn. "Y'all will thank me for this one day. Don't go back to that corner, understand?"

Despite the terrified, deflated stares that were the only response from both of them, he nodded and headed toward the mouth of the alley.

"Shit. Fuck. *Fuck!*" Mikey rocked on the ground, not oblivious to the coonhound standing in front of him.

"We *can't* go back!" Janice shrieked after the dwarf. "It took us two days to scrounge up enough for that bag, and you took everything we have!"

Johnny stopped beside Lisa and studied both ends of the street.

Agent Breyer bit her bottom lip, her hand still resting on her weapon, and frowned in sympathy at the addicts falling into despair at the loss of their stash. "We should help them, Johnny. Take them to get some help or something. This isn't—"

"They gotta help themselves, darlin'. That's the way it works." He cleared his throat and headed down the sidewalk.

"Johnny." She turned after him. "Aren't you gonna call your dogs?"

He didn't answer her.

"Don't worry about us, lady," Luther said as he paced in front of Janice when she sank to the ground and began to cry. "Johnny says we're on 'em, we're on 'em until he says stop."

"Got 'em right where you want 'em, Johnny!" Rex yipped at Mikey. The man jolted where he sat but didn't try to get away. Instead, he lowered his head and scratched vigorously through his greasy hair with both hands. "Damn. Gotta say, though, Johnny, these hamsters stink."

"Yeah, no wonder you don't want 'em around."

Johnny heard his hounds clearly enough in his head and didn't bother trying to reply.

Lisa stared at him and her frown deepened when the dwarf stopped in front of the closest food truck and held up two fingers. When he returned to the alley, he had a curved paper tray of street tacos in each hand. Rex and Luther whipped their heads toward him as he stepped into the alley, their tails wagging.

"Yes! Way to go, Johnny."

"I *knew* we'd start getting treats for doing what we already do anyway."

He approached Janice first and extended one of the trays toward her. "Come on now, darlin'. It's hard to eat when you're cryin' like that."

"What?" She looked up, her dirt-stained cheeks smeared with her tears, and sniffed. "For real?"

"Uh-huh."

"Quit playing this bad-cop, good-cop bullshit," Mikey muttered where he continued to rock and scratch his head with both hands. "We gave you what you wanted. So either arrest us or leave us the fuck alone."

"I'm givin' you what you *need*, Mikey." Johnny stopped in front of the man and held out the other tray of tacos. "So quit whinin' and take the stuff that ain't more likely to kill ya."

The man finally stopped his nervous withdrawal tics and looked at the dwarf and the tacos. He licked his lips.

So did Rex. "If he doesn't want it, Johnny…"

"Thanks." Mikey took the food and didn't touch it until the bounty hunter turned and headed out of the alley. When he did, he practically inhaled the food.

"Aw, *man*." Rex sniffed at the crumbs falling around the man's feet. "We were so close."

Luther shifted keenly in front of Janice, waiting for her to spill something big enough to grab and run. "Come on, lady. No, no. Not that bite. It was about to fall—"

Johnny whistled shrilly. "Let's go!"

With a final longing glance at the street tacos, the hounds turned and padded out of the alley.

Lisa forced herself to turn away from the homeless addicts eating a free meal and jogged to catch up. "I thought you said they have to help themselves."

Johnny shrugged. "That ain't the same as showin' a little kindness. Hey."

The couple looked quickly at him.

"There's an inpatient rehab center on Washington. They got open beds and work with self-pay patients."

"Uh…yeah." Mikey shoved the rest of his last taco into his mouth. "Yeah, okay."

Johnny nodded and continued down the sidewalk.

"How do you know that?" Lisa asked, glancing behind her as the hounds caught up.

"I saw it on a billboard. They're all over town. Now, where's my whisky?"

She scoffed and glanced at the half-full bottle in her hand. "Doesn't that feel a little hypocritical?"

"Nope. I ain't sold all my shit and put myself on the street for that. And I ain't shakin'."

With a shrug to concede the point, Lisa handed it to him. She smiled when he held the bottle at his side and didn't open it on the street.

CHAPTER FIFTEEN

They ordered room service for dinner and Johnny had to order a second time because the portions were way too small. When he called the front desk to ask what the problem was, a woman with a perky voice told him, "We have two of the finest chefs in Oregon, Mr. Walker—"

"Johnny. And I ain't talkin' 'bout the chefs. I'm talkin' 'bout the size of these meals."

"We serve locally sourced, skillfully crafted artisanal fare at this hotel. You're welcome to place another order for room service. If you'd like to sample some of our—"

"Nope. Thanks." He dropped the hotel phone onto the receiver and snorted. "For nothin'. I'm 'bout fed up with all this. Ar-*tee*-sinal. What is that?"

Lisa set her empty plate on the room service tray and opened an Old Town Brewery Pillowfist IPA she'd taken from his mini-fridge. "It means made in a traditional way."

"Traditional? Any tradition bent on starvin' a person and callin' it food needs to die out with the rest."

She took a long sip of beer and grinned appreciatively. "Hey, this is good."

"Don't even try it." He lifted his coffee mug of whisky from the nightstand and took a sip. "I ain't lookin' for none of that."

"You won't know unless you try—" She caught his warning glare and shrugged. "Or not."

"Johnny, where'd you hide the rest of the steak?" Luther licked the plate on the floor and pushed it inch by inch across the carpet. "There's usually more."

"Yeah, I'm all for saving some for later, but this is more like what we'd get later."

"Quit yer whinin'."

Lisa choked on her beer. *"Excuse* me?"

"Not you, darlin'." He paused. "I'm talkin' to the voices in my head."

Rex sniggered and stretched on his belly. "That's one way to put it, Johnny."

"Is this it? Huh? You finally gonna tell her?" Luther stared at his master and sat in anticipation.

Lisa set her beer down and turned to face the bed. "Do you... hear voices, or—"

"'Course not." The dwarf waved her off and sucked what little remained of his already pitifully sized dinner out of his teeth.

"Nope." Luther chuffed and slid his front paws forward until he stretched beside his brother. "No dice."

"It's a figure of speech, ain't it?"

"Not for everyone."

"Don't start on all that with me now, all right? We got bigger things to turn our minds to." Johnny shifted on the bed and reached into his pocket for the baggie of drugs with the red boar stamp on it. "Like this lil' bastard right here."

"That looks like heroin."

"It probably is." he stared at the red stamp on the small square of plastic, then dangled it toward Lisa for her to see. "Guess who?"

"No." She leaned forward in the armchair and squinted at the baggie. "Is the same as those in New York?"

"Exactly the same, even down the type of bag." He gritted his teeth. "The Red Boar has his distribution ring all over the damn country now. If it wasn't already here two months ago, he has some damn quick circuits under his thumb."

"Yeah, that doesn't seem…likely." Lisa picked her tablet up and tapped on it.

"But this shit made its way to Portland one way or the other, which means his operation's a helluva lot bigger than your people knew fifteen years ago. Bigger than I estimated, too."

"And that'll make it even harder to pin him down. He could be anywhere, not only New York."

"Uh-huh." Johnny slid off the bed and headed to the bathroom. He flushed all the brown powder down the toilet, rinsed the baggie out in the sink, and returned to the bed as he waved the red-stamped plastic around to dry.

"Have you found anything in that fancy-pad?"

Lisa ignored the moniker and scrolled slowly with a scowl on her face. "I already knew the drug problem here was bad. There are many different dealers on the streets, and the bags with the red boar are merely a tiny part of it—only two mentions of it in a sea of…well, hundreds."

He snorted and sat on the bed. "Merely another brand in a flooded market. That ain't helpful at all."

"Maybe not right now. But we know someone in Portland has connections to the Red Boar. It's a start."

"I have enough starts, darlin'. What I'm aimin' for is to finish it."

"We will."

CHAPTER SIXTEEN

The next morning, Lisa knocked on his hotel-room door at a quarter after seven and was greeted by a groggy, glaring Johnny, his auburn hair sticking up in all directions.

"What?" he demanded roughly.

She thrust the to-go cup of coffee toward him and studied him with a grin. "You owe me one."

"Hold on now—" He grunted when she brushed past him into the room, then shut the door and ran a hand through his hair. "It ain't even seven thirty yet."

"It's close enough. Take the coffee, Johnny."

His scowl deepened. "Where did you get that?"

"The hotel bar brews its own coffee."

"Uh-uh. Nope." He gestured a vehement refusal. "I ain't interested in anythin' that mixolojackass did to a good ol' cup o' joe."

"Trust me. You're interested in this."

Grumbling, he took the cup and popped the plastic lid off. He sniffed the steam, took a tentative sip, and widened his eyes. "Fuck."

"Right?"

He slurped a little more. "There ain't nothin' fancy done to it?"

"It's regular Portland java. Black."

"That makes me hate him even more."

Lisa snorted and took a white paper bag out from under her arm. "And I brought breakfast—or at least a start at breakfast. If we need to, we can go to one of the dozens of places here in the city."

Johnny closed his eyes for his next sip of coffee, then muttered, "Is this you tryin' to get me to like this place?"

"Why would I do that? You've made your mind up. Here." She handed him a smaller brown bag.

"What's this?"

"For Rex and Luther. I know to not even ask, so *you* can give it to them."

Both hounds' heads popped up over the far side of the bed. "Did she just call us by name?"

"Treats, Johnny?"

The dwarf ripped the bag open and shook out two smaller than average round biscuits. He frowned. "Biscuits."

"*Dog* biscuits. Cute, right?"

"Sure. I'm merely missin' the fried egg and sausage patty."

Rex licked his muzzle. "Sounds good to me."

"Darlin', I could market my old shoes as top-of-the-line dog toys in this city and probably make three times what I paid for 'em. You got ripped off."

Lisa set the extra pastry on the desk and bit into hers. "You are even more cynical."

"It's bread."

"Trust me, Johnny, it's for the dogs. The hotel bakery outsources stuff from this baked good-for-canines company. I thought I'd offer Rex and Luther the same courtesy of eating with us before we head out."

"It ain't a courtesy." Johnny wrinkled his nose at the biscuits. "They *have* to eat."

"You know what I mean. Oh, you probably don't want to—"

He bit into the biscuit, chewed once, then lowered his head toward his hand and spat it all out again. She almost choked on her scone at his disgusted grimace as he wiped soggy chunks of dog biscuit off his beard. "All right. I'll give you that one."

"So...Johnny." Luther padded around the bed toward his master. "How about a little—"

"Snooze, you lose!" Rex yipped and raced past his brother to snatch up the uneaten biscuit Johnny dropped on the floor. "Oh, and you *seriously* lost out on this one, Luther."

"Johnny. Johnny. You're not gonna eat it all, are you?"

As he snatched his coffee to wash out the taste, the dwarf lowered the other biscuit in his hand absently.

"Yeah. Yeah. Yeah." Luther's rear end wobbled as he waited for the treat to drop within mouth range. He gobbled the whole thing in one swallow and licked Johnny's hand until the dwarf finally pulled it away again. "You are the best."

"These *biscuit* are the best." Rex grunted and licked the crumbs off the carpet.

"Or maybe she's the best. I don't even care. This is the best."

The dwarf wiped his palm briskly on his jeans and sat on the edge of the bed again. "Remind me which human nutjob we were gonna go see first."

Lisa licked crumbs off her fingers. "You know you can't say stuff like that when we're there talking to them, right?"

"I can't, huh?"

"No, Johnny, I didn't mean it like that—"

"I'm yankin' your chain, darlin'." He pointed at the huge pastry on the desk. "Is this one mine?"

"Yep. I'm serious, though. Please try to be...you know, the opposite of brutally insulting."

Johnny smirked at the hounds. "She thinks I'm all curmudgeon and no heart, boys."

"Sure, Johnny."

"You bet."

"Got any more biscuits?"

Some loyalty. He bit into the pastry and squinted. *Now this is a meal.*

"I didn't say that." Lisa popped the last bite of scone into her mouth and nursed her coffee. "I know there's at least *one* thread of compassion in you. I'm merely asking you to use it. Far more than normal."

"I'll be fine." He shook the pastry at her. "Exactly like this—hey."

Both hounds lunged for the crumbs at his feet.

"Y'all better git." He waved them away and scattered more crumbs. They only half-obeyed. "All right. The boys love the treats, I'll give you that. But it's wipin' their brain cells out so that's the first and last time."

"No problem." She stood from the armchair and retrieved her tablet. "They cost more than both our pastries anyway."

"You shittin' me?"

"Are you ready to go?"

He shook his head and took his duffel bag from the closet. "Let me get a few things together. Then we can go have a chat with…"

"Christopher Folsum."

"Yeah. Him."

Lisa's eyes widened when he retrieved his utility belt strapped with at least a dozen explosive disks. "Oh, come on. Do you honestly need that?"

"You never know." Johnny strapped the belt around his waist and fastened it. "It's stupid to go in unarmed when you're facin' a demon, ain't it?"

"Because of the *demons*. Sure." She sipped her coffee and headed to the door.

Christopher Folsum lived twenty minutes away on foot, and Johnny finally consented to leave the SUV in the garage and walk there. After three minutes on the sidewalk, he wished he hadn't.

"It never ends, does it?"

"What's that?"

"All...this." He gestured at the busy street as they turned the corner and headed up toward Goose Hollow again. "Look. You got artsy fartsies paintin'—what is that? Coffee beans? Then that dude in the clogs yodelin' over there. Like full-on yodelin', and he thinks that'll draw folks into his shop."

"It's a good marketing tactic."

"Yeah, for yodelers."

Lisa perked up as they approached the next shop. "Hey, look at this. Bite the Bullet. That sounds cool."

Johnny's glance through the window told him all he needed to know. "That ain't what you think it is, darlin'."

"What do you mean? It's a—" She pulled away from the window and turned stiffly to continue down the sidewalk. "Never mind."

"Hey, Johnny." Luther stopped beside the shop to lick a stain on the window. "What's with all the underwear and strappy things in there?"

"They look like dog harnesses," Rex added and trotted past his brother.

"Huh."

The blocks faded from shops into houses renovated to be shops and eventually into purely residential neighborhoods. Johnny exhaled a heavy breath and straightened to place his hands on his hips. "Next time, darlin', you oughta check the geography with the map. I get enough runaround as it is. I don't need to pile on extra while we're workin' a case."

Lisa passed him at a steady pace up the steep hill lined with brightly painted single-family homes. "My bad." She flashed him an energetic grin, not even a little winded by the climb. "Next time, I'll check."

Yeah, and she won't tell me on purpose. With a grunt, he hurried after her again and managed to force his breathing to remain mostly calm.

"Whoa, check out these houses." Rex trotted casually up the hill. "Luther, how many rodents you think we could sniff out under those porches, huh? Like the rotting ones with all the moss."

"A lot. Maybe a whole den of hamsters, too."

"Yeah, then Johnny'd be *really* proud."

"Okay." Lisa stopped once the top of the hill leveled out and pointed up ahead. "Folsum's house should be the third one down. So do you want to do the talking or should I?"

Johnny darted her a sidelong glance. "Is that a rhetorical question?"

"Probably." A breeze blew over the hilltop, rustled the lush green branches hanging overhead, and cast their massive shadows across the road and the old, foliage-laden Portland front yards. A huge tree creaked as it swayed. Luther stopped to lift a leg on the thick bark, then padded along happily and stared into the fluttering branches.

Rex snorted. "Showoff."

"How about I start," Lisa said, "and if there's anything I leave out in the process, you can—"

"No. No, no. No!" A man's voice carried toward them from up the street. "You can't make me!"

"It sounds like one of the neighbors is havin' a little upset."

Lisa frowned and quickened her pace. "Or Christopher Folsum is."

They closed in on the man's house and the top of his driveway, which dipped down the other side of the hill into a thickly wooded yard with the house and garage built off to the side.

"Ha. You…you think you can take everything from me, huh?" the man shouted, followed by an admittedly mad-sounding cackle. "Think again. You *lose* this time. 'Cause you know what?

Where I'm going…ha. Well, let's see you try to follow me there, huh?"

A loud snap and choking noises issued up the hill from the garage, joined by what sounded much like a rope rubbing on timber although they were too far to tell.

"Shit." Johnny raced down the steep driveway, Lisa on his heels with her firearm drawn. He skidded across the rough asphalt and turned to see Christopher Nelson hanging by a rope from one of the garage's thick beams. A second later, he flicked his utility knife open, caught the point of the blade between his fingers, and threw it at the highest point of the rope where the most force was centered with the intention to weaken it. His blade sliced through three-quarters of the weave and clattered against the far wall and Folsum lowered by six inches. The man spun as his legs kicked beneath him. "Fuck."

"Johnny!"

"I know!" The dwarf snatched up the chair that had been kicked out and shoved it under the flailing legs. He stepped onto it quickly, slid one arm around the man to ease the full weight off the rope, and grasped the knot above his neck. With a grunt of effort, he gave it a sharp, powerful jerk.

The remainder of the cord snapped and they both fell when the chair gave out beneath them and they landed in a pile. The bounty hunter scrambled to right himself and immediately grappled with the rope around the man's neck. A series of coughs and splutters followed as the homemade noose loosened. Folsum dragged in a huge, rasping gasp and flopped on the floor to stare at the frayed end of the rope tied around the beam.

"Come on, man." Johnny patted his cheeks in what he hoped didn't feel like battery to the guy. "That ain't the way, man. It ain't the way to handle it."

Folsum swallowed thickly, felt the raw line around his neck, and began to sob.

"Oh, shit."

Lisa had already dialed nine-one-one and gave the emergency dispatcher the address. "Yeah, we'll stick around. Thanks." She slid her phone into her pocket and stepped tentatively into the garage.

The man on the floor sobbed incoherently, and Johnny sat back on his heels with a sigh.

"Is he okay?" she asked

"Well he's alive but I wouldn't call this okay." The dwarf gestured toward him. "All right, brother. You...you don't have to—"

"You shouldn't have done that." Folsum clenched his eyes shut and rocked slowly. "Why did you do that? I didn't ask for help."

"Christopher?" Lisa stepped closer and lowered her head to catch his attention. "It's Christopher, right? Or do you go by Chris?"

The man merely moaned again before his chest jerked with sob after hopeless sob.

"Listen, I know you feel there's no other way out of this. But taking your own life..." She squatted a foot behind Johnny and studied the man. "That's not the answer."

"You don't understand." Folsum thumped a limp arm against the floor. "It's my *only* way. I can't...I can't keep doing this."

"That's how it feels right now, but you can't give up before—"

"No, you don't get it." He gasped through his sobs and propped himself on one elbow to squint at her through his tears. "I love my life. I truly do. I was happy. It's *her* leaving me with no choice. Do you hear me? She wants to take everything from me. And if I'm still here, she wins."

Lisa and Johnny exchanged a concerned glance.

"Who?" he asked.

"The *demon*, man. It's all her!"

Shit. This guy's nowhere near well enough to answer questions now. The agent sighed inwardly.

"The paramedics are on their way," she said softly. "When the ambulance gets here, they'll help you get back on track."

"That's never gonna happen. I can't let her win." The man began to weep again and raised both hands to cover his face.

She nudged Johnny in the side and nodded at Folsum's left forearm. Immediately below his elbow was the thin oval mark with three diagonal lines slashed through it.

The bounty hunter grimaced and nodded slowly. "Now, I don't give my word on a whim, Folsum. You hear me?"

The man continued to cry.

"But Agent Breyer and I aim to get this...demon, whoever she is. We'll make her stop."

"You don't think I already *tried* that?" Folsum shrieked. "I don't have anything left. Nothing. I can't *do* this—"

"Yeah, well, you don't have to, brother." With his grim expression schooled into what he hoped was reassuring, he patted the man's shoulder with as much certainty as he could manage. When he received no reaction, he pushed to his feet and crossed the garage to retrieve his knife.

Rex and Luther sat at the entrance, their attention fixed on the man who continued to sob and run his fingers over the raw ring around his neck. Luther uttered a low whine. "You ever see someone look so unhappy to be saved?"

"Nope. Good thing Johnny knows how to throw a knife." They both looked at the severed rope that dangled from the garage ceiling, then at the other end that lay in a loose coil at Folsum's side. "Hey, look. Free rope. Wanna play tug-o-war?"

Johnny snapped his fingers and pointed at them. "Don't even think about it."

"Okay, okay. Jeez."

"Only trying to lighten the mood, Johnny."

Lisa approached the dwarf as the rising wail of sirens drew closer. "It seems to me like they're still behaving well."

For a moment, he considered telling her about the collars. *For what, huh? So she can say you're hallucinatin' and join Nelson in his campaign to make me an alcoholic?*

"Yeah, it seems like it." Johnny gestured toward the hounds as he closed his knife and hooked it onto his belt. "But they're my hounds. I can tell when they're thinkin' mischief. It's in the eyes."

"Right." She turned to study them speculatively.

Luther's tail thumped against the concrete and Rex's mouth popped open so his tongue lolled from the side of it as he panted. "Good goin', Johnny."

"Yeah, now she *seriously* thinks you're crazy."

CHAPTER SEVENTEEN

When the paramedics arrived, together with two Portland PD officers, a sobbing, raving Christopher Folsum was guided into the back of the ambulance, examined quickly, and taken to the hospital to have tests run as well as a psychiatric evaluation.

Lisa had no problem taking the lead in the discussion with the two officers and provided her statement as a witness and as a Federal Agent.

"What were you doing out here at Mr. Folsum's home?" Officer Millbrook asked.

"Coming to speak to the victim."

"You know he's one of the people who's been going off about this so-called Portland demon, right?" Officer Hennessey added.

"Yes. That is why we're here."

"Agent Breyer, these are all cases that engender concern, but there's no physical evidence of wrongdoing or that any of these individuals are actual victims."

She raised her chin obstinately and glanced at the officers in turn. "And that's why the case was sent to us. Are you familiar with the Bureau's Bounty Hunter Division?"

Millbrook grunted. "I've heard of it but we never had to call your people to this city as far as I know."

Hennessey sniffed and fisted both hands on his hips. "So you're the agent on this case, then. The one the Bureau thinks includes victims and...what? Some kind of magic?"

"That's right."

"Then I assume he's the bounty hunter." All three of them turned to where they'd left Johnny at the bottom of the driveway. Now, however, he had finished scouring Christopher Folsum's garage and strode across the concrete floor toward the door into the house. "Wait. Sir? Sir!"

"You can't go in there until we've finished—"

"Watch me." He grunted and waved a hand dismissively before he opened the door. "I have a license."

"Wait up, Johnny." The hounds trotted after him.

"I don't think those cops like hounds."

The door closed behind them.

The officers grumbled and shared a frustrated glance. "Do you take full responsibility for that guy?"

Lisa frowned at them. "That's my job. And while the attempted suicide remains under your jurisdiction, Folsum's house and any evidence we find that helps us solve this federal case falls under mine."

"Yeah, yeah. Nothing we haven't heard before." Millbrook thumped the back of his hand against his partner's arm and nodded toward their squad car. "I think we're done here."

"I think you're grasping at straws on this one, Agent Breyer," Hennessey muttered.

"Well, that's why they sent us in." She gave him a small, tight smile. "So you let us worry about the straws and the magic, huh?"

The officer scratched the back of his head, then turned to join his partner in the squad car. "That's a shitload more paperwork than I wanted to see on my desk today."

Millbrook started the engine. "It always is when the feds show up. There's no use in hoping for a good day now."

She watched the officers turn in the wide drive before she hurried down the steep hill toward the house. As she walked through the garage, she glanced at the frayed end of Folsum's homemade noose that still dangled from the beam. *This could have gone better. And it could have been so much worse.*

When she stepped into the house, the smell of mildew and rotting food hit her instantly. She wrinkled her nose, covered her mouth, and stepped slowly down the narrow hallway littered with dirty clothes. With her free hand, she groped in the back pocket of her jeans and retrieved the surgical gloves she'd stashed there. Unfortunately, she had to remove the hand from her mouth to slide one pair onto her hands. "Johnny?" she asked and waved the second pair as if that might conjure her partner.

"Livin' room," he muttered from her right.

Lisa moved the other way down the hall and stopped abruptly. The dwarf stood in the center of the room, his thumbs hooked through his belt loops, and studied the main wall in front of him.

"Oh, my God." With a deepening frown, she approached him slowly. Her foot kicked an empty beer can and it skittered across the hardwood floor littered with packaged food wrappers, empty cracker boxes, and open pizza boxes with most of the pizza uneaten and growing an impressive colony of mold.

Rex sniffed the spinning beer can when it slowed to a stop, then snorted and shook his head. "Not into beer."

"Hey, Rex." Luther sniffed the floor and followed the trail to an open can of Spaghetti-O's still half full. "I think I hit the jackpot."

Johnny snapped his fingers. "Y'all stay outta things, understand?"

"Aw, come on, Johnny. The guy's not gonna miss this stuff. It's not like he planned to come back inside for leftovers."

"Yeah, look at everything. It's all as ripe as hell."

"Too ripe."

"Just the way we like it."

With a grunt, he turned to glare at his hounds. They both hunched almost on their bellies and returned his stare. Luther inched closer to the Spaghetti-O's can.

"I said no."

"Fine…" Luther took a final sniff, padded toward his brother, and sat, licking his muzzle. "Party pooper."

"What is all this?" Lisa asked as she moved beside the dwarf to study the wall. When she extended the second pair of gloves toward him, he glanced down and shook his head. She returned them to her back pocket with a frown.

"If you were lookin' for evidence Folsum didn't lose his mind, this ain't it."

The entire wall was plastered with different sizes and colors of loose paper. Most of them were regular white printer paper, but a good portion was on lined notebook paper, sheets from a legal pad, graph paper, and eventually, pages ripped from magazines. Every single one of them had a drawing in thick, dark lines —pen, pencil, or sharpie—of the same round, dark image.

"These have to mean something." Lisa folded her arms and studied the drawings. "What do they look like to you?"

"Are you fishin', or do you have an actual idea?" Johnny darted her a sidelong glance. "I ain't an art critic, darlin'."

"You don't have to be for this." She stepped closer to the wall and her shoe crunched on a slice of dried bread that crumbled to dust beneath her. "Those look like tunnels."

"Huh." He narrowed his eyes to focus better. "You know, I think you're right. The question now is whether Folsum's artistic streak is part of the crazy or part of the magic."

Lisa stepped beside the armrest of the couch to move closer to the wall but her attention was drawn to the furniture itself. "Even if the report hadn't said it, Johnny, Folsum wasn't always crazy. It looks like he was successful as a contracted carpenter in Portland."

He stared at the couch. "You mean the nice house and all."

"Yeah. If you ignore the crumbs and the beer stains and the streaks of—what is that?"

"Cheeto dust, lady." Rex licked his muzzle.

"Uh-oh, Johnny. Red flag right there. She's never had Cheetos?"

"Neither have we."

"Yeah, but I know 'em when I smell 'em."

"Whatever he had on hand and he couldn't be bothered to clean up," Johnny muttered and ignored the canine peanut gallery. "On account of all his art."

"Well, it certainly looks like that took over at one point, yeah." Lisa looked at the drawings pinned, tacked, and taped to the wall. "Anyone else would characterize this as obsessive behavior."

"Ya think?"

"Johnny—look." She pointed at one of the drawings in front of her. "There's something else in this one."

He took one step forward and squinted to study it more intently. "It looks like a person."

"That's what I thought too."

"And there's another one 'bout two feet above the back of the couch. Dead center."

Lisa climbed onto the sofa and held her arms out at her sides for balance so she wouldn't have to touch anything unnecessarily. "That one?"

"Yep. The person's bigger in that. Folsum ain't one for details, is he?"

"The tunnels are more detailed than merely scribbles. That's for sure. Hey, see if you can find any others with a person. Even only a silhouette like this."

"All right." Johnny marched across the floor but was careful to step over the piles of rotting food and crumpled paper towels the man had discarded before he simply used the couch instead.

The hounds watched their master cross the room dutifully but made no more smart-ass remarks.

"Yep. One right there." The bounty hunter pointed at a large tunnel drawing tacked up too high for him to reach. "There's no real detail. It looks like one of them shadowy figures in the paranormal flicks."

"You mean *Paranormal Activity?*"

"Ain't they all the same?"

With a shrug, Lisa hopped off the couch to approach him and examine it for herself. "Yep. And there's another one way up high. None of them look any more detailed than the others."

"This one has more." Johnny pointed at a smaller drawing at the far-left side of the wall. "See the stone detail? And what's that? Some kinda handrail? And a broken wooden sign behind it, maybe."

"Truly?" She joined him to study the drawing. "Wow. Maybe he did have some talent."

"Eh...I think that's a fairly subjective assessment." The dwarf sniffed and scowled at the images. "Everythin' on this side looks like the inside of a pro's sketchbook."

"And the drawings on the right are more muddled. I know." She stepped back to look at the entire wall. "So either he started with the crappy drawings, tacked them up as he went, and produced better and better quality until the very end on the left—"

"Or he went in the other direction and lost his skillset with his marbles."

"Except the dark figure in the corner hasn't changed at all." She smirked and shook a finger at the wall. "No, I think he put these up from right to left. Everything's muddled and almost crazed on the right. Erratic."

"Yeah. Like somethin' a crazy person would draw after they

went crazy."

"Usually. If it weren't for that dark outline that looks like a person, I'd probably agree with you."

"Drawin' folk without faces don't make a person less insane, darlin'."

"It doesn't make them more insane, either. This fits the profile of someone with obsessive tendencies centered around one thing —like a nightmare or a dream. Sometimes, it could be a real person, like their face or their belongings."

Johnny snorted. "Are you 'bout to tell me you're a federal psychologist too? 'Cause whatever you're seein', I ain't."

"Okay. I worked with a criminal psychologist before I officially passed my exams. Don't ask me how long ago that was. Trust me, it was long enough."

He smirked at her. "All right."

"One of the patients we worked with was a six-year-old girl who… Well, let's say she needed to work through considerable trauma. She did the same thing with drawings. At the beginning of every session, Dr. Sanders had her sit with a box of crayons and paper and told her to draw whatever she wanted to. Yeah, at first, they were only scribbles, but the thing she was fixating on that caused so many problems for her—the trauma—manifested in the drawings over and over after maybe the first two sessions."

"Okay, I think we already covered that part with this."

"Just listen, Johnny." Lisa pointed at the drawings on the right side of the wall. "This little girl drew her bedroom each time. The first few times, it was rough—scattered lines and nothing more than blobs as the shape of her bed, the dresser, her bookshelf, and stuffed animals. But every time she came in for a session, the images became clearer. Granted, she was only six, but each new drawing took on more definition and detail." She trailed her pointing finger slowly across the wall toward the left. "Every time, she remembered more of what she'd suppressed until she was finally able to tell us about it."

The dwarf swallowed thickly and scowled at her. "In her own bedroom?"

She looked equally disturbed. "Yep. We arrested the asshole soon after that. By the time he's out of prison, she'll be an adult and living her own life, hopefully far away from where she had to grow up."

"Naw, if the sonofabitch did that to her is behind bars, he ain't never gettin' out alive."

"That's what I hope for." She exhaled a long sigh, then shook her head and stepped toward the wall again. "The point is that's exactly what's happening here. Look. These drawings take on more definition as they move across the wall. The one you pointed out is probably one of the last but the figure in it is still smudged and shadowy. There are no real details."

Johnny narrowed his eyes as his gaze traced the expanse of drawings. "Do you think he was bein' his own shrink with at least a hundred pictures?"

"I think he was trying to remember, Johnny—specifically, what that figure in the tunnel truly looks like."

"This demon, huh?"

"It makes sense. And I think he came close."

"Before he simply couldn't cope anymore and ditched the art gig for somethin' a little more permanent." The dwarf moved toward the far-left corner to peer at the more detailed drawings. His boot knocked against a pile of books stacked against the wall and scattered them across the floor. With a frown, he scanned the covers—*The Art of Happiness, How to Be Happy, The Power of Positivity*, and others with similar titles. "Maybe he didn't give up so easily after all."

"What do you mean?"

"All these self-help books on happiness and pullin' your despair outta the gutter." He nodded at them.

The agent frowned. "So a successful guy working for himself and living in a fairly nice house with nice things somehow gets this mark on him. He said he loved his life. That he was happy."

"And maybe he'd credit all the self-help readin'."

"Or he already knew of a few tools to try to help himself when things got bad and tried to work through a psychological block to remember what the hell he was trying to draw in the first place."

"Huh. It doesn't look like anythin' worked." Johnny strode across the living room and stopped in front of a large, obviously expensive entertainment center that supported a fifty-six-inch flatscreen TV. "He has a weird collection of DVDs if you ask me."

She snorted and turned. "I'm surprised you know what a DVD is."

"Careful, now." He nudged the top DVD case aside with the back of his hand to see the other titles beneath. "Okaay...a few standup shows and comedy films and Hallmark movies. All right, that's where I draw the line in good taste."

Lisa joined him and studied the titles. "I bet the point of all these was the same as the books."

"Fill his head with fluff to drown out all the crazy?"

"He was trying to *stay* happy," she explained and darted him a sidelong glance. "That's the point of watching comedy—and I assume the point of Hallmark movies. He said she—this demon—wants to take everything from him. That if she does and he's still alive, she wins."

"Yeah, I'd say that usually happens when someone loses their mind. There isn't much to be happy about at that point."

A little impatient, she rested her hands on her hips. "You don't honestly think it's a simple answer like that, do you?"

He shrugged. "It might be."

"Johnny, you saw that mark on his arm as clearly as I did. There's dark magic involved."

"I know. We oughta go see one of the other two names on the list. If we find more crazy drawin's and feel-good entertainment scattered 'round either of them, I'll be willin' to believe Folsum ain't simply one round shy of a full magazine."

"Right." Lisa regarded him with a small frown, then scoffed and shook her head. "Only Johnny Walker would use a bullet metaphor for mental illness."

"If the bullet fits…"

"We should check the rest of the house. Maybe there's something magic-related. Or a sign that Folsum tried to look into this on his own to find out more about demons, cults, or specific blocks to his memory."

"Yeah, all right." Johnny snapped his fingers and nodded at the hounds. "You heard the lady, boys. Time to move. You're sniffin' for magic."

Rex stood immediately and trotted across the living room toward the hall. "That's easy, Johnny. We find anything, we'll give the signal."

Luther stayed where he was and stared longingly at the half-empty can of Spaghetti-O's.

"Luther. Now."

The hound whined. "Johnny, it's just sitting there…"

"Is there somethin' wrong with you, boy? Leave it."

"Okay, okay." He padded slowly through the house after his brother. "Next snack we find after this, though, I want first dibs."

"Git." Johnny pointed down the hall and didn't lower his arm until Luther had disappeared into one of the open rooms. *I woulda said when I brought them home that Luther was the smarter one. Somethin' ain't right with him.*

"You're not going to tell me your dogs can sniff out the subjects of books or curated reading, are you?" Lisa asked.

"Nope. That's where our eyes come in."

"Right. Because dogs can't read, either."

"Mm-hmm." He sniffed and continued down the hall to search through Christopher Folsum's personal effects. *If I had a collar for every canine out there, I reckon they'd all prove her wrong.*

CHAPTER EIGHTEEN

After an hour spent going through every drawer, cabinet, closet, and bookshelf, they called off the search.

"There's nothin' but crusty clothes, rottin' food, and a sad fella's decline into madness." Johnny shook his head as they trudged up the steep driveway toward the street.

"The point is that we left no stone unturned," Lisa added. "Or moldy plate, as it were."

"I still ain't buyin' this demon nonsense." They turned left to descend the hill toward the center of downtown. "It could merely be poison makin' everyone lose it."

"It's not. They all had negative tox screens, remember?"

"Do any of the docs here have a degree in magical medicine?"

She brushed her hair out of her eyes. "Not here. But the department has at least three. All the blood samples were tested traditionally and by magical means. There was no poison, Johnny. Not even the magical kind."

"And there's still that mark."

"Right. Anyone who uses dark magic on humans is already playing with a double-edged sword. Magic is much easier to identify when it's dark. Whoever branded these victims knows what they're doing or we would have already found exactly what that mark means and what it's for."

Johnny raised an eyebrow at her in surprise. "Couldn't you even find it in your fancy doohickey?"

"No, Johnny. The Internet didn't pull up any clues about dark magic. The department couldn't find anything either."

"It wouldn't be a good sign if they did."

"Why's that?"

The dwarf cleared his throat. "You don't want a horde of federal employees with knowledge of dark magic on the payroll, darlin'. That's askin' for trouble."

"Fair." Lisa pulled her phone out and looked up restaurants in the area. "Do you know anyone on the west coast who specializes in runes and magical marks?"

He snorted. "I never needed that kinda contact. Runes and magic ain't exactly standard for the bounties I bring in."

"Oh, I get it. Because your type is the smarter than average criminal who decided they could do the most amount of damage on Earth with the least amount of magic."

"And that's why I'm so good at my job, darlin'." He shrugged. "Most amount of damage with the least amount of magic."

"If you say so." She scrolled through her phone and looked up at the next cross-street. "We still need to interview those other victims who aren't locked up, in a psych ward, or out of state. And I think it's a better idea if we don't go into it on an empty stomach."

"Yeah, Johnny." Luther trotted faster to catch up with them. "Hunger's a distraction."

"You want us to be sharp for the next hunt, right?" Rex added.

He glanced at the hounds and muttered, "She weren't talkin' to y'all."

"Well, not technically." Lisa turned her phone to show him the restaurant displayed on the screen. "But it doesn't mean they have to sit outside and wait for us to eat."

The bounty hunter squinted at her phone and scowled in bemusement. "You gotta be shittin' me."

"Nope. I found at least six within a few blocks of each other. This one looks appealing." Lisa grinned. "It has a good menu for all of us, don't you think?"

"That ain't dog-friendly, darlin'. That there is dog-servin'."

Rex whipped his head up from sniffing the sidewalk. "Say what?"

Luther's tongue lolled from the side of his mouth. "Did he say they serve dogs?"

"But we're hounds."

Johnny grumbled and finally shrugged. "What the hell. I could do with a meal. We'd better call and check their portions first, though. I ain't payin' thirty bucks for a mouse-sized lunch."

"It'll be fine." Lisa slid her phone into her pocket and pointed at the next intersection. "We'll turn here, and it's only another block or two after that."

"Uh-huh." The bounty hunter scowled at a mural in bright colors painted on the building they passed. It depicted weird geometric shapes and a pair of legs. "As long as I don't have to stare at somethin' like that while I'm eatin'."

When they reached the restaurant, the hostess greeted them with a huge smile. "Welcome to Water Dog. Table for two outside?"

"That would be great." Lisa glanced at Johnny and elbowed him in the side when she saw him glare at all the dog statues, photos of "doggie customers" plastered on the right wall, and the kitschy decorations of everything canine-themed hanging from the ceiling and stacked on the shelves. "Won't it?"

"Sure," he muttered gruffly.

"Perfect." The woman nodded, her grin unwavering. "I will have to ask you to leash your four-legged friends. When you're outside on the patio, feel free to let them loose. We have a little dog park out back."

"Dog park?" Luther whipped his head from side to side, overwhelmed by the dogginess of the restaurant's indoor seating. "For real?"

"Johnny, this place was *made* for us!" Rex uttered a high-pitched whine. "Let's go. Let's go."

The dwarf snapped his fingers. "I ain't got leashes but the hounds will be fine."

"It's merely restaurant policy. Here." The hostess ducked behind the counter and popped up again with two thin nylon leashes in her hand. "And we have extras."

"Uh-huh." He scowled at the items.

"It's only to walk across the restaurant," Lisa muttered.

"Fine." The hounds sat immediately when he snapped his fingers, and he snatched the leashes from the hostess' hands. "We'd already be sittin' at a table by now, but fine."

"Thank you." she gathered their menus and silverware while Johnny hooked the leashes to the collars of his perfectly behaved coonhounds. When he finished and held both nylon ropes with enough slack that they draped on the floor, she nodded. "Right this way, please."

"Whoa. Hey, Johnny. Look." Rex stared at the canine sculpture as they passed. "It's a bear."

"Where are all the hounds?" Luther asked. They headed through the restaurant full of Portlanders eating in tasteless canine heaven, most of them without dogs. "Hey, I found one—"

An old, gray-muzzled poodle lay at his master's feet at a table on their right. He looked at Rex and Luther and uttered a low, raspy growl.

"Jeez." Luther whined and gave the table a wide berth. "You don't have to be that mean about it."

Rex snorted and trotted at his master's side. "Johnny, if that's the only other hound in here, I don't think they've got their marketing right. It's supposed to be hound-friendly, isn't it?"

He said nothing and followed Lisa and the hostess to the back patio.

"Oh, yeah!" Rex yipped when he saw the large green lawn behind the dining patio and the half-dozen other dogs running around in play. "This is more like it!"

"How's this table here?" The woman set their menus and silverware down without waiting for a reply.

"It's great." Lisa pulled a chair out. "Thank you."

"Of course. Charlie will be your server. And here's the doggie menu."

Johnny snorted. "The what?"

"It's great, right?" The hostess tapped the third paper menu on the table. "Our chefs are brought in specifically with working knowledge of canine nutrition, and we have the largest selection of doggie meals in Portland. Enjoy."

She turned and left them on the half-full dining patio and Rex and Luther sat and waited to be unleashed. Their tails thumped madly on the concrete.

"Come on, Johnny. Come on."

"We wanna go play!" Luther yipped at a black lab that darted across the lawn and it stopped to look at him before it snorted and raced after two French bulldogs. "Oh, you think you're too good for us, huh?"

"Your loss!" Rex shouted after the lab.

The dwarf removed the leashes and dropped them on the ground. "Go on, then."

"Yes!"

"This is the best!"

"Who wants to race? I'll take on every single one of you mutts at the same time!"

The hounds raced onto the lawn. Luther sprinted after the black lab anyway, and Rex headed to the huge metal tub filled with water in the shade. "Holy crap. They put ice in the water? Johnny, how come we don't get ice?"

Johnny shook his head and sat, then scowled at the menu.

Lisa chuckled and handed him the doggie menu. "This is very creative."

"Naw, I ain't entertainin' that nonsense." He waved the menu away, and she set it aside with a playful frown. "They can have what I'm havin'."

"But it's made specifically for—"

"Darlin', I don't trust folks with 'knowledge of canine nutrition' to know better 'bout my hounds than I do."

She shrugged and studied the menu for humans. "It's your call."

"Damn right." He studied the choices available to him and snorted. *Canine chefs. Who the hell thought that was a good idea?*

"Hey, look." Rex trotted up to another metal container, this one filled with water, ice, and cold glass bottles. "Johnny, they serve beer to hounds too? Oh, wait. No, it says soda."

"Wait, hound soda?" Luther asked as he joined his brother.

"I don't know. Hey, how about you try to turn one of those around, and I'll read the label?"

"I can do both." Luther plunged his whole head into the tub of ice water but withdrew it quickly. "Yeah, I saw a hound on that bottle."

"Are you sure it wasn't your reflection?" Rex lapped the water that dripped from his brother's muzzle.

"Totally. Not sure I can read, though. Johnny!" he barked. "Come help us out with this."

He pointed at the small yard of the dog park. "I ain't openin' bottles for hounds. Y'all go run it off."

"Ooh. Ooh. Rex." Luther spun and sniffed the air. "See that retriever?"

"Yeah, check out the tail on that one."

"Let's go!"

Shaking his head, the bounty hunter returned his focus to the menu. "Fifteen bucks for avocado toast?"

"It's one of their signature recipes," Lisa muttered.

"They had better be some magical fuckin' avocadoes at that price."

She looked at him with a coy smile. "Is that what you're getting?"

"Hell no." He stabbed the menu. "Three burgers. Easy choice. Simple. Can't screw that up and charge too much. Look at that. Burgers are cheaper than the damn toast."

"And you need three."

"The hounds gotta eat too." He leaned back in his chair and folded his arms. "And I get extra fries."

CHAPTER NINETEEN

After they had all enjoyed a lunch of acceptable portions, they left Water Dog with full stomachs and two more human victims to visit.

"Who's next?" Johnny asked as he tossed the borrowed leashes through the restaurant's front door.

"Gina McKinney." Lisa scrolled through her phone. "She lives in Irvington but came to stay with her sister Alexis after she started seeing demons."

"Sure. She lost her mind and decided she needed help." He nodded, his expression grim but satisfied with the logic. "It's a better option than what Folsum had available."

"Probably, yeah. Poor guy. Her sister lives only a few blocks east."

"Well then, let's get on." He stared at the group of downtown Portland locals that approached. Three people walked their bikes on the outsides of the group, steered with one hand, and held to-go coffee cups in the other. "Now what's the point of that, huh?"

"Walking?"

"Bikes—if they ain't gonna get on and ride."

She shrugged. "I don't have an answer for that. But can we stick to the actual mystery here and focus on the case?"

"Uh-huh." He turned to stare after the group as they passed and continued to talk and laugh as they sipped their overpriced coffee. He jerked a thumb toward them and widened his eyes at Lisa. "It's like some kinda damn fashion accessory."

"Come on." She rolled her eyes with a mixture of exasperation and amusement and crossed the street.

It took them ten minutes to reach the house only a few blocks beyond the center of downtown. Johnny studied the tall, narrow duplex for a moment and shrugged. "At least she ain't out here cryin' 'demon' with no one to hear."

Lisa ascended the front porch steps and slid her phone into her pocket. "You'd better let me start the conversation."

"Sure. You're the psychologist understudy."

Her quick look was almost a glare when he joined her on the porch.

The hounds padded after them and Luther squeezed between them to sniff the bottom edge of the front door. "I smell more hounds, Johnny."

"No, that's only one." Rex joined him at the door, where he sniffed and snorted.

The dwarf snapped his fingers and pointed at the porch floor. "This ain't the hound hotel, boys. Wait."

"Yeah, yeah. But when you go in there to interrogate the two-legs, Johnny, can we interrogate the hound inside?"

"We'll ask her all the questions, Johnny."

"Like where she keeps all the snacks."

"Why she's holdin' out on us."

"Ooh, if she likes playing fetch."

"If this one's got any bones buried in the backyard, Johnny, we'll find 'em."

He stared at the front door as Lisa stepped forward to knock briskly. *Wrong kinda bones, boys.*

A sharp bark came from inside the two-story duplex, followed by the sound of a back door sliding open and shut again. The barking continued, this time from outside.

"Yeah, we'll be there in a minute!" Luther shouted.

"Just a friendly check-in." Rex licked his muzzle. "As soon as your two-legs lets us in."

The front door opened slowly and a woman in her early thirties with thick, curly brown hair peered out. Her brown eyes widened when she saw Johnny, Lisa, and two hounds on the front porch. "Can I help you?"

"Alexis McKinney?" Lisa asked.

Her eyebrows drew together in a pained frown. "Yes. I'm sorry, who are you?"

"Agent Breyer with the Federal Bureau of Investigation." The agent flashed her badge. "And this is Johnny Walker. We were hoping to find your sister Gina here."

"Oh." Alexis glanced over her shoulder but didn't open the door any wider for them to have a good look inside. "Well, she's here but I don't know if now's a good time—"

"Is she still talkin' 'bout the demon?" Johnny asked.

Both women looked at him in surprise.

"That's what this is about?"

Lisa nodded. "We have a few questions that weren't covered by the Portland PD when they wrote their report of Gina's...situation."

"Situation." Alexis wrinkled her nose. "That euphemism still rubs me the wrong way."

"I ain't a fan of tryin' to sugarcoat somethin' with a different name either." The bounty hunter gestured beyond the woman with his head. "You might be able to help us answer some of these questions too. Do you mind if we come in?"

"Um..." Alexis glanced at Rex and Luther who sat obediently at the dwarf's sides and stared at her. A small smile bloomed on her lips. "Your dogs have that 'pleading eyes' look to perfection."

"Johnny, I like her," Luther said.

"Yeah, and I bet her hound's even cooler."

He ignored them. "I can't say they don't know exactly what they're doin'."

"I'm sorry. Of course you can come in." Alexis stepped back and opened the door fully.

"Thank you." Lisa stepped inside first.

The hounds waited until Johnny followed her before they practically leapt over the threshold. "Oh, yeah. Definitely another hound here."

"A hairy one too." Luther sniffed at a forgotten wad of fluffy white hair in the corner. "How does anyone handle the heat with that much fur on 'em?"

Alexis shut the door and smiled wearily at the hounds. "I have a Great Pyrenees, Lakshmi. She's in the back yard right now, but these guys are more than welcome to go out there with her."

"Yeah, Johnny, can we?" Luther panted at his master.

"Can't interrogate a Great Pyrenees if there's a door between us, Johnny."

The dwarf cleared his throat. "That'd be fine."

"And they're good with other dogs?" The woman headed across her living room toward the sliding glass door in the back.

"Yep."

"We're good with everyone, lady." Rex trotted after her. "It's the squirrels that have to worry."

"And the hamsters." Luther stopped short when the Great Pyrenees stopped on the other side of the glass door, panted through a doggy grin, and wagged her tail to swish the long white fur. "Oh, man. Look at her, Rex."

"I know. I'd interrogate that bitch all damn day!"

"Look at you two." Alexis chuckled. "You're so excited. This'll be great. Lakshmi needs new friends."

"Yeah, yeah, yeah." Luther almost bounced in excitement. "We're *real* friendly."

The glass door slid open and they barreled into the yard to circle the other dog.

"Hey, there. How ya doin'?" Luther moved closer to sniff beneath her tail. "Well, *yeah*, we're here for a reason."

"Don't listen to him until we've started this off right," Rex added as he joined the round of mutual canine butt-sniffing. "I'm Rex."

"And I'm the good-looking one," Luther added before Alexis slid the glass door shut again.

Johnny stared at his hounds through the back door and folded his arms. *It's gonna be a hell of a job to tune them out when they're still in range.*

"It looks like everyone's getting along." The woman turned to her visitors who waited in her living room and she gestured toward the couches. "Please. Have a seat. Can I get you anything to drink?"

"We just came from lunch," Johnny muttered. "I'm fine for now, darlin'."

She regarded him a little warily and frowned like she couldn't decide how to feel about a dwarf in all black with the odd disks on his belt beside the utility knife. "Okay. What about you, Agent Breyer?"

"Lisa, please." She sat on the couch opposite their hostess and shook her head. "And no thank you. I'm fine."

Alexis shifted on the couch and looked from one to the other. "So. You're here to look into what happened to my sister, then. Right?"

"That's right." The agent nodded. "What did the Portland PD have to say about what Gina's been going through?"

"Oh. Um…" She frowned at her lap. "They tested her for drugs, which I already knew wasn't the issue. So did she. She was evaluated by two different psychiatrists too, and all they gave us was some unconvincing diagnosis of PTSD. And the police simply went with that, I guess."

"But you don't think that's what happened." Johnny leaned forward on the cushion beside Lisa. "Right?"

"No, I don't." Alexis glanced across the living room at the staircase leading to the second story. "My sister hasn't gone through anything that would trigger PTSD—at least not that I know of. And she's...she's not herself, you know? She's such a happy, outgoing person, always moving and very extroverted. Seeing her now, though, it's like someone else in there who I don't recognize. I don't understand what's going on with her."

"Well, that's why we're here," Lisa said calmly. "We think something else is going on here—something the district police department simply isn't...equipped to handle."

"So they sent the FBI." The woman frowned.

The dwarf sniffed. "And me."

"You're not with—"

"I'm a bounty hunter, darlin'."

"Oh." The woman stiffened. "But you're not here for Gina, right? Because she hasn't done anything to anyone. I promise. I've been with her almost the whole time—"

"It's nothing like that," Lisa reassured her. "We're merely trying to determine what happened to her."

"So we can apprehend the asshole who did this to her and seven other folks in the area," Johnny added. "Most of 'em ain't fortunate enough to have someone like you carin' for 'em through the whole ordeal. As far as I can see, you're doin' a hell of a job."

"It doesn't much feel like it, but thanks." The woman tucked her thick curly hair behind one ear but it instantly bounced free again. "Do you think this was some kind of attack?"

The agent turned to him and raised her eyebrows.

'Course she wants to hear me say it out loud. He grunted. "Yep. Agent Breyer's with the Department of Magicals and Monsters, Bounty Hunter Division."

"Wait—you're saying this is some kind of magical attack?" Alexis shook her head. "I don't understand. We're normal."

Lisa chuckled. "You're humans, yes. But that doesn't mean you're immune to magic—if it turns out that's what this is. Which we do think is the case." She darted her partner a sidelong glance and tried to hold a smirk in check.

He scratched the side of his face through his thick beard and gazed around the living room. *Yeah, okay. I took the bait but we still gotta prove this is what we're workin' with.*

"So to start, Alexis," the agent continued, "can you tell us more about the day Gina started acting...unlike herself?"

"Sure. Um... It was about four weeks ago. We went out that Friday night, only the two of us. I'd cleared my weekend schedule and wanted to do something fun."

"What d'ya do for a livin'?" Johnny asked.

"I'm a web designer so I work from home for my clients and set my own hours, for the most part."

"And your sister?"

She laughed wryly. "Don't ask me for specifics because it all goes right over my head. She works in insurance. Or...at least she did. She called in sick that Monday morning after she spent the rest of the weekend holed up here with me. The sick leave extended indefinitely so I'm fairly sure she lost that job."

"And you were with her the entire weekend?"

"Yeah. She was a mess. Saturday morning was weird and she looked constantly out the front windows and was totally paranoid. It got even worse the next day. She started talking about someone harassing her—this...demon, I guess. Even worse, she hardly slept and I was up most of the night trying to calm her. Night terrors, I think. But she screamed and yelled throughout and had a hard time recognizing me when she finally woke up."

Lisa frowned. "Well, looking at it from only that perspective, the PTSD diagnosis makes sense."

"But that suddenly?" Alexis shook her head. "If she'd gone through some horrible ordeal, I would have at least heard something about it. Maybe not all the details, but she never mentioned having a bad experience with anything. Okay, she wasn't exactly in love with her job and I heard her complain about that fairly often."

"I'd say it's fairly standard with that kinda job," Johnny muttered.

"But I honestly don't think that had anything to do with it. If something had happened to her at work, she wouldn't have tried to keep the job by calling in sick, right?"

"We can't answer that." Lisa clasped her hands in her lap. "But if you think there's any way her job had something to do with it—"

"I don't. Gina has so many friends. Like I said, she wasn't in love with her job but that's normal, right? And she has hobbies and a healthy social life. She plays racquetball at the rec center every Wednesday night. None of that changed at all since we went out on Friday—although she doesn't go out, the interest and desire to live her life is still there."

Johnny stroked his beard, his eyes narrowed in thought. "What did y'all do?"

"The usual Friday-night stuff. We went out to eat at a Chinese place we've gone to for years. After that, we did a little bar hopping, but the police already asked if we'd had anything we don't usually have. We didn't. Yeah, we were a little drunk, but it was a normal Friday. I dropped her at her apartment at around one am and came home. The next morning, she called me, freaking out about how she didn't feel safe at her apartment and needed to get out. She asked if she could stay with me and of course, I told her she could. I went to pick her up, brought her here, and she's been in the guestroom for the last month."

"Does she get out at all?" Johnny asked.

"No." The woman's pained frown deepened. "I can't get her to leave the house for anything. She won't even go into the back yard with Lakshmi, and she loves that dog."

"Huh." He sniffed and pointed at the staircase. "Is she upstairs?"

"Yeah. Both our bedrooms are up there."

"I wanna talk to her."

"Um…" Alexis sighed. "I'm not sure that's a good idea. The psychiatrists put her on medication to calm her. At least that's what they said it's supposed to do but it doesn't always work."

Lisa leaned forward and gave her a reassuring smile. "Would it help if you went upstairs and told her who we are and why we're here? Ask her if she'd be willing to talk to us."

"It might." She gazed at the staircase. "I can't make any promises, though."

"That's okay. If there's a chance she's willing to talk to us so we can ask her a few questions ourselves, that would be very helpful. We want to help you both and any little detail might be exactly what we need to find the truth. We're not ruling anything out yet."

Johnny snorted. *Except for PTSD, poison, and mental illness.*

She ignored him. "It's worth a try, right?"

"Yeah… Yeah, you're right." Alexis stood and tugged the hem of her t-shirt down. "I'll be back in a few minutes. Are you sure I can't get you something to drink?"

"We're fine. Thank you."

"Okay." The woman moved quickly toward the stairs, paused as if she had something else to say, then continued across the living room to ascend the slightly creaking staircase.

Outside, all three dogs barked and raced across the lawn in huge circles.

"Oh, you think you're fast, huh?" Luther shouted after the Great Pyrenees. "Well, I got news for ya, beautiful. I'm faster than—"

"A snail!" Rex howled and darted past his brother. "And I win!

Hey, Lakshmi, hold still. We haven't finished interrogating you yet—whoa! No, I'm not blaming you for anything. Come on!"

"Rex, get that squirrel!"

Johnny startled and shook his head.

"Are you okay?"

"I'm thinkin'." He rubbed his mouth. *I gotta find a way to tune those hounds out so I can do the thinkin' that needs to be done.*

CHAPTER TWENTY

Ten minutes later, Alexis' footsteps creaked down the stairs. She stopped a little over halfway down and cleared her throat. "She seems okay with it so I guess you guys can come up."

"Good." Lisa stood. "Thanks for checking with her."

"Well, it's more like she didn't freak out when I said you wanted to talk to her." The woman watched Johnny cross the room toward the stairs with a hesitant frown. "But if she gets too worried or overly excited about something, we'll have to give her space. Just so you know beforehand."

"That's fine." He reached the bottom step and nodded. "All I want is a few words and we'll go from there."

She led them up the stairs a glanced over her shoulder at least three times to make sure they were following her. At the top, she turned to the right and pointed down the hall. "It's the first door on the left. Let me go in first, okay?"

"That's a good idea." Lisa nodded and followed them tentatively toward the guestroom.

Alexis knocked on the open door. "Gina, it's me again and I've brought the people I told you about. They're here to help you." She paused and when there was no response, she sighed and stepped back to let Lisa and Johnny through. "I don't know how much you'll get out of her right now, honestly. Please, be gentle."

"Not a problem." The bounty hunter stepped into the room and paused.

Gina McKinney sat on her bed, huddled against the headboard in an oversized t-shirt and sweatpants with her knees pulled up to her chest. She had the same thick, curly dark hair and wide brown eyes as her sister, although hers were dulled by the dark, baggy circles beneath them. Her curls fell across her shoulders in an unwashed, tangled mess, and she stared at the bedspread in front of her. She didn't look up when the dwarf entered or when Lisa followed him and stepped aside to give Alexis a view into the room.

"Gina?" Agent Breyer called softly. "My name's Lisa. This is Johnny. We wanted to ask you a few questions about the night you went out with your sister. Is that okay?"

The woman nodded vaguely but still didn't look up. Her lips parted and moved like she was whispering something, but no sound came out.

"Anythin' you can tell us will help us to help you, Gina," he added.

Slowly, the woman raised her head and gazed at each of them. "You're not from the hospital?"

"No." Lisa took another step toward the bed centered along the opposite wall. "We're with the FBI."

Gina's eyes widened and she raised her head even more to study the newcomers. "So you're trying to find her? Do you think you can?

"Who might that be?" Johnny asked.

"*Her*." The woman glanced briefly at the window where the shades were closed completely against the bright summer day. "She's trying to find me. That's why I came to stay with Alexis."

"Who is she?"

"You don't know? No, of course you don't. You're supposed to be good at finding people, right? And you came here to talk to me about finding her." She scoffed. "The FBI can't find a demon. I don't think you can help."

"But you've managed to avoid her by staying with Alexis for the last month," Lisa said to play into the delusion while she tried to not make it sound condescending. "That's more than many other people managed so far."

Gina grimaced. "There are others?"

"Yep. Seven other folks we're tryin' to help too," Johnny confirmed and narrowed his eyes as he studied the room. "Exactly like you."

"Not exactly like me. I can't—" The woman exhaled a heavy, helpless sigh and pulled her tangled mess of curls away from one side of her neck to push them over the opposite shoulder. "They gave me meds I don't need. Did you know that? They don't keep her away and all they do is make it so hard to think. I'm not normally...this slow."

The two visitors exchanged and glance when the side of her now-exposed neck revealed the same mark they'd seen on Christopher Folsum. Lisa nodded.

As he stepped toward the bed, Johnny pointed at his neck. "What's that there below your ear?"

"What?" The woman's hand brushed against the mark before she looked at her fingers and shook her head. "There's nothing there."

"There's a small mark, darlin'. Have you taken a good look in the mirror recently?"

"No, mirrors are the worst." Gina shrank against the head-board again. "That's where she can see me—where she can look inside me the easiest."

"Did anyone mention that mark to you, though?" He pointed at her neck this time. "Maybe your sister said somethin' 'bout it? It's hard to miss when your hair ain't coverin' it."

"I don't have any marks," she whispered. "I don't even have tattoos. What are you doing? No. Stop. Don't come any closer."

"I only wanna get a better look." Johnny raised both hands. "Is that all right with you?"

"No, it's not okay. You don't need to look at my body. The doctors already did that."

Lisa spread her arms placatingly and remained where she was. "Gina, if we can have a closer look, we might be able to—"

"She sent you, didn't she?"

"Now, that ain't anywhere close to the—"

"She did. She sent you!" Gina pressed herself against the headboard and pointed a shaking finger at one, then the other. "Alexis can't tell the difference, but I can. You're here to take everything from me. Tell that demon I won't fall for it. I won't! If she can't find me at my apartment, good. And you can't make me go back."

"Gina, we're not working for anyone but the FBI," the agent said quietly and lowered her hands.

"You're lying!" The woman clamped her hands against her ears and clenched her eyes shut. A low, anxious moan escaped her as she began to rock against the headboard. "Don't listen. Don't listen to the lies. My name is Gina McKinney. I'm thirty-two. I have a good life. I'm happy. I have friends, I'm talented, I'm funny, I can…I can handle anything."

"Gina?" Alexis stepped into the room with them and pressed a hand to her mouth as she watched her sister descend into another episode. "Hey, sweetie, it's me. Can you hear me?"

"I like fuzzy socks and vanilla candles. My sister loves me."

"That's right. I'm right here."

"Alexis! *Alexis!*" Gina hunched over, her eyes still tightly shut, and screamed at the top of her lungs. She removed her hands from her ears and batted violently at the air in front of her as she shook her head vigorously. "Alexis! She's trying to get in! She's gonna find me!"

"No, no. I'm right here." Her sister darted toward the bed,

climbed onto it, and shuffled toward her sister. "Hey, it's me. It's okay. Everything's okay."

She avoided the wildly slapping hands and managed to pin her sister's arms at her side in a tight hug.

Johnny frowned and watched the terrified outburst. "You see that mark on her neck too, right?"

"He's lying!" Gina screamed.

Alexis shushed her and hugged her even more tightly as she stroked her hair. "I think you guys should go downstairs."

The bounty hunter gestured toward the terrified woman. "Do you have any idea what this demon lady looks like—"

"*Now.* Please." The woman darted a warning glance at him before her features softened when Gina subsided into sobs in her arms. "I need to calm her. Wait for me downstairs and we can talk. Shh, sweetie. It's okay. Everything's fine. No one's trying to break in, I promise."

"Johnny." Lisa nodded toward the hallway. "Come on."

With a grunt, the dwarf turned grudgingly and followed her into the hall. "Don't it smell a little funny to you that she can't even acknowledge that mark on her neck?"

"A little." She gestured down the stairs for him to go first. "That doesn't mean we need to push her on it."

"It makes it seem like she's hidin' somethin'."

"Johnny, she's terrified. And it's not hiding something if she can't remember what happened to her."

"Huh. She could talk fine."

They reached the main floor and turned toward the couches in the living room. "I think the issue with that mark on her neck is one of those traumatic blocks," she continued. "Like with Folsum. He made all those drawings because he wanted to remember the figure in the tunnels but couldn't. I think subconsciously, Gina knows about the mark."

"Are you sayin' we should get her to draw it?"

They sat on the couches and she shook her head. "No. For her,

I think that would simply make it worse. It would push her again and that's not the right way to go. But I'm starting to think the marks are more related to the victims' memories than anything else—like a wrench thrown into the gears."

"It made Folsum explode, draw the same thing over 'bout a hundred times, then try to kill himself. And it makes this lady upstairs refuse to look at what's right in front of her?"

"I don't think she'd be able to see it even if she were looking for it, Johnny. That's the block."

He grunted and tugged at his beard. "Well, she's certainly the same level of crazy he is but a different kind. No drawings. No obsessive whatever-you-call-it."

"No, hers manifested differently. Folsum didn't have any fear of leaving his house. He didn't struggle with the paramedics when they took him to the ambulance."

"Naw, his issue was still bein' alive."

Lisa glanced warningly at him. "There's a better way to say that without making it sound so heartless."

"The truth is what it is, darlin'." He shrugged. "I ain't tryin' to make it anythin' different."

With a sigh of acknowledgment, she leaned back against the couch cushions.

"So he had a fear of everythin' he loved bein' taken from him. Of not bein' happy. And Gina McKinney's afraid to go outside."

"She's afraid of being followed and found. She thinks she's safer here than in her apartment." Lisa drummed her fingers on her thighs. "The curtains are closed and no one comes in or out. She won't go out back with the dog—"

"And how is that like the other cases, huh? Other than the fact that these folks are scared outta their minds and blamin' it on a demon lady?"

Her grim frown was determined. "That's why we're here."

The bedroom door upstairs shut softly, followed by Alexis' slow, hesitant footsteps down the stairs. When she reached the bottom, she pulled her curly hair away from her neck and shoulders and let it fall down her back. "I think I have her down for now, although I had to give her another dose of the benzodiazepines the doctors prescribed. She hates them but it's the only thing that works."

"Alexis, we didn't mean to upset her so much," Lisa said as she started to stand.

"No, it's okay. And you don't have to go if you still have questions." With a final glance at the staircase, she sat on the couch across the coffee table and sighed. "Trust me, that was mild compared to some of the worst days."

"Has she ever said anythin' 'bout that mark?" Johnny asked.

"No. And I learned very quickly to not ask about it. She did the same thing when I tried to work out what it was. I spent an entire day trying to convince her I was truly her sister and not some demon lackey in disguise. She'll be okay." She looked at them with tired but hopeful eyes. "Did you get any of your answers?"

"Well, we do know she ain't drawin' on the walls."

"I'm sorry?"

Lisa frowned at him and shook her head. "It was certainly helpful, Alexis. Thank you."

They fell silent for a moment. Johnny rubbed his mouth, then pointed at the woman. "I'd like to have the names of all the places y'all went to that night. Do you think you can remember them?"

Alexis' tiny smile broke through her obvious exhaustion. "We didn't get that drunk. But I already told the police everywhere we went."

"Well, it's possible they missed somethin', darlin'. And like Agent Breyer said, we ain't writin' anythin' off yet."

"Okay. Sure."

Lisa retrieved her phone. "Whenever you're ready, I'll make a list."

"Yeah. Um... Let me see. Well, we went to Mandarin House

first for dinner and a few drinks. Then we stopped at Dixie Tavern and The Barrel Room. We saw some of Gina's friends there and hung out for a while. Oh, before that, she wanted to take one of those tours in Old Town. I'm not a fan of horror stories or scary movies or anything, but I thought I could shake off the scare with a decent buzz after dinner, you know? Gina loves that stuff."

The agent looked up from her phone. "What tours?"

"The, uh...the tunnels. The Shanghai Tunnels under Old Town." Alexis shrugged. "They revamped it a few months ago. It seems they discovered some other access tunnels and changed part of their story when they lead you through them to include some new information they found about all the awful stuff that happened down there in the 1800s, I think."

Johnny tilted his head slowly. "Are they still runnin' these tours?"

"As far as I know, yeah. They're very popular with people who come through Portland from out of town, but it's something fun to do if you're local, too, especially if they change the story. It's a PG tour, but they don't exactly try to hide the worst parts. They merely don't go into too much detail, but it's easy enough to imagine all the rest."

"What time were you down there?"

"We took the very last tour of the night. So...I don't know. Five, I guess."

Lisa finished typing her notes into her phone and slipped the device into her back pocket. "That's great, Alexis. Thank you. I think we have everything we need. Johnny?"

"Yep." The dwarf stood and nodded at the woman, who looked quickly from one to the other. "Thanks for your time."

"Sure." Alexis stood and seemed almost disappointed that the visit was concluded. "That's it?"

"For now, yes." The agent shook her hand. "We'll let you know what we find."

Johnny raised an eyebrow. "We will?"

"Of course we will. Because once we know what's going on, we'll know how to help Gina return to her normal, happy, outgoing self." She widened her eyes at him and warned him to not say anything else.

"Right." He cleared his throat. "Yeah, you'll hear about it."

"Thank you." Alexis moved toward the glass sliding door. "I'm merely glad to know that someone's still looking into this and trying to help her. My sister doesn't deserve any of this, especially not being drugged for the rest of her life because no one believed me when I said it wasn't a mental breakdown."

"We don't think that's the answer either," Lisa assured her.

The dwarf joined their hostess at the back door and peered through the glass, looking for the hounds. "Where'd they run off to now?"

The woman opened the door and stepped outside. "Lakshmi? Come here, girl." She clapped and walked into the yard.

"Johnny!" Rex darted from the other side of the storage shed. "Hey, Johnny. You gotta do something! I can't stop it."

Without a word, Johnny stormed across the yard and rounded the side of the storage shed. "Luther!"

A low growl and a sharp yip greeted him before he reached the other side of the building.

"Whoa, whoa, whoa!" The younger hound struggled to get out from beneath the female Great Pyrenees who'd mounted him from behind. "Ever heard of privacy, Johnny?"

He stared at the spectacle. "What the hell?"

"All right, all right. Jeez. Can't get two minutes alone."

"Lakshmi!" Alexis joined him behind the shed and looked both horrified and highly amused. "I'm so sorry. She doesn't normally do this."

"Ain't your fault." Johnny folded his arms. "There might be somethin' wrong with one of my hounds, though."

"Get off!" The woman stepped toward her dog and swatted the animal before she managed to push Lakshmi aside.

Luther scrambled away and slipped behind Johnny, laughing. "Good times, L. Nice knowin' ya."

"Go on, Luther. Git." Johnny pointed toward the back of the duplex, and the hound skittered away across the grass to join his brother. "Thanks again for your time."

"Of course. Let me walk you to the door."

"Naw, that's fine." He looked at the Great Pyrenees who rolled happily on her back in the grass. "I think that ball of fluff might be a little more than my boys can handle. We'll see ourselves out."

He strode quickly toward the open back door, where Lisa waited for him. "What happened?"

"Hound done got himself mixed up with that other one. In more than one way."

"Dude, I *told* you she's faster than you," Rex muttered as he and Luther trotted beside their master through the house. "Why didn't you listen to me?"

Luther panted and paused to sniff the edge of the couch before Johnny snapped his fingers and opened the front door. "Who said that wasn't the plan all along?"

"Wait, *what*? That's not what interrogating means, Luther."

The bounty hunter pointed through the front door. "Both of y'all. Now."

His hounds bolted through the door and he shook his head as Lisa stepped out after them.

"Next time, y'all are stayin' inside with us."

CHAPTER TWENTY-ONE

"Okay, Johnny," Lisa said beside him on the sidewalk as they walked toward the center of downtown. "You can't say these cases don't have anything in common now."

"You mean other than the fact that all eight lost their damn minds?"

She glanced at him in exasperation.

"Yeah, all right. We were handed one more connection on a silver platter. Folsum drew all them tunnels, and I reckon he's drawin' the same ones the McKinney sisters took a damn tour through."

"So whoever's attacking these humans is...what? Attacking them during the tours? We didn't see anything in Folsum's house about tunnels under Portland."

"Naw, he pulled 'em all aboveground and plastered 'em to his wall. I call that a lead."

"And the demon part?"

"I still think that's merely a side effect at this point."

Lisa smirked and cast him a sidelong glance. "It's good to have you back in the game, Johnny."

The dwarf stopped on the sidewalk and turned to face her. "I've been back."

"No, you've been distracted." She nodded slowly and held his gaze. "And now you're ready to go after this scumbag terrorizing humans and their sanity."

He sniffed and resumed his steady pace. "Damn straight. 'Cause now, this case ain't simply all hooey. Forget the demon part. I aim to get in those tunnels and see who the hell's been carvin' out a little trap for unsuspecting folk."

The hounds trotted along beside him. "We're going underground, Johnny?"

Rex sniffed at a stray cheeseburger wrapper blown down the sidewalk toward them. "You know how many critters live underground? Even in tunnels?"

"Yeah, lots."

"Rats."

"Moles."

"Mice."

"Hamsters."

"Hush up," Johnny muttered and peered hastily over his shoulder at Lisa. She'd stopped on the sidewalk to scroll through her phone and didn't seem to have heard him. *If these hounds keep up all this talk, I'm bound to let slip more than I can cover up as talkin' to myself.*

"You don't want us to go after the hamsters, Johnny?" Luther looked at where he expected Johnny to be, then realized his master had also stopped on the sidewalk. "Johnny?"

Rex trotted toward the dwarf and sat, his tongue lolling from his mouth. "Yeah, I thought that was one of your biggest reasons for coming here."

He ignored them and studied Agent Breyer. "Is somethin' holdin' you up, darlin'?"

"What?" She looked at him, then glanced at her phone again before she hurried to catch up. "I'm looking at the

Shanghai Tunnel tours. We missed the last one by about half an hour."

"Is that the last of the day?"

"Yep. Five o'clock. They are open tomorrow and slots are still available."

The dwarf nodded. "Then that's the one we'll take. Last stop on a Friday night. I ain't goin' down in them tunnels without recreatin' exactly how the McKinney sisters did it."

Her knowing smile widened and she inclined her head to fix him with a teasing look. "So do you want to take me to Chinese for dinner and hop a few bars after this tunnel tour?"

He scratched his head. "I didn't say that."

"Well, if we're recreating it—"

"Yeah, well, we ain't sisters, neither. Get us a place on the tour tomorrow, darlin'. We'll decide on the rest from there."

She smirked and returned her attention to her phone. "Done and done."

"Good." Johnny cleared his throat and glanced at the hounds. Rex stared across the street at a group of adults in tight, dark clothing who kicked a hacky sac around in front of a headshop. Luther was busy licking between his legs.

"So now what?" Lisa stashed her phone in her pocket and glanced around the street. "We have the rest of the night to do whatever we want."

"Uh-huh. And I know exactly how to fill the time." He strode away without looking at her.

Laughing, she hurried after him and caught up before he turned the corner. "Well, I certainly didn't expect that."

"What?"

"Johnny, for someone who's so adamant about not enjoying his time in Portland, you look like a bounty hunter on a mission."

He snorted. "I took the case, didn't I?"

"Hey, Johnny," Rex called. "What do you think—Johnny? Shit."

"Johnny, where'd you go?" Luther howled. "Johnny!"

The dwarf whistled and both hounds darted around the corner after him.

"You can't leave us on the street like that. What gives?"

"Whew. We were this close to being lost dogs."

He glanced down at them and grumbled, "Y'all need to pay attention."

"You can count on us, Johnny."

"Yeah, we're sharp as sticks."

Lisa smiled at the hounds and shook her head. "And now you're the one with a plan to fill our time while we wait for that last tour tomorrow." She turned to study the mural of a lady with a rabbit mask beside them. "So spill it. Where are we going?"

"Park and Salmon."

Her smile faded. "The drug dealer's location? Seriously?"

"You sound disappointed."

"No…uh, I merely thought you had something fun in mind."

The dwarf chuckled. "Shakin' a drug dealer down to hopefully bring us closer to the Red Boar? What part of that ain't fun?"

"Okay, I get it." She ran a hand through her hair and drew a deep breath. "Don't you think we should focus on the actual case in Portland, though?"

"I can multi-task, darlin'. I thought I already told you that."

"Yes, Johnny. I'm well aware of your vast skill set."

"And I'm well aware of your sarcasm."

"I have no problem tracking the assholes pumping city streets full of that poison, Johnny, as long as you can promise me you'll keep your head in this case tomorrow night."

"I'll be sharper than a tack tomorrow night. Don't you worry 'bout that. Grabbin' one of these dealers and givin' 'em a good what-for does a hell of a number on a guy's optimism."

"I'm sure it does."

They reached the intersection Mikey had told them about in the alley the day before and stopped across the street to watch. On the corner was a rundown-looking deli with the marquee broken off one hinge and so it slanted at a precarious angle. The neon *Open* sign flickered in the window, and not a single pedestrian approached the entrance for either the cold cuts or an obnoxiously large pickle from the jar.

Johnny folded his arms across his chest and leaned against a tree that grew in the small park square they'd chosen as a vantage point. "Seriously? This whole damn city's overrun with coffee shops and craft bars and goddamn dog bakeries, but no one comes to the one place that looks legit."

Lisa frowned at the building in question. "How does that look legit to you?"

"It's a hole in the wall, darlin'. You can't get better than that."

"I think in Portland, hole in the wall stands for, 'We're about to go out of business.'"

"Fuckin' Portland." He shook his head. "Ain't no one 'round here who knows a good thing when they see it."

"Well, feel free to mosey on over and grab yourself a soggy sandwich."

He frowned at her. "I ain't here for a sandwich."

"Oh, I know."

Rex and Luther sniffed around the tree behind their master. "Hey, Johnny. You might wanna move out the way for a second."

"Uh-oh. Johnny, he can't hold it."

The dwarf glanced at Luther, who stared at him with pleading eyes while he cavorted in an urgent canine dance. Rolling his eyes, he stepped away from the tree, and the dog sniffed madly around the base of the trunk.

"Thanks, Johnny." Luther lifted his leg and his satisfied sigh filled Johnny's mind. "Oh, yeah. That's more like it."

"You had to pick the tree I was usin', huh?" the dwarf muttered.

"Look, Johnny. It's nothin' personal. I would have used another tree…"

Rex sniffed at the wet stain on the bark, then lifted his leg too. "All the others are already taken. By strangers."

"Yeah, and they look like they need those trees more than we do, Johnny."

The bounty hunter turned to glance across the small park square and frowned. A group of six homeless people had gathered on the grass and hunkered there to dig through their worn packs and coat pockets. Two of them talked in low, muttered voices, and the other four stared blankly in front of them.

"It's a big thing out here too, ain't it?"

Lisa turned to scan the group. "Homelessness? Yeah, Johnny. It's been a problem in Portland for a while."

"Do you think one of them's gonna try to meet this guy on the corner?"

"Maybe. It's hard to tell until someone makes a move." She turned to study the sidewalk outside the deli. "But I don't see anyone at the corner or even hiding behind it."

"We'll move 'round. Try a different angle."

With a shrug, she gestured for him to go ahead. "You've got the lead on this one."

"Uh-huh. To me, boys. And leave the damn tree alone, huh?"

"It's a good tree, Johnny."

"Strong tree."

"You should try it sometime."

The dwarf snapped his fingers and strode down the street. Lisa and the hounds followed him across the next intersection, where they stopped outside a convenience store that looked like it had seen better days than the deli, but barely. Two bearded men in baggy, stained shirts sat against the brick wall but their full beards and weather-beaten faces made it impossible to tell their age.

"Hey, look." Luther stopped on the sidewalk and stared at the men. "Johnny, you should tell these two-legs their people are over there in the park."

"Yeah, they smell the same too."

Johnny ignored the hounds and nodded at the men who merely looked wearily at him.

One of them cleared his throat. "Hey, man. Nice dogs. Real pretty, all right."

"Thanks." He stayed where he was and stared across the street at the side of the deli. *No damn dealers steppin' out on this side either.*

"Any chance you could spare a few bucks, man? Anything helps."

"I ain't got any spare change, brother. Sorry." He glanced at Lisa, who widened her eyes at him. *Oh, so now I'm the dwarf shellin' out for the homeless, huh? You help one so gotta help 'em all?*

"Even a nickel or a coupla pennies," the other man added. "A little goes a long way."

He sighed, scanned the wall of the deli again, then turned to nod at the homeless men. "I tell ya what. My hounds have been walkin' the city all afternoon. They are probably thirsty."

"Yeah, we feel that, man."

"I bet. Lisa?"

"Johnny?" She smiled at the homeless men and turned toward the dwarf.

"Do you mind goin' inside and grabbin' a couple of waters while I keep an eye out for our friend?"

Her smile widened. "Sure, Johnny."

"And maybe some snacks. You know, the kind that ain't gonna go bad if we wanna carry it 'round with us."

"I'll be right back." The bell jingled on the convenience store door as she stepped inside.

"Johnny. Hey, Johnny." Luther spun to face his master and his tail wagged dangerously close to one of the homeless men's faces. The guy leaned away and stared at the dwarf. "Did you say snacks?"

"Oh, man." Rex whipped his head up from where he'd sniffed the other man's worn boot where a hole had begun to form under the big toe. "We made a stop for dog snacks? Way to go, Johnny."

"We're gonna have a snack party!"

He ignored them and focused on the other side of the street. *It ain't a party until I find this dealer. That's it.*

Lisa emerged five minutes later with four bottles of water, a large bag of beef jerky, and an even larger bag of trail mix. "Is this what you had in mind?"

"That'll do fine, darlin'." He took two water bottles and the bag of beef jerky and ripped it open there on the street.

"Oh-ho-ho, *shit*, Johnny." Luther licked his muzzle. "That smells amazing."

"Good find, lady." Rex sat between Lisa and Johnny and gazed hopefully from one to the other.

The dwarf took two pieces of beef jerky and handed one each to the hounds. The strips disappeared in seconds before Rex and Luther sniffed the cracked asphalt for more.

Johnny turned toward the homeless men and lifted the bag. "Y'all like jerky?"

They both looked at him with wide eyes and nodded, hesitant and uncertain. "Hell of a meal, if you ask me."

"Keeps a while too."

"Sure does." Pretending to consider it, he sniffed, then stepped toward them and proffered the bag. "Y'all are welcome to it."

The man with the hole in his boot grinned through his unkempt beard and took it quickly. "Thanks, man. That's kind of you."

"Much appreciated," the other added and took a strip his friend offered him.

The bounty hunter looked at the bottles of water in his hand. "Shit. You gonna need somethin' to wash it down."

"Aren't those for your dogs?"

"Naw. We can share the other two—can't we, Lisa?"

"Yeah, I think it's enough."

With a grin, he handed them bottles of water, and the men gazed at him in disbelief as they took the gifts.

"You know how to make a man's day, brother. For real."

"Naw, y'all would do the same for me. A group of folks standin' outside this store waitin' for whoever we're waitin' for, right?"

The men nodded and focused on the beef jerky, ripping it off between their teeth.

Rex and Luther sat in front of them, their tails wagging, and watched each piece lift out of the bag and enter mouths that weren't theirs. They said nothing, however, although both seemed poised to pounce on any stray pieces.

"How long do you think we'll have to wait here?" Lisa asked as she held the bag of trail mix absently in one hand.

"I can't say." Johnny folded his arms and studied the side of the deli and the narrow alley behind it. *Do you wish it were sooner rather than later?*

"You said you're waiting for a friend?" one of the homeless men asked.

"That's right. I was told to meet him there on the corner."

The other man finished another long drink of water, then wiped the drops from his beard and shook his head. "I think your friend told you wrong, man."

"Oh, yeah? How's that?"

"Nothing but no-good dealers stepping out on that sidewalk during the last few weeks. It's a terrible thing too, pumping out all that shit into the streets. This is a good city."

"Yeah, you don't want to mess around with the kind of people who stand on that side."

"Do y'all see these deals goin' down?" Johnny asked.

"Uh-huh."

"Yep. Every damn day. We stop here around this time and wait for Remy to go on break."

"He's a real nice man—like you. Most days, he's got leftover breakfast sandwiches he can't sell anymore 'cause they've been in there two days already or whatever. Real good man."

"He sounds like it." Johnny glanced at Lisa and she tilted her head. "I wonder if our friend got the times mixed up, though. Did y'all see anyone standin' out here today lookin' like he was waitin' for someone?"

The man with the hole in his boot shook his head and stared across the street. "Nope. It's weird when I think about it."

"Yeah, they're usually out there selling at all hours but nothing today at all."

"Is that right?" The bounty hunter frowned as he considered this and sighed heavily. "Well, shit. It looks like we've been stood up, Lisa."

"We'll have to have a talk with our friend after this." She glanced at the bag of trail mix in her hand.

"I think we will. Thanks for the updates, fellas."

"Aw, don't mention it. Thanks for the jerky."

"And the water."

One of the men looked at Rex staring at him and snorted. "These dogs look about as hungry as we did five minutes ago."

"Boys." Johnny snapped his fingers. "Y'all give these gentlemen some space now."

"Aw, Johnny. They've got the whole bag."

"Yeah, we're only waiting for leftovers. Every two-legs drops something."

The man holding the bag of jerky pulled out a piece and smiled at Rex. "Very pretty dogs, man. Is it okay if I share with this one?"

Luther whipped his head back to look at his master. "Seriously? Only Rex? I'm a pretty dog too, Johnny."

Lisa bit her lip and expected her partner to explode about his no feeding the hounds rule.

"Hmm." The dwarf frowned at Rex, who stared intently at the jerky strip between the homeless man's dirt-encrusted fingers. "I suppose one more ain't gonna hurt him. Only one, mind."

"Read you loud and clear." The man handed a strip to his friend and nodded at Luther. "You get that one, Bill."

"Sure."

"Oh man, oh man, oh man." Luther stretched his neck out to take the jerky politely.

"You sure are a good-looking dog." The man with the hole in his boot offered a piece to Rex, who swallowed it in a single gulp and licked his hand in gratitude. "Sure. Look at you. A big ol' sweetheart, aren't you?"

"Johnny, I like these two-legs." Rex panted and closed his eyes to enjoy a good head rub.

"Very nice two-legs," Luther agreed and sniffed the other man's boots.

Lisa stared at the dwarf in disbelief and a small smile played at the corner of her mouth.

He cleared his throat and pretended to ignore her. "All right, boys. We have a friend to find and these fellas have their own business to attend to."

"Many thanks for the refreshments, brother." One man lifted his bottle of water. "What's your name?"

"Johnny."

"Right on, Johnny. I'm Bill. And this is Mack. Best lawyer you'll find on the streets."

Mack burst out laughing. "Oh, sure. Pro bono's the only way to get it done."

They chuckled and nodded at the bounty hunter. "Good luck finding your friend, Johnny."

"I'll take the luck and say thanks." He smiled and glanced at Lisa. "It looks like this ain't the place we were hopin' for."

"Then it's time to go." She glanced at the bag of trail mix and frowned. "Oh, no."

"What?"

"I can't believe I didn't look at the ingredients in here. Dang. Hey, are either of you allergic to anything?"

Bill shook his head. "Not that I know of."

Mack nudged his friend's shoulder. "Except for a bath, maybe."

"Very funny. If I could smell anymore, I'd say the same thing about you."

"Trust me. You smell."

Lisa chuckled and extended the bag toward them. "I'm allergic to raisins so I can't touch any of this. Do you want it?"

"Raisins, huh?" Mack grinned at her and his weathered eyes crinkled at the corner. "I bet you could go inside and exchange that for something you can eat."

"I have water." She brandished the other two bottles in her hand. "And we have that friend to find."

"Time is of the essence. That's what I always say." Mack took the bag from her. "Thank you."

"No problem. Hey, if you happen to see those dealers here on the corner, we'd appreciate anything else you might be able to tell us. You know, if our paths ever cross again."

"We're here every day," Bill said. "And we cross paths with more people than you might believe."

"Not many of them are as decent as you two. Or have such beautiful dogs with them," Mack added. "We'll keep an eye out."

"'Preciate it, fellas. Enjoy the sunshine, huh?" Johnny turned to step across the street toward the park square. "I heard it don't stick 'round here all that much."

"Summer days, right?" Bill lifted a hand in farewell. "Take care, Johnny."

"Yeah, you too."

Lisa smiled at the men as they turned their attention to the trail mix, then followed Johnny and the hounds across the street. "I thought you never let anyone feed your dogs."

"It's all about the intention, darlin'. A coupla fellas down on their luck wanna share the little they have with my hounds? There ain't nothin' but kindness in that."

Luther sniffed at the same tree as they passed. "I bet they would've shared more if you let 'em, Johnny."

"But we're not complaining," Rex added. "Maybe next time, you can buy them a steak, Johnny."

"Ooh, yeah. We *love* to share steak."

CHAPTER TWENTY-TWO

"So no dealer on the corner selling drugs stamped with the red boar." Lisa paused briefly to stare at the same rabbit-mask-lady mural when they passed it again en route to the center of downtown. "I'd say Mikey and Janice were lying to us if Mack and Bill hadn't confirmed that someone does usually deal at that corner."

"Uh-huh." Johnny frowned up the street at the rising clamor of music and shouted chants that approached. "The question now is why ain't that dealer in his regular location?"

"Do you think he was tipped off?"

"I ain't sure what to think, darlin'. Especially 'bout all that damn noise. What the hell is that?" He gestured up the street at a group of people who waved flags and banners. Someone in the front played a banjo as he walked, followed by other musicians in a row behind him.

"It looks like a parade to me." Lisa shrugged.

"I don't like the looks of it."

They continued to walk and the words on the banners became easier to read.

"Oh." Lisa grinned. "I've heard about this. It's the Portland Blues Festival this weekend."

He pointed at the banners and raised an eyebrow at her. "The one at Waterfront Park?"

"Yeah! How did you know?"

"It says it right there on the banner, darlin'. I can read too."

She shook her head. "That could be something fun to do tomorrow while we're waiting for that five o'clock tour."

He snorted. "If you wanna go listen to all that clangin' and bangin', be my guest."

"Johnny, it's blues, not folk music."

"Same difference. If it ain't metal, I ain't goin'."

"Isn't blues very big down in the South?"

"Not in my neck o' the woods." The dwarf trudged down the sidewalk and shook his head vigorously. The parade celebrating the start of the Blues Festival took up most of the street before they turned at the next intersection.

"Hey, Johnny." Luther stepped off the sidewalk after the group but immediately turned when he realized his master wasn't moving. "Do we know any magicals who play music at home?"

"Oh, yeah," Rex added. "Well, there's Ronnie. Doesn't he do something with spoons?"

"You mean like eat with them?"

"No, as an instrument."

Johnny glanced at his hounds. *What are they goin' on about now?*

"Look at all the magicals in that parade, Johnny." Luther sniffed the air. "Couple dwarves in there. And a…at least two witches."

"Three," Rex corrected. "Weird to see 'em marching around like that, don't you think? Johnny?"

The bounty hunter turned toward Lisa. "Did you notice any magicals in that little display?"

"A few." She shrugged. "The dwarves are easy enough to identify—no offense."

"Why would I find that offensive?"

208

She shook her head and looked down the cross-street at the last of the parade. "No reason. Why are you asking about magicals?"

Johnny shrugged as if he thought the answer was obvious. "Well, there ain't no shortage of 'em in Portland. It's a shame they ain't done nothin' to fix the city up the way it oughta be."

"Like that deli?"

"Like the whole damn place."

Stifling a laugh, she scanned the downtown streets that grew busier as the day wound down and the nightlife geared up. "So what's your point?"

"This demon-lady whoever has eight victims under her belt, all human. How come we don't have any reports of magicals with the same thing?"

Her eyes widened. "Do you think humans are being targeted specifically?"

"They might be. I wanna know why."

"They're more susceptible to magic, depending on what it is. At least as targets. Yes, they all know it's there, but how many humans run around looking for magicals or try to get involved?"

"Exactly. What d'ya think the ratio is of magicals to humans runnin' 'round in those tunnels oohin' and ahin' over whatever they find down there?"

"I have no idea, Johnny. But when we're down there tomorrow, we'll get our answers."

"Yeah, I guess we will. If we do it right, we'll get every last damn one." He sniffed and pointed at the intersection with 3rd Avenue. "It's time for a drink."

"Are you sure?"

He darted her an exasperated glance.

"Okay, yeah. You haven't had your drink today and it's after five o'clock."

"That ain't got nothin' to do with it. I'll choose the bar this time, darlin'. If they ain't got what I'm drinkin', there's still the bottle at the hotel." He strode across the street, followed closely by the hounds.

"Music sounds good, though, Johnny."

"Yeah, I bet all those people dancing and bluesing drop a *lot* of snacks."

"No festivals." He shook his head and stepped onto the sidewalk before another cyclist raced down the street without slowing. *Not in this city.*

They wandered down 3rd Avenue in the general direction of their hotel. Johnny scowled at all the open doorways filled with schmoozing Portlanders, their drinks in hand as they mingled outside. It seemed every other bar had some kind of live musical performance either inside or out on the patio, and the sound of it all at the same time made his scowl deepen.

"For a city tryin' to be some kinda progressive haven, you'd think they'd learn how to progress without the noise. How are folks supposed to choose where to go when they can't hear themselves think?"

Lisa shook her head and strolled casually beside him. "Hey, there's a saloon."

"Do I look like a cowboy?"

"Okay, that's a no. Look at this one—whisky distillery. It has your name on it, right?"

"Unless it has my actual name on the label, darlin', I ain't buyin'."

She sighed heavily and approached the front door, where the distillery posted a list of their different barrels available to sample and buy on the premises. "You don't even want to try—"

"Nope." He didn't stop walking.

"It shouldn't be this hard to find somewhere to buy a drink," Lisa muttered as she jogged to catch up with him. "Have you ever tried anything else?"

"Liquor?"

"Yeah."

"Nope."

"I get it. You're set in your ways." She gestured ahead of them in the direction of their hotel only a few more blocks down. "I feel like you'll simply be disappointed again. Why don't we go to the hotel and look over the file again? Now that we have this connection with the tunnels, I think it might be a good idea to look for—"

The bounty hunter had stopped listening almost as soon as she'd started to talk. He now stared at a bar entrance in the alley beside him—The Death Trap—with grungy neon signs and heavy metal pumping from the huge speakers, and the shredded guitar and wild drumming reverberated in his chest. *Now this is what I wanted to see.*

The hounds sniffed the entrance to the alley. "Whoa, this place stinks."

"Smells like blood and sweat, Johnny. And booze."

"Exactly. Y'all go stay with Lisa." With a broad grin, he stepped into the alley.

"Wait, what?"

"Go on."

The dogs stared after their master for a moment, then turned and trotted to catch up with the agent. "Does he want us to tell her where he went?"

"She can't hear us, bro."

"Then what's the point?"

Johnny cocked his head and listened to the pounding music spilling into the alley. A man in black jeans, a tight black t-shirt, and a silver-studded black band around his wrist and a five-inch mohawk stood in front of the door, smoking a cigarette. He pulled the last of it away from his lips, blew out a thick plume of smoke in the waning daylight, and jerked his chin at Johnny. The dwarf returned the gesture before his gaze settled on the tattoo on the man's wrist that peeked out from beneath the black band.

A red boar.

The man crushed the cigarette butt beneath his thick black boot, turned swiftly, and disappeared inside The Death Trap.

The bounty hunter quickened his pace and jerked his head away from the last whiff of cigarette smoke as he stepped inside. *Two birds with one damn stone. It might be my lucky night.*

The bar was packed with metalheads, even those who didn't traditionally look the part. Three women in their late twenties with their hair and makeup all done up for a night on the town and wearing weather-appropriate short skirts and shorter shorts stood in a huddle inside the front door. They nodded their heads to the music and studied him with coy smiles. The blonde in the middle raised her drink toward him and her gaze roved over him slowly.

Johnny jerked his chin at her and moved through the bar, keeping an eye on the man in black with the boar tattoo. *The idiot ain't makin' it easy to blend in with that hair. Perfect.*

He glanced at the bar as he passed it. The customers paid for their drinks and moved on without congregating and taking up all the space. *They are slingin' simple drinks. Folks move on to make room and everyone's feelin' the vibe. It sure as shit is my kinda place.*

As he moved through the crowd of half-dancing, half-drinking people with his gaze on the mohawk, a woman with four different dog collars dangling around her neck stepped in front of him and cut him off. "Nice knife."

"Sure is." He nodded and peered around her as the mohawk returned to a table with two other guys and threw back two shots in a row.

"Do you know how to use it?" she asked and tossed her black-dyed hair over her shoulder as she gave him a long, slow look of appraisal.

"'Course I do, but now ain't the time, darlin'. 'Scuse me."

The woman smirked as he stepped around her and turned to watch him stalk toward his target and his pals. They'd chosen the table closest to the narrow hallway leading to the bathroom and the back door. The man with the tattoo caught sight of Johnny coming toward him and nodded again.

"Yeah, hey. How's it goin'?" The bounty hunter extended his hand for a shake.

"What's up?" The man grunted and grasped his hand, willing to placate someone who looked like he belonged there too.

As soon as their hands met, he crushed the guy's fingers in an iron grasp and twisted his wrist to expose the red boar tattoo.

"Fuck! What are you—"

"Nice ink, shitface." He yanked him from his seat and thrust him against the wall forcefully enough to drive the breath out of him. "We gotta have us a little talk."

"What the hell's wrong with you, man? Dude, I don't even know you—"

"It don't matter. Let's go." He jerked him away from the wall and shoved him down the hall. After a couple of steps, he leaned back to look at the man's buddies, who watched him with wide eyes. "Yeah, y'all got the right idea. You sit tight. He'll be back in a few."

"What's this about, man?" His quarry spread his arms in the narrow hallway and regarded him with a trace of panic. "You wanna tell me—"

Johnny drew his utility knife and flicked it open.

"Whoa, whoa. Hey. You don't have to—"

"No, you're the one who's gonna tell me what I wanna know. Back door, and don't try anythin' unless you're sure you can outrun a thrown blade."

"Fuck. Okay, okay." He raised his hands in surrender and stepped backward down the hall.

The dwarf stalked after him. "Keep movin'."

The door to the ladies' restroom opened and a tall woman in a black leather jumper and four-inch platform shoes stood in the doorway to watch. "I honestly didn't expect the night to start like this."

"It ain't over yet, darlin'. Go enjoy yourself." Johnny nodded toward the bar and practically shoved the other man into the back door before it opened and let them out into a medium-sized lot behind the building, complete with a dumpster and fire escape ladders along the other buildings.

"Okay, man. What's—"

He caught the man by the back of his black t-shirt and shoved him forward against the brick wall. "I'm askin' the questions here."

"You haven't asked me anything!"

After spinning him again, he pushed him against the wall and pointed the knife at his gut. "If I'm bein' honest—which is one of those things I value very highly—you're only the bottom of the barrel, pal." He nodded at the guy's wrist. "But I saw that tattoo."

"What?"

"Who do you work for?"

"I have no fucking clue what you're talking about!"

The back door burst open beside them and two women poked their heads out, laughing.

"Not now, ladies." Johnny wiggled the blade tip at them. "Go on back inside."

The woman with her hair cut in a short bob leaned her head farther out and stared at the apparent victim.

"Vanessa!" her friend whispered harshly, followed by another giggle. "Christ, it's like you go around looking for trouble." She dragged her drunk friend inside and pulled the door closed behind them.

Scowling, the bounty hunter turned toward the other man, who'd bent quickly to remove a knife from the inside of his boot. The sucker realized immediately, though, that he'd lost his planned element of surprise and straightened, wide-eyed, before he tried to rush his interrogator.

With a low growl of annoyance, Johnny ducked the poorly aimed swipe and came up on the other side of his opponent. With his knife still in one hand, he slipped the other between the man's arms and pounded his wrist with both fists, each moving in opposite directions.

"Aw, *shit*!" His adversary clutched his wrist and stumbled against the wall as his tiny blade skittered across the cracked asphalt. "You broke my fucking wrist!"

Johnny sniffed and nodded unsympathetically. "It might be fractured. Come on. I told you not to try anything."

"What the hell do you want?"

The dwarf shoved him against the wall again and held the point of his blade under his chin. "I told you what I want. Who the fuck do you work for?"

"The...t-the Portland Nursery. Out near Centennial!"

"Wrong answer." He smacked the man across the face with his left hand, grasped a fistful of his black t-shirt, and swept the knife in his other hand to the guy's ribcage. "Your fucking ink gave you away, dumbass. You marked yourself with the red boar and I wanna know where the fuck that shit comes from before it lands in your grubby little hands."

"What?" His captive tried to look at his wrist but there was too much bounty hunter in the way. "That's it? It's only a tattoo, man. You're crazy."

"Okay, we can do this on a three-strike system." Johnny hauled him away from the wall, turned, and threw him against the dumpster. He made impact with a loud clang and a pained grunt. "You pulled a knife on me and you're still lyin'. Who do you work for?"

The man huddled against the dumpster and raised both hands in surrender. "I have no idea what you're talking about. I swear. I'm a regular guy."

"Then why did you get that tattoo?"

"Because it's fucking cool. Why else?"

"Is this strike three?" He waved his blade in the air and stalked toward his quarry, feeling far more optimistic with the heavy metal music rising in a muffled beat from the other side of The Death Trap's back door.

CHAPTER TWENTY-THREE

"Johnny!" Lisa shouted and spun on the sidewalk. Her gaze settled on every person walking through downtown Portland wearing all black, but none of them were Johnny. *Jesus. How many people wear black in the middle of the summer?*

Gritting her teeth, she pulled her phone out and dialed his number. "You have some serious explaining to do, Johnny Walker."

She looked at Rex and Luther, who sniffed the sidewalk at her feet. "We told you where he went, lady."

"Yeah, if you'd only *listen*." Luther looked at her and chuffed. "Great. You're on the phone."

"Dammit." She pocketed her phone again and studied the street. "Fine. I'll retrace my steps and—"

Rex yipped. "You hear that?"

Luther's ears flopped against his head when he turned toward his brother. "Johnny found something."

"Come on, lady. Come on!" Rex darted down the sidewalk, then stopped and turned. "Shit. Luther. How do we get a lady two-legs' attention?"

"I don't know. Sniff up her skirt?"

"She's not wearing a skirt."

"Damn."

"Lisa!" Rex barked at her and took two more urgent steps forward. "Come on! We're gonna miss it."

"Don't you run off on me too." She pointed at the hounds. "And you don't even have leashes. What the hell was he thinking?" She stared at the dogs, who returned it impatiently. *It's worth a shot to get them moving, right?* She snapped her fingers and pointed at the sidewalk in front of her. "Rex. Luther. Come."

Luther sniggered. "Look at that, Rex. Ha-ha. She's trying so hard."

"Lady, do you wanna find Johnny or not? 'Cause it sounds like he's bashing someone's face against a brick wall right now." Rex barked again and took two more steps forward.

"Oh, my God. Fine. Come here." Lisa moved toward them, and the hounds bounded away down the sidewalk before they turned to look at her again. "If anything happens to either of you, I'm very sure I'm dead. So please…be good dogs and stick with me until I find Johnny."

"That's what we're *saying*." Rex barked twice. "Johnny."

Luther's tongue flopped out of his mouth and he looked up the sidewalk with a low whine. "He's this way."

Lisa frowned at them. "Do you know where he is?"

"Oh, my God. *Finally*." Rex barked twice again and Luther trotted up the sidewalk to join his brother.

"No. No, this is crazy." Lisa spun and tried to smile at a young couple who strolled past her with their arms around each other.

"Hey, those your dogs?" the guy asked.

"Kind of…"

"You have to keep them on a leash in public," the woman said with a concerned frown.

"I'm working on it," she muttered through clenched teeth and settled her attention on the hounds again, who remained exactly where they were and waited for her. *I'm not talking to two coon-hounds. Real life does not work like* Lassie*.*

"Aw, come *on.* Luther, do something."

"What? Why me? You're the smart one."

Rex snorted and stepped urgently down the sidewalk. "Let's *go,* lady. You wanna hold this whole thing up because you don't trust Johnny's hounds to know what they're talking about?"

Luther whined. "We should leave her here."

"Johnny wouldn't have told us to stay with her if that was the plan, bozo."

"Oh."

Lisa stepped toward them and cast wary glances around the much larger number of pedestrians and locals who now began to mill around downtown. The hounds yipped and darted away from her.

"Shit, this is gonna take all night."

"Yeah, lady. Johnny might be dead by the time we find him. And I mean from natural causes."

"Ha-ha. Good one."

"You guys are making this very hard right now." She gestured with her hands in frustration. "We need to find Johnny."

Rex barked twice. "Duh. Listen to yourself. Jeez."

She squinted at him. *That's the third time he's done that. And I'm either crazy or these dogs can understand me. Screw it.* "Do you know where he is?"

Luther barked twice. "That's what we're saying. Hey, I thought Light Elves were supposed to be smart."

"Can you—" Lisa rolled her eyes. "Jesus, I can't believe I'm saying this. Can you understand me?"

Two barks issued from Rex. "Yes! For the love of raw beef, lady. *Come on!*"

"Luther?"

"Wow, you're dense!" He barked twice and pranced anxiously down the sidewalk. "Can we go now?"

I'm going insane. Lisa's eyes widened and she tilted her head slowly. "Bark once if you can understand—"

Both hounds barked once, which made several pedestrians step away and watch them warily.

She jolted and took a step back. "Do it again."

"You're wasting our time, lady."

"Yeah, how many times do you have to ask?"

She sighed. "Okay. Okay, I'm reading into things. Of course they can't understand me."

The hounds glanced at each other, then each barked once. She jumped and shook her head quickly. "No way."

"All right, that's it. Luther, if she doesn't get it by now, she's the worst partner Johnny's ever had."

"Isn't she his only partner?"

"Does it matter? Come on." Rex uttered a warbled bay and raced down the sidewalk. "Keep up, lady!"

"Yeah, you might wanna pick your jaw up off the sidewalk." Luther darted after his brother and wove deftly around pedestrians.

"Holy shit." Lisa stared after them until she realized they were getting away. *Dogs. Dogs can understand me. What?*

She raced after them and had to slide sideways to avoid knocking into a group of women with neon-dyed hair in different colors. "Hey, wait!"

"Look at that, Rex. She's not as dumb as we thought."

"Only took half a lifetime." Rex darted left into an alley, followed quickly by his brother.

The agent skidded to a stop in front of the entrance and sighed heavily. *I'm gonna have to turn my badge in if this doesn't pan out.*

She raced past two restaurant employees standing in the alley on a smoke break. Another man rummaged through a pile of black trash bags as she followed the hounds, and he looked slowly at her in suspicion when she hurried around him.

"Yeah, this is it," Rex said and sniffed the air. "He's close."

"Only guy around that smells like whisky and gunpowder," Luther added. "And dwarf."

"Rex! Luther!" Lisa barreled down the alley after them and tried to maintain her momentum when they made a sharp right turn into another intersecting alley. "Get back here!"

Luther bayed and yipped once. "Johnny!"

"We found you, all right." Rex growled and stepped forward. "Who's your friend?"

The agent finally rounded the corner and stopped when she saw Johnny pinning someone with a mohawk against the dumpster. "Holy shit."

"No, no, man. Come on." The guy groaned and raised his hands. "You're insane! All this shit about strikes."

"And you're one of the worst liars I ever questioned," the dwarf retorted coldly.

"Johnny." Lisa drew her service weapon from her shoulder holster and aimed it at the stranger's head, just in case. "What's going on?"

"This bastard don't wanna give up the goods."

"Now you're trying to rob me?" the man shrieked.

"What?" Lisa shouted.

The bounty hunter pressed his knife insistently against the man's ribcage. "You don't know when to give up, do ya?"

Lisa stepped toward them as the hounds growled and closed in around the dumpster. *He looks like he's lost his mind.* "Johnny, I can't help you if you don't tell me what the hell this is about."

"He has a red boar tattoo on his goddamn wrist," the dwarf all but snarled. "And I aim to make this little piggy start squealin'. Last chance, asshole."

"I have no idea what you're—"

A fireball streaked down the side of the building from behind the dumpster. Lisa turned to watch it crash against the wall of the building behind her, and Luther snarled fiercely.

"We got incoming, Johnny," the hound shouted.

"Three," Rex added. "Nope. Four."

"Is that you, Dennis?" A low, growling voice echoed in the wide alley, accompanied by heavy footsteps from multiple pairs of feet.

The captive sneered at Johnny and shouted, "How could you tell?"

"'Cause you're always getting your dumbass whooped behind bars is how." A massive Kilomea with glowing yellow eyes strode down the alley, followed by a human man and two wizards.

Lisa's eyes widened when she saw the next fireball surrounded by red sparks in the Kilomea's hand. *He shouldn't be able to do all that.*

"Well, you know me." Dennis struggled to free himself from his captor's grasp but the dwarf held fast. "Popular as shit and all that."

"Huh." The Kilomea stopped and stared at Johnny and his glowing eyes narrowed into slits. "What does a dwarf want with this pain in my ass?"

Johnny shoved the man against the dumpster again but finally released him. Dennis grunted and tried unsuccessfully to rearrange his severely stretched shirt. "You know him better than I do. Might be you can answer both our questions."

The Kilomea chuckled. "Does he owe you money or something?"

"Nope. Only a name." He changed his grip on the knife and glanced at the wizards, who summoned attack spells while they waited for the word. "It might be yours."

"And who's the broad?" The huge magical who'd completely shed his human illusion nodded toward Lisa and his tongue protruded between his huge teeth.

"She's with me. And yeah, that gun's loaded." Johnny spread his arms and held the knife out to one side. "Do y'all work together?"

The Kilomea glanced at Dennis with a sneer. "This little shit works for me."

"See?" He pointed his blade at the man again. "Now how fuckin' hard was that?"

"What do you want?" the wizard in cut-off jeans asked.

"I'm workin' my way up the ladder." He nodded at the Kilomea. "It looks like you're the big dog in this alley."

"Hey." Rex snorted. "Low blow, Johnny."

The hairy magical beast glanced at the hounds, then at Lisa again. "It depends on what you're looking for."

The dwarf lowered his empty hand slowly to his belt and the black explosive disks hanging from it. "Lemonhead. Does that ring any bells?"

The Kilomea's eyes widened for only a split-second before he attacked with a snarl.

Johnny ducked the massive swinging fist, activated an exploding disk as he drew it from his belt, and lobbed the device down the alley toward the wizards and their human tagalong.

"What the—" It exploded and the wizards were hurled into the brick wall while chunks of building material broke off and rained around them.

The huge magical summoned a fireball in one hand and his eyes glowed even more fiercely as he launched it at his much smaller adversary. Johnny dropped to his knees beneath the flaming spell and uttered a piercing whistle.

"Hell yes!" Rex snarled and leapt at the wizards who still tried to recover against the wall.

Luther pounced on Dennis and knocked the man down to pin him beneath both front paws. "This one's not going anywhere, Johnny."

The Kilomea spun to face him again, this time with red sparks flaring in both his hands. They grew and gave way to dark-red energy that filled the alley with an eerie glow. "You're asking all the wrong questions, dwarf, and should have stopped while you were ahead—"

Lisa's fireball caught him squarely in the back and he staggered forward with a roar. "You too, asshole."

"Bitch!" The hulking creature turned and stalked toward her and the red energy flared in his hands again.

The bounty hunter lunged after him, but the other human with the wizards barreled into him from behind and tried to wrap his arms around him and drag him off his feet.

"What the fuck?" He slapped a hand on his attacker's arm and bent forward to throw the guy over his shoulder. The man landed on the asphalt with a grunt and remained on his back in a daze as he stared at the tops of the buildings around them. Johnny delivered a fist into his gut, then stepped over him. "You got a lotta work to do on that move."

"FBI," Lisa shouted and aimed her pistol at the Kilomea's head. "Stop or I will shoot."

"A Light Elf with the FBI." The huge magical chuckled. "Not for much longer."

Johnny tossed another exploding disk at the creature's back. It bounced off but made the intended target turn in confusion, and everyone stared at the blinking red light on the top of the disk.

"It's all about timing," the bounty hunter muttered.

His adversary snorted. "You gotta be kid—"

The disk exploded at the magical's feet and Johnny threw another one behind him as he ran toward the stunned Kilomea. "Rex! Out!"

With a snarl, Rex jerked on the jeans caught between his jaws, ripped them all the way to the crotch, and leapt away with a mouthful as the second disk sailed toward the wizards.

They scrambled away from the flying explosive but were launched forward into a pile of trash bags on the other side of the dumpster.

Johnny lunged toward the Kilomea with his blade and slashed at the huge magical's inner thigh.

"Fuck off!" His massive opponent whirled and battered his huge, hairy forearm against the dwarf's chest.

The blow was sufficient to catapult him across the alley until his back thumped against the wall. He grunted, shook his head, and pointed his knife at the magical. "All I want is a little information."

"You ain't gettin' shit!"

Lisa launched another fireball at the Kilomea's face, but it sailed past him and over the heads of the wizards who tried to clamber out of the pile of trash. The next one she threw caught him in the chest and made him stagger back with another roar. Calmly, she leveled her gun at him again. "I don't like to shoot someone unless I have a good reason. We can overlook whatever this stupid alley fight is if you simply tell us what we want to know."

The alley settled into a tense silence broken only by Dennis' feeble attempts to slap Luther off him while the hound whipped a mouthful of his shirt from side to side. "Get this fucking dog off me, man. What the hell's wrong with you people?"

"Shut up," the Kilomea snarled at him, breathing heavily.

Sirens blared in the distance and drew steadily closer.

Johnny stepped away from the wall. "We can do this all night if we have to. But know that my hounds are real good at sniffin' out bullshit—and the idiots dishin' it out."

The large magical rubbed his seared chest around the charred hole Lisa's fireball had made. "You're dead already if that's the name you're after."

"Then give me a better one."

The sirens wailed at high volume on the other side of the bar and red and blue lights threw scattered shadows across the far end of the alley. The wizards finally extricated themselves and stood beside the dumpster to brush trash off their clothes and glare at Rex, who snarled at them in warning.

Luther growled at Dennis, who raised both hands and stared at the hound's slavering jaws. "Want me to rip this one apart, Johnny?"

"These wizards can't fight for shit," Rex added.

The Kilomea grunted and opened his mouth. In the next moment, the shouting started.

The back door of The Death Trap burst open and a stream of half-drunk people spilled out into the alley.

"The cops are bustin' the place up," a short man with a shaved head and studded suspenders shouted. "Anyone with anything on them should get out."

Luther snarled and leapt away from the crowd of people that streamed through the door. "What is this?"

"Fuck the police!" It was the same woman who'd popped her head through the back door when Johnny had first started his interrogation of Dennis. She threw devil horns into the air and whooped before her friend dragged her along the alley, moving with the tide of bodies.

Heavy metal pumped through the open door, accompanied by more shouts.

Johnny tried to push through the bodies to reach the Kilmoea, but he couldn't cover ground fast enough. "Y'all need to move!"

"Yeah, you too, man. Unless you got nothing to hide."

The dwarf grumbled as person after person darted out of the back door until the alley almost overflowed with them. He caught a glimpse of his target's glowing yellow eyes beneath the restored human illusion before the magical and his cohorts vanished in the haze of drunk bodies that scattered through the back alleys of downtown Portland.

Even Dennis was gone.

"Shit."

Lisa had holstered her weapon the second the back door

opened and now pushed down the alley toward him. "I have so many questions right now. Like why you thought it was a good idea to—"

"We need to go after 'em," he growled.

"Johnny…"

"Why do you wanna do that?" Rex asked as he sat at his master's feet. "They didn't have anything on 'em."

The dwarf glanced at his hound and frowned.

"He's right, Johnny," Luther added. "I shook that two-leg with the spikey hair up and down, and there wasn't even a whiff of drugs on him. Or common sense, now that I think about it."

"That hairy one was kind of a beast, but no drugs."

"Nope. Not even a little."

Johnny gritted his teeth. *Then why the hell did they fight us?*

"They recognized the name Lemonhead," Lisa interjected. "Even if they've only heard the name and not met the guy. But I don't think—"

"Forget it. They're gone. But if I see those assholes again, I'll pull the real damn answer out from between their teeth if I have to." He flipped his utility knife shut and slipped it onto his belt. Without warning, he pushed toward the back door and wove around the last few stragglers escaping from the bar who stumbled over themselves and laughed as they looked back drunkenly to make sure they weren't being followed. He caught the edge of the door and threw it open before he stormed inside.

"Johnny. Hey, come on!" Lisa lunged at the door but missed it by an inch before it clicked shut. There was no handle. "Seriously?"

She turned and looked at the hounds seated dutifully behind her.

"Don't worry, lady." Luther panted and stared at her. "He probably went in for a drink. Or two."

Rex lowered his head to lick beneath one leg. "He'll be back. Hey, maybe with snacks."

She folded her arms and frowned at them. "You two look like you're up to something. And I might be losing my mind. Come on. I bet we'll find him out front after his drink."

Inside the bar, Johnny nodded to the shredding guitar solo that blared over the speakers as two Portland police officers finished cuffing two men in baggy hoodies before they steered them toward the front door. The other two officers glanced around the half-empty bar with their hands on the butts of their holstered service pistols. After a moment, they exited after their colleagues.

Red and blue police lights flashed through the front door. The static crackle of a radio rose faintly through the blaring music.

The bounty hunter smirked at the crowd of hardcore metal-heads who thrashed at the far side of the bar and formed their own mosh pit without a live band anywhere in sight. He sniffed and approached the counter to lean over it to shout at the bartender, "You got Johnny Walker Black?"

The man with long dark hair pulled back in a ponytail nodded and turned swiftly to take the bottle off the shelf.

Johnny grinned. "Neat."

He watched while his drink was poured swiftly and expertly, nodded in time to the music, and jerked his chin at two women who approached the bar. With a small smirk, he slapped a ten-dollar bill on the wood in exchange for his drink and knocked it back. The women at the bar scrutinized him thoroughly and constantly darted glances at him as they ordered their drinks.

A fight broke out at the far side of the amateur mosh pit—two skinny guys with baggy pants wrestled each other to the table and threw wild fists that mostly caught only thin air. A glass shattered somewhere but the music continued to play.

The bartender returned and shouted, "Want another?"

"Naw, I'm good. Keep the change." Johnny grinned. "You know, I thought this city was a real shithole. After comin' here, though, I think maybe it ain't so bad."

"Okay, man."

The dwarf threw devil horns with one hand, and the man returned the gesture swiftly before he leaned toward his next customers.

With a chuckle, the dwarf pushed through the bar patrons who hadn't felt the need to run from the cops. The wrestlers thumped against the wall beside the front door before one of them hauled the other to the floor and began to batter him with his fists. Johnny stepped around them without a word and entered the alley.

The police lights still flashed from the two squad cars pulled up on the curb in front of the other bars. He stepped out of the alley, sniffed, and turned to find Lisa and the hounds waiting for him. "Perfect timin'."

"That's twice in under an hour." She held two fingers up. "We're working this case together, Johnny. I'm not here to chase you all over Portland and lose my mind thinking your dogs can understand what I'm saying."

He glanced at the hounds, who both licked their muzzles and stared at him. *How the hell did they manage that?*

"Do you have anything to say?"

With a grunt, he gestured up the street in the direction of their hotel. "Do you still have beer in your room?"

"What?" She fell into step beside him and Rex and Luther trailed a few paces behind them. "I thought you didn't drink beer."

"I don't. But I reckon you could do with a few after tonight."

She scoffed and fixed him a condescending frown. "I don't need to drink after every confrontation with a couple of thugs in an alley."

"I know. But if you're thinkin' my hounds can understand you…"

"Stop." She glanced over her shoulder at the animals padding along behind them, who panted and gazed at her with huge eyes.

"They did know exactly where to find you, though. Which is a little weird now that I think about it."

"No, it ain't. They can sniff a 'gator out from miles upriver. I think I'm a hell of a lot easier to find." *And she's cuttin' awfully close to the truth here.*

"Kind of an understatement, Johnny," Rex said.

"Yeah." Luther stopped to sniff a bench on the sidewalk. "You're no 'gator but you have your own kinda Johnny stink, you know?"

The bounty hunter snorted and shook his head.

"What's so funny?" Lisa asked.

"You did good back there, darlin'—showin' up with the hounds and tossin' a few fireballs."

"You know, I appreciate the pat on the back but I can't shake this feeling that you're keeping something from me."

He shrugged under her scrutinizing stare and simply grinned. "You're the fed. If I'm hidin' somethin', you're bound to find out sooner or later."

Lisa rolled her eyes. "Does that have anything to do with why you simply disappeared without a word to go beat up a guy with a red boar tattoo?"

"Nope. That was only me tryin' to get a lead. That little gang back there has somethin' to do with the drug ring. No one gets the same tattoo as that red stamp simply 'cause they think it's cool."

"Okay. I get that you wanted to catch the guy before he disappeared. And that all four of us walking into that bar together might have drawn more attention than you wanted. Fine." She shook her head and focused down the street to search for the marquee above their hotel. "But don't do it again."

"All right. Sorry for steppin' on your toes, Agent Breyer. Next time, I'll shout it out in the open where everyone can hear."

She punched him in the shoulder and he staggered sideways

along the sidewalk with a snort. "And don't leave me in a back alley on the other side of a door with no handle either."

"Fine."

"Did you at least get your damn drink?"

"You bet."

CHAPTER TWENTY-FOUR

The next morning, Johnny sat on the bed in his hotel room, searching through his phone for information about the Shanghai Tunnels tours. He tried to swipe up again to refresh the Internet search and his screen shifted to the last page he'd been reading instead. "Damn smartphones. Has anyone ever managed to pin down what the hell makes 'em so smart?"

Rex raised his head from his forepaws and yawned widely. "Have you tried asking it questions?"

"Yeah, Johnny." Luther gnawed between the toes of one paw, then settled for licking it repeatedly. "That's how we test something's smarts. If it can't answer a question, it's dumb enough to be chased."

Johnny waved his phone at the hound. "You wanna chase my phone now?"

"Uh..."

Rex chuckled. "Yeah, you passed the smarts test, all right."

A knock caught his attention.

"Yeah?"

"It's Lisa."

"'Course it is."

"What was that?"

"Nothin'." Johnny tossed his phone onto the bed and slid off to open the door.

"Morning." Lisa shoved another to-go cup of coffee toward him. He took it gratefully and closed the door behind her as she waltzed into his room.

"Don't tell me you wasted any more money on those dog biscuits."

"Nope. Only coffee. I assumed that if you wanted breakfast, you'd get it yourself. Which I see you've already done."

"I was up early." He slurped the coffee, swallowed, and glared at the cup. "Damn. It's still good."

She pulled her tablet out from under her arm and sat in her usual place on the round lime-green armchair. "And you decided to wait inside?"

"I was tryin' to read about those tunnels but the damn phone won't do what I want."

Biting back a laugh, she settled more comfortably. "What did you find?"

"Tour times. All kinds of back story about the tunnels. Unfortunately, they ain't advertisin' the extra thrill of gettin' marked by dark magic and hallucinatin' demons."

The agent took another sip of coffee. "So you're completely sure you still want to wait for the last tour of the day?"

"Did somethin' change in the last fourteen hours?"

"No." She placed her coffee down and looked at him with a barely concealed smile. "But if that's the case, it means we have all day to poke around the area—"

Johnny snorted. "If you made another one of those damn wish lists, Lisa, you can forget it right now."

"No, I don't have a list." She glanced at her tablet and cleared her throat. "But I did find a great park not too far from here."

Rex and Luther both jerked their heads up again to stare at her. "She said park, Johnny."

"Yeah, that's what I heard."

"We're in."

"I ain't goin' to no stupid Blues Festival." The dwarf sipped his coffee and sat on the edge of the bed.

"Johnny, you can't hole yourself up in a hotel room with two hounds for the next eight hours."

"Watch me."

"I'd rather not." She pulled up pictures of the park and leaned over the chair's armrest to show him the tablet. "And I wasn't talking about the Blues Festival. You made your opinion perfectly clear on that one."

"Uh-huh." He studied her warily for a moment before he took the device. "So what's this?"

"A hiking trail with green space and fresh air. It's not downtown Portland. If that doesn't do it for you, I know two coon hounds who look like they could use a nice hike."

Rex and Luther gazed at her with wide eyes. "Johnny, she's onto something."

Luther pawed at the carpet and inched toward her. "Yeah, yeah, yeah. She's on her way to bein' a better two-legs than you, Johnny."

The dwarf grunted and frowned at the smaller hound, who looked quickly at him and stopped belly-crawling. "I mean, it's not like she could *do* that."

"We don't wanna stay in a hotel room all day, Johnny."

"No way. A park sounds good."

"Really good."

"We can run."

"Don't you wanna let us run, Johnny?"

"Enough." Johnny handed the tablet to her and caught her frowning at him in surprise. "What?"

"That's what I was about to ask. Enough what?"

He sniffed and muttered into his coffee cup, "The damn hounds are starin' me down."

Lisa glanced at Rex and Luther, who now stared at her with their pleading puppy-dog eyes. "Not anymore."

His loud slurping filled the hotel room. "Fine. We'll go for a hike."

"Yes!" Luther leapt to his feet and yipped. "We get to *run*!"

"But I ain't payin' to walk around outside."

"It's a public park, Johnny." She chuckled at the younger dog's excited tight circles and stood. "They're free."

"The way this city's runnin' things, it wouldn't surprise me."

Rex reached the door first and spun to stare at his master, panting madly. "Let's go, Johnny. I'm ready!"

"Not if I'm ready first." Luther raced toward his brother, misjudged his skid to a halt, and thunked his head against the door. He shook himself and turned in another tight circle. "Totally ready."

"The park ain't on the other side of this door, boys. Y'all need to rein it in."

They took the SUV to Forest Park and pulled into the parking lot twenty minutes later. Lisa slid out, shut the door behind her, and took a deep breath of the warming morning air. "This is beautiful."

"It ain't the Everglades, darlin', but it ain't the city, neither." Johnny walked to the back to open the cargo area for the hounds. Rex and Luther bounded out and trotted toward the trailhead, sniffing furiously.

"Johnny, this is awesome."

"Everything's so *green*."

"Kinda like home, right?"

"No, it ain't."

"What?" Lisa joined them at the trailhead.

Johnny cleared his throat. "It ain't like home."

"Yeah, you said that already."

"Well, it bears sayin' again." He rubbed his mouth and trudged down the dirt path. *This ain't gonna last. I gotta tell her about the collars.*

"Hey, what was that?" Luther dove into the thick foliage on the side of the path, rustled around in the ferns, and yanked his head up to search the forest floor frantically. "Where'd it go?"

"You mean that squirrel?" Rex raced past his brother into the underbrush, baying wildly.

"Don't you have a problem letting them run like that without being able to see them?" Lisa asked.

"Why would I?"

"Like you said. It's not the Everglades."

"They're fine."

"What about you?" She looked directly at him as they moved up the first small hill.

"As long as no one tells me I gotta leash my hounds in an open space, I'll be fine too."

When they reached the top, they had a full view of most of the path stretching out in front of them down the middle of a valley. Tree branches covered in moss and creeping vines grew everywhere along the mountainside and other hikers were out on a warm summer morning.

Lisa smiled. "It looks like a popular place."

"Uh-huh." Johnny frowned as he studied the people moving up and down the path and even between the trees. All of them were couples holding hands or with their arms around each other, laughing, kissing, and gazing into their partner's eyes. "I think you might have chosen the wrong place."

"What do you mean?"

They passed a young couple seated on a fallen moss-covered log.

"Look at that. They're all over each other like it's their own private park." He turned around and leaned toward them. "Y'all know there's other folks out here, don'tcha?"

The couple didn't come up for air to respond.

Yeah, they're not hearin' anythin'.

Lisa shrugged and looked at the overhanging branches above them. "Maybe it's the sunshine. I know it's summer, but aren't nice days like this still rare out here?"

"Rare or not, that ain't an excuse for all this…" He swept a hand across the valley to include all the couples.

She smirked at him. "You have a bone to pick with PDA, huh?"

"PD what?"

"Public displays of affection." She laughed. "We both know you're the best at what you do, Johnny, but sometimes, I wonder about your social skills."

He clicked his tongue and uttered a noncommittal grumble. "I have no need for social skills when I'd rather be huntin'."

"Or you could simply enjoy some fresh air and decent company. It's not a bad alternative, right?"

"No, I suppose it ain't."

They walked in silence for a while and tried to ignore the oddly increasing number of couples who came out to the hiking trail for public canoodling. The hounds raced out of the underbrush and glanced behind them as they rejoined him briefly on the path.

"Hey, Johnny. Whatever you do, don't go back that way."

Rex snorted and trotted in front of his master. "That was *not* an image I wanted burned in my mind."

The dwarf frowned and peered at the thick foliage from which the hounds had emerged. A soft rustling on the other side was followed by heavy breathing.

"What's wrong?" Lisa stopped and studied the same area.

"Does that sound like a struggle to you?"

"Well…there are wild animals out on a hiking trail…"

A woman's high-pitched giggle traveled faintly toward them, followed by a man's deep laughter and a low, barely concealed moan.

Her eyes widened. "Oh…"

"Told you, Johnny." Luther stared at the rustling bushes and cocked his head. "Wild animals, all right."

"Hey, weren't you the one who wanted *privacy* with that Great Pyrenees?" Rex sniffed the ferns on the other side of the path and inched slowly into the foliage again.

"That's different, Rex."

"Yeah, in more ways than one."

As the hounds disappeared in the woods again, Johnny cleared his throat and kept walking.

Lisa tucked her hair behind her ear, shook her head, and hurried away from the not so private rendezvous. "So."

"Yep."

"You know, we...haven't had a chance to talk about Amanda starting at the academy."

"We don't need to go there right now, darlin'."

"Why not?"

The dwarf sniffed and turned away from her to gaze into the trees. "You spent time talkin' to her before she left for that school. I can't say much you ain't already heard straight from her."

"Oh, I know she was excited to get started." She chuckled but her smile faded when he still wouldn't look at her. "Johnny, I was talking about you."

He released a slow, heavy sigh and darted her a sidelong glance. "What about me?"

"I know how much she means to you." She shrugged. "Anyone who saw you two together could see it immediately, no matter how hard you tried to hide it."

"I didn't try to hide a thing."

With her hands clasped behind her back, she studied his frowning profile. "Except for how much you miss her already."

Johnny scoffed. "I'm fine."

"You clam up every time her name's mentioned. And as soon as she started at that school, we found you drunker than I thought you could get. I know it was hard enough to go through Dawn's case and I also know how quickly you and Amanda—"

"I don't need any of that head-shrinkin', all right? I said I'm fine. She's in good hands at that school. She wants to be there. We're all movin' on. Simple as that."

"I'm not trying to be your therapist—"

"Then stop pryin' into my personal affairs and leave it."

She stared at him and slowed on the path.

The dwarf kept walking, then slowed and gritted his teeth. *Now you're bein' an asshole. Fix it.* He turned to look at her and grimaced when she frowned at him in disbelief. "Sorry. I shouldn't have said it like that."

"Well, that's a start."

"Look, darlin', I—"

"You're ridiculously dense sometimes, you know that?"

He gaped and his eyebrows drew closer together. "Say what now?"

"Do you honestly think I'm asking all this because I'm trying to pick you apart?" Lisa stepped toward him. "Or get enough juicy details to add to my reports to the Department? Is that it?"

Johnny scratched the side of his face. "Well, now I don't know what to think."

"I'm asking because I *care*, Johnny." She stopped directly in front of him, gestured a little helplessly with her arms, and pursed her lips in an attempt to hold back a small smile as she studied his face. "About you. And before you say something about how I don't know you enough or that you're not worth caring about, let me go ahead and remind you that I'm your partner. We broke into an armed warehouse to steal a gold-plated invitation. We bid on a dark-Web auction for a girl we didn't know. With your money."

He snorted.

"I'm not finished. We sat through the most despicable display of greed and power-mongering until we found Amanda, and then we crashed a Monsters Ball to get her out of there. Together. Not to mention running around the Everglades after a Logree that turned out to be another parent mourning the loss of her kid. Offspring. Whatever."

Johnny's mustache twitched above a smirk. "You're leavin' out the part where you let some kidnappin' bastards get away with the girl—"

"To save—"

"To save my hounds instead. I wasn't finished neither."

They stared at each other, and she finally laughed self-consciously. "Yeah. I guess I did forget that part."

"It's a big thing to leave outta the equation."

She shrugged. "Well, you taking that Logree case saved me my job, so there's that too."

"Uh-huh. You gonna come out and say what you're tryin' to say, darlin'?"

Lisa pressed her lips together and shook her head. "I'm only saying that if you want someone to talk to, I'm here. And you don't have to keep those walls up all the time. Trust me, things are much easier when you realize it's okay to let them down sometimes."

The bounty hunter sniffed and studied her face. "Well, I appreciate it."

"Right." Her smile returned as she lowered her head and tucked her hair behind her ear. "Any time."

"Now let me ask you somethin'."

She rolled her eyes teasingly. "What, Johnny?"

"Do you think there's any—"

"Stop! Oh, my God—Eddie, *stop!*"

The woman's shriek rose from the path behind them. They both turned toward the sound as the rustling foliage from the hidden couple took on a whole different tone.

"Hey, what's wrong?" the man asked.

"Something's wrong. I can't...I don't know. I have to—"

"Babe, come on—"

"I have to get out of here!" Branches and twigs snapped and a woman in her mid-twenties stumbled out of the bushes as she slipped her arm through the sleeve of her t-shirt. Her gaze darted wildly around the woods as she searched the trees and the dark shadows beneath the thick green flora. "It's not right."

"Emily, hold on." The man—she'd called him Eddie—emerged from the bushes after her, buckling his belt. "What's going on?"

"I…" The woman spun to look at him and swallowed thickly. "I saw something."

He smirked. "Come on. It's nothing you haven't seen before."

"Fuck off. I'm serious." A bird swooped across the path to land in a tree and Emily flinched beneath the shadow before she whirled again, breathing heavily. "I swear something was watching us."

"So? Let 'em watch. Come here."

"No, some*thing*, Eddie. Something…awful."

"Babe—"

"I know it sounds crazy, okay? I wanna go home." She hugged herself and shuddered even in the summer heat as she rubbed her arms.

"Yeah, okay. Okay. We'll go." The man pulled her toward him for a hug.

Neither one of them noticed the bounty hunter and the federal agent watching them from fifteen feet away.

Johnny leaned toward Lisa and muttered, "Did you see that on her arm?"

"It looked like the same mark to me," she whispered.

"Uh-huh. Hey, folks." He hurried toward the startled couple as Emily burst into tears. "I couldn't help but overhear y'all sayin' you saw somethin' threw you off a little. Is everythin' okay?"

"We're fine, man. Thanks. We're heading back to the car." The man pulled his girlfriend down the path.

"Hey, have you guys been on one of those Shanghai Tunnel tours?" Lisa asked from a few paces behind them.

Johnny and Eddie both frowned at her with varying levels of confusion.

She shrugged. "We're only in town for a few days. You look like you know the area."

The man tightened his arms around his girlfriend and wrinkled his nose at her. "Uh…yeah. It's a big drawcard for tourists, so have fun. Bye."

Shaking his head, he turned and led Emily along the path toward the trailhead. All the while, he rubbed her arms and lowered his head to whisper reassurances.

Johnny snorted. "Well, that's one way to get the answer."

"Don't look so surprised. You're usually the one who asks the blunt questions."

"Yeah, 'cause I'm the one who looks like he ain't messin' around."

"Hey, I'm dangerous when I have to be."

The dwarf scratched the side of his head as she passed him on the trail toward the parking lot. "I never said you weren't."

"Well, I'm not finished. When you find your dogs, meet me at the car." Lisa jogged up the path to catch up with the couple.

He whistled shrilly, then strode after her. "Time's up, boys!"

Branches snapped, leaves rustled, and both hounds bounded out of the underbrush and skidded across the dirt path behind their master. Rex shook himself from head to toe. "What happened?"

"Johnny, we had this big ol' thing cornered in its hole," Luther added. "Might've been a hamster."

"Don't matter. Let's go." Johnny nodded up the hill toward Lisa, who'd managed to stop the confused couple in their hasty escape from the hiking trail.

"Aw, man. Now we'll *never* know." Luther sat to scratch behind his ear, then leapt up when Rex passed him.

"Agent Lisa Breyer with the FBI." Lisa flashed her badge at the couple. Emily looked up at it briefly through her panicked tears.

"Seriously?" Eddie frowned at it in surprise. "What...uh, what's going on?"

The agent glanced at her partner when he caught up to her. "I won't keep you long. I'd merely like to get your full names and phone numbers."

"Uh...sure. I guess." The man rubbed his girlfriend's shoulders. "Why?"

"There have been some attacks in the Portland area over the last few months. I can see your girlfriend's shaken and I don't want to leave anything up to chance."

"What, you think we were almost attacked?"

"It's very possible." She nodded and pulled her phone out to store their numbers. "This man's been terrorizing young couples. You know, in the peeping-Tom kinda way. What she said earlier fits the perpetrator's MO, and I'd like to check on you both from time to time to make sure nothing else...strange has happened."

"Yeah, sure. Okay. Jesus Christ." Eddie scowled at the path. "Some people are fucking sick."

"Yes, they are." Lisa saved both their numbers in her phone, took a business card from her back pocket, and proffered it. "And if anything else happens, no matter how weird or unlikely it seems, give me a call."

"Right. Okay." Eddie took the card and swallowed uncomfortably. "Thanks."

"Eddie, I wanna go," Emily whispered.

"Yeah, we should—"

"By all means. Thanks for your time." Lisa nodded sternly and slipped her phone into her pocket.

Johnny folded his arms as they watched the couple hurry up the hillside toward the trailhead. "That was beautiful."

She glanced sharply at him. "What are you talking about?"

"Now I ain't sayin' I bend the truth from time to time if it fits a purpose, but you turned it into an art form."

A slow smile spread across her lips, but she didn't look at him. "Well, now we know the tunnels are connected to at least three victims. It's a good thing you have a partner who can think on her feet, huh?"

The agent continued up the trail without waiting for a reply.

Johnny sniffed, chuckled softly, and followed her with the hounds obediently at his heels.

"She's saying she's your partner again, Johnny," Luther muttered.

"And you didn't say anything." Rex cocked his head to look at his master. "You feelin' okay?"

He smirked. *It ain't worth arguin' right now.*

CHAPTER TWENTY-FIVE

Across the street from the Shanghai Tunnels Tours storefront, Johnny picked through the paper tray of food they'd purchased from one of the food trucks. "What is this again?"

"Tabouli." Lisa took a mouthful of hers and watched him warily. "Is something wrong?"

"Yeah. There's no meat."

"Johnny, you said you wanted whatever I was getting. I even double-checked to make sure that was what you wanted. Twice."

"It doesn't make it taste any better." He wrinkled his nose and glanced at the hounds.

"We'll eat it for ya, Johnny."

"Oh, yeah. Totally. You want to get food eaten, we're your hounds!"

"Does this have onions?" He held his paper tray toward Lisa.

"Most likely, yeah. I wouldn't feed it to the dogs."

"Do you want it, then?"

Her eyes widened as she took his dinner from him. "Sure. I love this stuff. Falafel and everything."

"Gesundheit."

She rolled her eyes and balanced both trays in one hand so she could use her fork with the other.

"Aw, come on, Johnny." Luther lowered his head and whined. "There was enough to go around."

"Sorry, boys. With all the extra who-knows-what y'all get into on the regular, I ain't addin' to the list with onions in the farfar or whatever." Johnny glanced at his watch. "All right. It's ten minutes —time to make this five o'clock tour."

"On an empty stomach, Johnny?" Rex hurried after his master and sniffed the dwarf's fingers.

"Come on. We haven't eaten in *days*."

"Y'all had chicken fingers two hours ago. Hush up." Johnny finished with a sharp whistle and stepped onto the sidewalk.

Chuckling, the agent shoveled more tabouli into her mouth and hurried across the street after them.

Ten people had signed up for the five o'clock tour with them and everyone waited in an eager group to get started.

"Oh, good." The tour guide with a mess of blonde curls and a pierced lip clapped briskly. "It looks like you're the last in our group tonight. I'm glad you made it."

Johnny grunted. Lisa dropped her empty paper trays in the trashcan.

"My name's Stephan. I'll be your guide through the Shanghai tunnels beneath Old Town, Portland. Now, while this tour is intended to be PG, please be aware that some of the stories you'll hear tonight as we traverse the underground network from the 1800s are disturbing. It helps to keep in mind that these are no longer in use for anything but these tours and for educational purposes. We've recently discovered a few new aspects to round out the history that exists beneath Portland, so for those of you who've been here before, you'll most certainly find a few changes. Is everyone ready?"

Nods and smiles followed and he nodded enthusiastically.

"Wonderful. If you could step over here for a moment, we'll get started shortly." Stephan stepped toward Johnny and Lisa and glanced briefly at the hounds. "I'm sorry, sir. We don't allow dogs in the tunnels."

The dwarf sucked stray tabouli out of his teeth. "The hounds stay with me."

"I'm sure they do most of the time, yes." The man inclined his head and smiled in full hospitality style as he clapped again. "But not in the tunnels."

"How 'bout I buy two more full-priced tickets for 'em and hand you two hundred for your troubles?"

The man chuckled uncertainly. "Sir, I'm sorry. It's only our policy—"

"Five hundred."

"I… Well." The guide looked at the dogs. "They need to be leashed, at the very least."

"And you folks wanna call this city dog-friendly." Johnny glanced around the storefront and shook his head. "Do you have any leashes?"

"No, sir. We don't allow dogs in the tunnels."

"Well, you do now, don'tcha?" He sniffed and looked at Luther, who was busy licking spilled sauce off his master's boot. "Shit. All right. I got leashes. Gimme a minute."

"You have five before the tour officially starts." Stephan grinned. "After you purchase the extra tickets, of course."

With a grunt, Johnny retrieved his wallet and paid the negotiated six hundred-dollars. "Don't worry 'bout breakin' any of it. We're good."

"Excellent. I'll see you over there in five minutes. With your dogs on leashes." Stephan turned and practically floated toward the group of people who waited anxiously at the start of the tour.

With a despondent sigh, Johnny bent and waved Luther away from his boot. "What else is there to lick, boy? Get off."

Luther sat. "Oh, there's plenty left."

"What're you doin', Johnny?" Rex tilted his head as the dwarf untied his shoelaces.

"Gettin' us into these damn tunnels however I can."

"Well, that's certainly creative," Lisa said as she stepped up behind him. "Do you think they'll hold up?"

"If I'm holdin' 'em, yeah." He pulled the lace free from his right boot, then started on the left. "I ain't do this to keep my hounds close."

"Of course not." She looked at Stephan and grinned.

Half an hour later, they had fallen behind the rest of the tour by at least six feet while Stephan droned on in his vivid recounting of the Shanghai Tunnel's morbid and nefarious history. The dwarf's hold on his shoelaces-turned-dog-leashes was practically nonexistent. "Is he seriously gonna talk the entire time?"

Lisa leaned toward him and whispered, "I'm very sure that's what tour guides do."

"Well, it ain't helpin'." He scratched his head and peered into the dark shadows of the branching tunnels, which were sectioned off by gates meant to keep tour participants on the right path. "Do you pick up on anythin' unusual down here?"

"Besides the fact that these tunnels exist and were used to transport men captured and sold into slavery?"

"Well, yeah."

"No, Johnny. Not a thing."

"No scent of magicals either, Johnny," Rex said. "And it's real easy to smell things down here without much wind. For instance, all those stains on the walls—what are you *doing*?"

Luther stood facing the wall with his nose pressed to the rough surface and dragged his tongue up one of the aforementioned stains. "Hey, this is *good*. Rex, you should try it."

"Nope."

"Kinda salty. Kinda bitter. You know, it almost tastes like…"

"If these walls could talk," Stephan continued at the head of the tour, "they'd have countless terrifying stories of all the violent acts performed down here. Torture aimed to make the captured men compliant. Drugging the victims. Death and bloodshed when prisoners wouldn't comply. Bodies piled up against the walls."

Luther whipped his head away from the stone wall and licked his muzzle. "Oh."

Johnny snapped his fingers. "Stay sharp, boys. We have a gaggle of potential human victims in front of us, so be on the lookout for anythin' movin' here that ain't part of the tour."

"Got it, Johnny."

Luther gazed at the walls and whipped his head from side to side. "You mean like all the shadows?"

Scowling, the dwarf shook his head and peered into the rotting remains of what had once been an actual hotel below the city. *I can't say things have improved much 'round here in the last few hundred years.*

His optimism didn't increase when they reached the end of the mile-long trek through the tunnels and emerged on the other side.

"And that concludes our tour." Stephan clapped yet again and nodded at each of the customers. "Any questions?"

A woman in full tourist garb—baseball hat, sweater tied around her waist, money-purse strapped over her shoulder, and an actual camera hung around her neck—raised a hand in the air and didn't wait to be called on before she launched into an elaborate question Johnny didn't have the patience to listen to.

"Yeah, I have a question," he muttered under his breath. "Why the hell wasn't this more useful?"

Lisa grimaced and scrunched her eyes in thought. "No demon attacks."

"Not a one."

"No magic."

"Nope."

"Nothing."

"Any other variations you wanna try, darlin'?" Johnny frowned at her.

"I'm merely thinking out loud. You know, taking a page out of Johnny Walker's book."

"Uh-huh." *And that's another stab at me talkin' to a couple of coonhounds. I ain't bitin', Lisa.*

As the tour participants who didn't want to listen through the camera lady's intense interrogation of their guide filtered away from the end of the tour, Johnny untied the lace-leashes from the hounds' collars and balled them into one hand.

Stephan caught his eye on the way out and nodded. "Thank you so much for visiting the Shanghai Tunnels. Have a great evening."

"Not yet," he grumbled.

The tour had taken them to the other side of Old Town, where the Friday-night action had only begun.

"So what now?" Lisa asked.

He snorted and made a wide circle to avoid a woman on the sidewalk behind a folding table she'd set up to read Tarot cards. "We get off the streets for now."

"Because we've gone through Plan A and don't have a Plan B?"

"Come on, darlin'. You know me better than that." Johnny gave her a sidelong glance and his mustache twitched above a mischievous smirk. "We ain't done with these tunnels. I plan to wait a few hours and come back for a private tour without Stephan."

She glanced around to make sure no one heard them, leaned toward him, and lowered her voice. "Are you seriously telling me you want to break in and go…demon-hunting with a flashlight?"

"Aw, you make it sound so cute."

"Johnny, we can't—"

"Lisa, we can. And we will. 'Cause I ain't droppin' this until we find the asshole attackin' humans and ruinin' their lives. Whatever's goin' on, it's happenin' down there. And I aim to flush it out." He opened his hand and grunted. "After I get these damn laces in my boots."

CHAPTER TWENTY-SIX

Portland wasn't necessarily dead-asleep at almost three o'clock in the morning, but it was certainly easier to navigate without being seen. *And there ain't no one to tell me to leash the hounds either.*

Johnny poked his head around the corner of the Shanghai Tunnel Tours' main building and glanced up and down the street. "All right. We're clear."

Lisa made a hasty check in each direction before she followed him toward the tunnel entrance. She looked at the black canvas case strapped over his head and shoulder that bounced against his thigh with every step. "I still think you went way overboard with the gear."

"Oh, yeah? What makes you think that?" They stopped at the large storm-cellar doors closed and padlocked over the stairs leading underground. He knelt and unzipped the case. "'Cause I could have opted to bring my pieced-apart rifle in this here case."

"And instead, you filled it with explosives and...I don't even know what else." Despite the hounds keeping a careful watch on the street, she turned her back to the tunnel entrance and scanned the area herself. "And I'm not sure explosives in tunnels that are hundreds of years old are the smartest way to go here."

"You're worryin' too much, darlin'."

"When there's a chance that you'd bring half of Portland down on our heads by playing with bombs? I don't think so."

The dwarf removed a handful of the small black explosive beads he'd stashed in the case and crushed two of them between his fingers. "Come on, now. Have I ever put us in danger with my gear?"

Lisa turned slowly to stare at him. "Was that a rhetorical question?"

"The correct answer is no. At least not anythin' we couldn't get ourselves out of." He pressed the detonating beads against the padlock, reached into the bag again, and pulled out a black bowl, which he turned quickly to cup around the padlock. A soft pop was followed by a clink of breaking metal as the lock burst open.

She frowned at the black bowl as he returned it to the case. "What's that?"

"It's for sound-proofin' a break-in." He grinned at her as he removed the padlock and tossed it aside. "A little somethin' I put together about…oh, twenty-five years ago. Of course, the explosions have only become louder since then but it does fine for the little guys."

"You know, it wouldn't surprise me if you were a bank robber in another life."

"I've been one in this life too."

"What?"

The bounty hunter lifted one of the cellar doors, then the other, and dusted his hands off. "It's a long story. Would you like to head into the darkness first, or shall I take the—"

"Come on." She yanked her phone out to turn the flashlight app on and moved down the wooden steps.

"Yes, ma'am." With a smirk, Johnny nodded at the hounds and followed. "Y'all stay sharp, now. I reckon there's much more to find down here the second time around."

"You got it, Johnny." Rex's back end wiggled as he passed his master down the stairs and gained on Lisa. "We'll sniff 'em out."

"And we won't even stop to lick the walls—hey… Look at this." Luther stopped to sniff at the wall and Johnny snapped his fingers.

"Focus."

The smaller hound snorted and ran down the stairs after his brother.

The dwarf slid his hand to the case strapped across his shoulder, withdrew a three-inch rectangular LED light, and slipped it onto the strap over his shoulder before he punched the top. A bright white glow spilled through the tunnels around them.

Lisa turned quickly and blinked against the sudden light. "What is that?"

"Hands-free." He raised both hands and wiggled his fingers. "You can put your phone away. It won't work this far underground anyway."

"That's only the cell service. Or lack thereof." She turned the flashlight off and slid her phone into her back pocket. "Which might be an issue if we need to make any calls."

"Naw. We're good." He sniffed and rummaged in his case again before he found the tiny metal spider newly fitted with reinforced armor along the body.

Her eyes widened. "Didn't you throw one of those at Lemonhead's face in New York?"

"Hey, you remembered."

"Yeah, because it was weird and didn't seem like the most effective use of your skills."

He slipped the headset he'd synced with the metal critter over his ear, turned it on, and tapped the top of the spider. "I ain't always sure what I'll use these little fellas for. It's different every time, I suppose, but this is what I made 'em for."

Carefully, he set the metal spider on the tunnel floor and flicked its back. Lisa jumped when it came alive and skittered down the tunnel to vanish quickly in the darkness at the edge of his portable shoulder lamp. "Is it supposed to be that quiet?" she whispered.

"It wouldn't be a very good spy-bug otherwise."

"Spy-bug."

"Yeah, it's a simple name and easy to remember." Johnny gestured toward the tunnel. "Shall we?"

With a sigh, she drew her service pistol and held it with both hands. "I'm ready when you are."

"Don't worry, Johnny." Rex padded softly down the tunnel in front of them. "We'll scope it out."

"Nothin' gets past us." Luther leapt away from his master's shadow that bounced along the wall, uttered a high-pitched dog-like giggle, and hurried after his brother.

"Did you have anywhere in particular in mind?" the agent whispered. "Or are we making this up as we go?"

"That half-standin' hotel was all kinds of blocked off. I think it's a good place to start."

"Right."

They moved silently through the tunnels while they listened warily and peered into every dark corner they passed. Many of the branching tunnels were covered by grates or otherwise sectioned off, as well as rough cells carved into the walls.

"Coming up on that hotel soon, Johnny," Rex said.

"Yeah, maybe you should turn that light off. We can see it all the way from here."

The dwarf slapped the LED light strapped to his shoulder and plunged the tunnel into darkness again.

"Johnny?" Lisa whispered.

He tilted his head and hushed her softly. "I think I hear somethin'."

They waited for a minute that felt like an hour, but not even the hounds made a sound wherever they were up ahead in the tunnels.

"Oh, shit, Johnny," Rex muttered.

The bounty hunter squinted into the darkness. *It still sounds like they're here next to me.*

"There's totally someone down there," Luther added.

"Yeah, yeah. In the hotel like you said."

He felt furtively in the black case at his side for a pair of night-vision goggles he'd modified to fit in small spaces like that. His movements slow and smooth, he raised them to his face, hooked one loop over his ear followed by the other, and blinked to adjust his focus as the outline of the tunnel took form again. When he caught Lisa's hand, she jumped and tried to pull away. "What are you doing?"

"Being both our eyes for now, darlin'." He said it so softly, he could barely hear his voice. "I think we found 'em."

They edged down the tunnel and stepped carefully to avoid the more uneven parts of the worn stone. The agent followed him blindly. His headset hummed with a low mutter, followed by a crackle of static. Finally, his spy-bug sent the voices through loud and clear.

"I don't care about what you have now," a woman snapped in a low, menacing voice. "What I want to know is how you ran out of it three days ahead of schedule."

"Well, it's not like every shot is a direct hit," a man muttered. "Sometimes, they miss."

"It's magic, you idiot. It was crafted to not miss!"

"I...I wouldn't say that's entirely true—"

"Shut up! Just shut up. You've wasted so much time already. I couldn't be here today because you failed to tell me you'd run out of the only thing you're responsible for keeping fully stocked. No, don't try to distract me with excuses, Val. Open the damn crate."

"Ooh, Johnny..." Luther spoke in a low whisper in the bounty hunter's mind. "That's one pissed-off witch."

Witch? That's who's behind all this? It's a little disappointin'.

"She's got a gnome down there with her," Rex added. "And…I think another wizard. Maybe two. Hard to tell, Johnny. They all smell like some *weird* kinda magic."

"Yeah, not in the good way."

Johnny tapped Lisa's shoulder and leaned toward her ear to whisper, "At least four. In the hotel."

She nodded and they moved around the bend in the tunnel. Once they rounded the steep curve, pale yellow light spilled through the slats in the rotting wooden planks that served as the old hotel's walls. Rex and Luther poked their heads slowly out of the shadows surrounding the entrance.

"That's gotta be them. Right, Johnny?"

"Has to be. Who else would think it was a good idea to come here in the middle of the night? Want us to go in after 'em, Johnny?"

The dwarf raised an open hand toward the hounds, then stripped the headset and the night-vision goggles off before he stowed them in his pocket. In the pale light, he glanced at Lisa and held up five fingers. She nodded and he counted down slowly with his fingers, taking one slow, silent step after another toward the door of the hotel that was little more than a slanted piece of flimsy wood.

Three… Two…

"Boss, you hear something?" the nervous gnome asked.

"Go check it out," the woman hissed.

One.

Johnny thrust his boot through the rotting wooden door. Splinters exploded in all directions, and the gnome on the other side shrieked and flinched instinctively. The bounty hunter yanked an exploding disk off his belt with one hand and drew his knife with the other. Lisa and the hounds hurried through after him. "It sounds like a bad night just got worse for you, huh?"

The room on the other side was small, lit by lanterns hanging from hooks on the ceiling, and filled with magical light. The witch wore a dark-purple dress with her red hair pulled into a tight bun. She stepped away from the destroyed door and the dwarf and slid her fingers along the surface of the wood table beside her. A slow, calculating smile graced her lips. "And who might you be?"

"FBI," Lisa said and stepped forward with her gun leveled unflinchingly. "What's in the crate?"

The woman chuckled softly and pointed at the wooden crate beside her. One long, manicured fingernail glistened in the light. "You mean this crate?"

"Don't play dumb," Johnny growled. "Are you the magical attackin' all the humans in these tunnels?"

"Well, in this century, yes." She flashed them a mad grin and darted a commanding glance at the cowering gnome. He nodded and tried to skitter away, but Luther bounded in front of him and growled. Val the gnome squeaked, leapt away, and flung his hands up in immediate surrender. His boss rolled her eyes. "You're so useless."

"He's not going anywhere, Johnny. I got him."

The bounty hunter nodded at the crate beside the witch. "Step away from the table."

"Oh, no. I can't do that." The grinning woman gestured expansively. "I plan to use these very soon...whoever you are." Her smile vanished and one dark eye twitched. "And I've put far too much into this to let a few idiots stand in my way. I'm sorry, did you say you were federal agents?"

Lisa stepped forward. "Hands up."

"No."

"Uh...Johnny?" Rex glanced around the small room. "We're missing the two wizards, at least."

He gritted his teeth. "What's in the crate?"

The witch reached slowly inside it with one hand while her gaze darted around the edges of the rotting room to scan the shadows. She withdrew a small vial filled with slightly glowing purple liquid. "My answer."

"That ain't an answer at all." He growled his annoyance. "Put it down."

"No, I think I'll hang onto this one and maybe use the full dose with the casting. I'm not exactly sure what the right ratio is for a dwarf and a disappointingly skinny half-Light Elf, but so much of this has been trial and error."

Rex sniffed at the dusty, dank air. "Johnny, something's wrong—"

The far wall of the hotel shattered and flung pieces of splintered wood and centuries of dust all over the room. A huge shifter barreled through and his eyes flashed before he transformed and bounded toward Johnny.

Lisa squeezed a shot off that nicked the massive gray wolf in the shoulder, and he snarled and landed awkwardly before he lunged toward her instead of her partner. At least a dozen other magicals streamed through the hole in the wall and another five emerged from the shadows. A Crystal woman's blast of frigid air peppered with shards of ice blew through the underground hotel like a blizzard.

The bounty hunter raised his forearm to shield his eyes, still holding the knife. *Shit.*

"Johnny!" Luther shouted and snarled as he leapt at the shifter who showed no signs of slowing even after he'd been shot. "They've got something else in the crate!"

Lisa squeezed off another round at what she thought was a magical storming toward her, but the bullet streaked through the shadows that danced along the Crystal's blizzard spell and cracked deafeningly against the stone wall of the tunnels beyond the hotel.

"Double it on these assholes, Val," the witch shouted. "I want to see how far they fall."

"Shit, Johnny. Look out! They've got something else in that

crate" Rex shouted and jerked his head with his jaws clamped around a wizard's ankle.

A sharp pinch nicked the back of Johnny's neck. His inactive disk fell from his hand and clattered to the ground as he slapped the sting on his neck. He couldn't see his fingers through the haze of Crystal magic when he lowered them in front of his face. "What the—"

The dwarf staggered forward, his eyes suddenly heavy, and tried to shake off the dizziness that washed over him with unbelievable speed. *Goddamnit. The bitch fucking drugged me.*

The Crystal's spell cleared and he saw four versions of all the magicals in the abandoned underground hotel staring at him. Or at least he thought they were. He couldn't be sure. *Where are the hounds? Where's—*

"Johnny?" Lisa's voice came from somewhere very far away.

He tried to call her but he couldn't make his lips move. His vision darkened and his hearing faded into a dull, indecipherable drone before a dark-purple light flared in front of him.

A female figure stood within the strange illumination, which burst away from her like dark sun flares. When she spread her arms, two massive wings of black smoke unfolded to overshadow everything else. Horns emerged from her head, and two glowing red eyes burned within the shadowy, featureless face. A dark, reverberating chuckle blasted into his head and made his eyes water. "Oh, this will be fun."

The ground trembled beneath him and the bounty hunter groaned heavily as he tried to keep his balance. *Oh, that demon. Fuck.*

CHAPTER TWENTY-SEVEN

Johnny tried to shake the dizziness off as he trudged toward what he thought was only a hallucination. *It has to be. There's no way this shit is real.*

But before he could manage more than two steps, everything changed around him. The darkness faded, the glowing demon-lady was gone, and he stood in his living room. *What the hell?*

A choking sound rose behind him, and he whirled with his utility knife in hand to see Amanda sprawled on the floor, her hand stretched toward him. Her blood spread in a crimson pool around her as her wide eyes shimmered. The girl's mouth gaped open and closed, and she raised a hand in a plea. "Help me. Johnny, I can't—"

More blood gurgled from her mouth.

"Jesus Christ." He leapt toward her and another wave of vertigo wracked him. The living room disappeared, replaced by the scattered lawn and gravel drive in front of his cabin. "Amanda!"

He spun wildly, searching for her in the darkness beneath the starry sky hanging over the Everglades. A crackling roar made him turn again, and he froze.

His cabin was on fire and the flames surged ten feet into the air. The screen door on the front porch cracked, fell from its hinges, and was engulfed in seconds by the flames. "No, no, no. What the fuck is this? My fucking home!"

The second he pushed toward the blaze of heat he could feel on his skin and the plumes of smoke stinging his nostrils, his world tilted upside down. When it righted again, he stood in a dark alley lit by a blazing neon-red sign shaped like the Red Boar. A gunshot cracked through the narrow space between buildings, followed by a scream. "Papa!"

"Dawn!" He didn't even care that it was impossible. *That's my daughter. She fuckin' needs me.*

"Johnny!" Rex's shout in his mind was so intense, it stopped him in his tracks. "Don't believe any of it!"

A canine snarl and the snapping of jaws came from somewhere very far away, and he shook his head. "Where are you, boy?"

"Right here next to you, Johnny," Luther said. "These assholes aren't gonna know what hit 'em."

"Where…" The dwarf glanced around the alley.

"Trust us."

"We got you."

"And you're probably gonna have to get a lot of these fuckers on your own."

"We'll be your eyes, Johnny. Just—shit! Duck!"

He dropped into a crouch and winced when the searing heat from a spell streaked over his head, but he saw nothing. *That was a damn fireball.*

"Okay, two feet to the right." Rex snarled and another scream Johnny didn't recognize came from even farther away.

The walls of the alley trembled before the shadowy form of the demon stepped forward out of the shadows. "You're trying so hard, dwarf." The voice echoed in a hundred different tones, and the glowing purple aura around the woman shuddered. "Stop fighting. I'm only here to take what you love."

"Johnny, snap out of it!" Luther shouted. "And move your ass. Hey, hey, behind you!"

The bounty hunter whirled and caught the briefest glimpse of a wavering shadow and an arm that swung toward him. He ducked the arm he couldn't see with any degree of certainty, then swiped his blade into where a person's ribcage would have been. The knife stuck in solid, warm flesh, and a wizard materialized in front of him and gaped in disbelief as he sagged to the floor.

He jerked the knife free, stepped back, and shook his head again. *None of this is real except for these bastards tryin' to kill me.*

"Good aim, Johnny!" Rex barked. "We got these shitheads on your right."

"Yeah, but turn left at three o'clock," Luther added. "Shit! Your other left!"

Johnny spun right and slashed at another shadow with his knife. Blood sprayed against his face. With a hiss, he squinted at the alley he knew wasn't real and tried to clear the hallucination.

The vision faded and he stood in front of his burning cabin again. The demon flashed into existence in front of him, laughing in her inhuman voice. "You're watching it all fall apart, aren't you? Yes…I can feel it. Oh, you *do* keep it all bottled up inside, don't you, dwarf?"

He lunged forward and swung his blade at the glowing purple figure. She disappeared, shrieking with laughter. When he turned quickly, the terrifyingly huge wings were fully extended in front of him again.

"But there's more you haven't shown me. I can smell it."

With a roar of effort, he surged toward her and slashed again but she was suddenly six feet too far out of reach.

"What is it? What are you so afraid of?"

"Johnny!" Rex shouted. "You're facing the wrong way."

"He can't fight like that," Luther added. "Johnny, the rest are over here!"

The bounty hunter turned more slowly this time, breathing heavily, and scanned the dark grass in front of his burning cabin. *Listen to them. That's it. Listen to their voices, Johnny.*

Lisa knelt on the grass, her hands tied behind her back. A faceless figure stood behind her and held her tightly with one arm while the other hand pressed a knife to her throat.

"No."

"Johnny." She stared at him with wide eyes. "Johnny, don't let him—"

"Oh, yes…" The demon's voice echoed from everywhere all at once and she drew in a long, hissing breath. "It's so predictable but I guess I should have seen it."

"No, no, Johnny," Rex said and snarled again. A sound like ripping flesh barely registered in the bounty hunter's mind. "Whatever you see, it's not real."

"Get her, Johnny. The witch! Right in front of you!"

"*Do* something," Lisa begged and tears streamed down her cheeks as the shadowy bastard's knife pressed harder against her throat. "Johnny, don't stand there and—"

The knife glinted in a blur to open a wide gash in her flesh and spill her blood over the grass.

Johnny roared in anger and tried to run to her, but the world tilted and pushed him off balance. "Lisa—"

"*It's not her!*" Rex and Luther shouted at the same time.

That snapped him out of his horrified shock long enough for his instincts to kick in. *'Course it ain't. We're in fuckin' Portland.*

He tossed his knife, caught it by the blade, and hurled it at the fake Lisa Breyer who knelt in the grass with blood pouring from her slashed throat. The blade struck true with a wet thunk, buried to the hilt in not-Lisa's chest. She coughed, lurched forward, and toppled without a sound.

"Fuck..." He staggered sideways and his hand flailed to find something to grasp to stop his fall but with no success.

The bounty hunter landed heavily in the dust and his ears rang as his senses returned slowly. Reluctantly, he shifted his gaze to where he half-expected Lisa to be sprawled on the floor in front of him. The body was there but it was the witch, her dark eyes wide and staring at him as blood seeped slowly from around his utility knife buried in her chest.

"All *right*, Johnny!" Rex limped toward him with a sharp yip. "Now that's what you call a kill-shot, huh? Johnny?"

Luther sniffed his master's face, then gave it a tentative lick. "You don't look so good. Are you still in there?"

"Johnny, it's us."

He responded with an unintelligible groan as his vision narrowed into darkness.

"Uh-oh, Luther. There he goes..."

The dwarf woke with a pounding headache and rolled onto his back. *I swear I didn't drink enough to feel this shitty.*

"Hey! He's up!" Luther skittered toward him across the dusty floor and shoved his nose into his master's face. "Shit, Johnny. We thought you were dead."

Rex snorted. "No, we didn't. But it's a good thing you're waking up now. So is everyone else, I think."

Luther sniggered. "Well, except for the dead ones."

He pushed to a seated position and grunted as the dizziness began to clear. "Lisa?"

"Yep." Rex trotted across the destroyed hotel. "Over here, Johnny. She's been kinda curled in a ball since you both keeled over and passed out."

"Yeah, that was weird."

"Hey." He forced his limbs to move so he could crawl across

the floor toward her. Sure enough, she was still curled huddled into herself, whimpering and trembling. He cleared his throat when he reached her and placed a gentle hand on her shoulder. "Aw, come on, darlin'. Come on out of it—"

Lisa gasped, jerked upright, and delivered a blistering slap to the side of his face. "Back the fuck up!"

"Shit." The bounty hunter turned his head away and gritted his teeth through the sting. "It's me."

"Johnny? Oh, my God." She covered her mouth with both hands, then reached toward his face. "I'm so sorry. I thought—"

"You thought I was some scary fuck tryin' to do somethin' scary to ya?" He chuckled and wiggled his jaw. "I get it but it's only me."

She caught his face in both hands and studied it intently. "I don't even… Okay, it sounds crazy, but is this—"

"Is it real?" He took her hands in his and lowered them gently from his face. "If it ain't, I'm all outta ideas, darlin'."

She stared at him, breathing heavily. "That was awful."

"Yep. Are you okay?"

"Well…physically? Maybe."

"Hey, sorry to break up your little moment and stuff." Rex leapt on the chest of a groaning wizard and elicited a sharp grunt before he snarled in the man's face. "But we got a bunch of dipshits waking up."

"Yeah, now would be a good time to—" Luther clamped his jaws around the gnome's twitching hand. His prisoner shrieked, and the hound spat him out again with a warning growl. "Call in the cleaning crew. You got your demon, Johnny."

"Got the demon," Johnny muttered.

Lisa frowned at him. "What?"

He turned to look at the witch lying face-down beside the wooden table and the crate of purple vials. "The witch. Same thing."

"We need to call this in." She pulled her phone out of her

pocket with a shaking hand and unlocked the screen. "Shit. There's no service down here."

"Hold on." He reached for the black case and frowned when he didn't feel it at his side.

"Lookin' for this?" Luther trotted toward him with the nylon strap between his teeth.

"Good boy." It took him five seconds to remove the small black square from between the random items in his case, and he dropped the rest to punch the buttons on the side of the device.

Lisa tilted her head with a disbelieving expression. "You brought a pager?"

"It ain't a pager." His fingers felt stiff and clumsy but he finally managed to turn it on and a pale green circle illuminated at the top. "It's a service box."

"What?"

"I made two of 'em. Amanda has the other one with her at school for emergencies."

She chuckled weakly. "Wow."

"Check your phone."

The agent looked at the screen and raised her eyebrows. "Well, this is the last time I have my doubts about anything you make."

"That's good to know."

She raised her phone to her ear, stared at him, and smiled at the faint pressure when he squeezed her other hand. "Yeah. It's Breyer." She cleared her throat and studied the floor littered with bodies of dead and unconscious criminals alike. "We found the dem—uh...the perp in the human attacks. We could use backup. Yeah, the, uh... The Shanghai Tunnels under Old Town. Yes, I know. Send a team out. Thanks."

The hounds made their rounds among the bodies. Luther stopped in front of the witch and sniffed her outstretched hand. "Hey, Johnny. You want your knife back?"

"Naw. She earned it."

Lisa cleared her throat. "Johnny, that does not sound like you're talking to yourself."

His eyes widened.

"Looks like you're busted, Johnny." Luther sat and thumped his tail across the dead witch's face. "About time, too."

"So you gonna tell her?" Rex licked a small cut on his forepaw. "Now or never, right?"

"Seriously, what's going on?" she demanded.

He sniffed and toyed with the spy-bug he'd found lying close by and which would undoubtedly need a few repairs. "All right, darlin' There's, uh...there's somethin' I oughtta tell you 'bout them hounds. And it ain't gonna sound exactly sane."

"After all this?" She gave him a tired, crooked smile. "Try me."

CHAPTER TWENTY-EIGHT

Four days later.

"Here you go, Johnny." Darlene set the glass of Johnny Walker Black on the bar and slid it toward the bounty hunter. "You let me know when you want another."

"Thanks. I'll stick with only the one today." He took the glass and stared into the whisky, then knocked it back.

The door to the trailer-diner opened and closed, and Darlene smirked before she nodded. "Your friend's here."

He turned on the stool as Lisa walked toward him with a knowing smile. "Well, there's a surprise."

"Is it?" She took the stool next to him. "Hey, Darlene."

"What can I getcha, honey?"

"Nothing. I'm good, thanks."

"Mm-hmm." The woman darted them a sideways glance and chuckled before she moved down the bar.

"How you doin'?" Johnny asked.

Lisa ran a hand through her hair and took a deep breath. "Better. Things have settled, relatively speaking. You?"

He stared at his empty glass. *I should've asked for another.* "I'm fine."

"Good. Listen, I went ahead and handled the debriefing for both of us this morning. And got the rest of the reports from the labs."

"You don't say?"

"You were right. Maya Carroway—the demon-witch—was feeding off human fears and using it to power her magic."

The dwarf grunted. "Not only human, though."

"Well, for the most part." She folded her arms on the bar. "It took our team a little longer than expected, but they managed to create a type of antidote potion for the one Carroway used to buoy her psyche spells. All victims have been given it and we're working to clear things a little for those who were locked up while under her influence. Hopefully, it helps."

"Did they say anythin' 'bout you and me?" He turned slowly to meet her gaze.

"Yeah. The spells she used were tailored to humans specifically because most of them have an incredibly low tolerance for magic. It seems she gave you and I way more than the regular dose, but we snapped out of it far quicker too."

"Yeah, I assumed it was somethin' like that. The hounds were immune."

"As it turns out." Lisa tucked her hair behind her ear and nodded slowly. "They were amazing, Johnny. I don't think we would've made it out of there without them."

He snorted. "Don't tell them that."

"We can totally hear you, by the way," Rex said.

Luther giggled. "Can't hide from us, Johnny. Tell her she should've stayed outside for a longer belly rub."

The dwarf wrinkled his nose.

Lisa tried to hide a laugh. "What?"

"They already heard. And you gave 'em belly rubs?"

"Hey, no belly rubs isn't one of your rules." With a shrug, she gazed at the back of the bar. "And they deserve it."

"Uh-huh. As long as they don't let it go to their heads."

"It's probably a little late for that."

They both stared across the bar. Johnny inched his fingers closer to the empty rocks glass in the silence. *Uh-huh. I need another.*

Lisa drew a deep breath. "You know, I understand what happened and that it's over. That nothing I saw was real. But I keep going back to all the awful things that spell pulled up in me. Losing my job was one of them. And I saw an old friend of mine get…hurt. I had to call her to make sure she was still okay."

"And she is, right?"

"Oh, yeah. She's doing as well as the last time I talked to her. What about you?"

He grunted. "What about me?"

"You know, if you wanted to talk about anything you saw when we were drugged by dark magic and you fought off a group of criminals based on Rex and Luther's instructions."

"Ha. Funny."

She shook her head. "I wasn't trying to be."

"I know." With a sniff, he tilted his head and stared at the bar. "I saw Amanda."

"Oh, wow."

"Yep. And my cabin burnin' to the ground. I heard Dawn callin' for me too."

She stared at him in surprise. "I—"

"And a few other things. Hey, Darlene!"

"Yeah, honey?"

"How 'bout another drink and two fried catfish plates?"

"You got it." The woman smiled at him and turned the coy look onto his companion as she poured another four fingers of whisky into his glass. "Those'll be right up."

"Thanks."

When the woman disappeared through the door into the kitchen, the agent leaned forward to catch his attention. "A few other things?"

"Yep." He snatched the glass and slid it toward him, still staring at the back of the bar. *If she pushes, I ain't gonna be able to keep it down.*

"Like what?"

Shit. He cleared his throat. "You." He immediately lifted the glass to his lips and gulped half of it.

Lisa laughed in surprise. "Johnny Walker. Are you afraid of me?"

A slow smile spread across his lips despite how hard he tried to keep it at bay. The bounty hunter turned toward her and met her gaze. "You know that ain't what I meant."

Continue the adventures of Johnny Walker and his coonhounds in *Zero Dwarfs Given.*

The story continues in book 4, *Zero Dwarfs Given*, coming in early January.

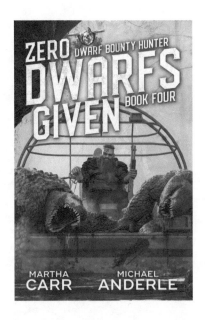

Pre-order today to have your copy delivered at midnight on January 3, 2021

Get sneak peeks, exclusive giveaways, behind the scenes content, and more. PLUS you'll be notified of special **one day only fan pricing** on new releases.

Sign up today to get free stories.

Visit: https://marthacarr.com/read-free-stories/

The garden of my dreams is approved and all set to be installed in the spring in the backyard of the dream house. It's gonna be the bomb. It's also the first time I've really done something that says, I'm putting down solid roots – both figuratively and literally.

I've always had a thing about owning too much stuff. I don't like it. For a long time, I thought it was because I just couldn't buy that much anyway. I was a journalist, author and single mother. That combo kind of screams, 'I have no money'. (I still look back and marvel at how I could stretch a dollar till it sang.)

I was used to doing more with less for decades while building a career and raising a son. But then, the Great Recession happened and frankly, I was worn out from dealing with agents and publishers and marketing and I just wanted a break. I came in out of the cold and looked for a corporate job.

After sending out hundreds or resumes (I promise, not an exaggeration), I finally got a job. I was an editor in brand compliance for a large health care company. The shorthand of that is I was part of the 'word police' team. We checked everything to make sure it was copacetic before it left the building.

I was probably the happiest person in a building with a thousand people. I had an insurance card in my pocket. There were not one, but two Starbucks – one for each building, and a large cafeteria with chefs, not cooks.

I had my own cubicle that had walls where I could put up a calendar and a few pictures. After so many years of hustling and making do, I could predict what would happen tomorrow and the next day and the day after that. And every two weeks the same amount of money popped up in my checking account. It was heaven.

And, after I had caught up on all the bills and put a little money aside for emergencies, it also meant I could upgrade my lifestyle. Go from that used couch from a friend's friend and buy a new one. It was heady times.

This would be the first time I would own something that had some real value to it. It would be harder to leave it behind or sell it at a loss. That thought left me sitting on the couch taking deep breaths. I realized I could no longer just decide to go. I would have to actually plan or maybe even stay.

This all started with an unusual childhood that I'll leave at that, but the upshot is I had learned to stay small, be invisible. Owning nice things, creating large gardens and staying in one place where people get to know you really well makes you visible.

I know I've got a lot of best selling books and you'd think that would be the definition of visible, but it's not. It's the life we create on a local level, with the people right around us and at long last, I'm getting around to doing just that.

Wait till you see this garden, too. It's like I'm kind of home... at last. More adventures to follow.

Thank you for finding Martha and me here at the back of the book!

Well, it is the week after Thanksgiving and just starting December. I had expected to be back from Texas a couple of days ago.

No need, we didn't go. *Thank you a lot, COVID, for that.*

Since we didn't go, and due to a general malaise, we decided to not make a large turkey, but I have to admit I am still grateful for so many things.

Including you!

It doesn't matter if I have one story inside me or one thousand. Without readers, it is a pretty desolate wind-swept prairie where my words catch in the breeze and are gone. It's a pretty lonely existence at that point for an author.

Enter, reader!

With you involved, we get to know that our words have homes in your imagination, and the characters live on in ways that encourage us to continue what we do. We might (or might not) be individuals the wider world will know about, but in the end, it doesn't matter.

What matters and what I am thankful for is that you will know our characters, for in each of them, perhaps in a small part, is a piece of me and Martha and those who work with us on all of these projects.

At some point, raise a glass of your favorite beverage and toast a character in a book or story you love. In essence, you are raising a toast to us.

In there somewhere, you will find me toasting you right back.

Ad Aeternitatem,

Michael Anderle

Solve a murder, save her mother, and stop the apocalypse?

What would you do when elves ask you to investigate a prince's murder and you didn't even know elves, or magic, was real?

Meet Leira Berens, Austin homicide detective who's good at what she does – track down the bad guys and lock them away.

Which is why the elves want her to solve this murder – fast. It's not just about tracking down the killer and bringing them to justice. It's about saving the world!

If you're looking for a heroine who prefers fighting to flirting, check out The Leira Chronicles today!

<u>AVAILABLE ON AMAZON AND IN KINDLE UNLIMITED!</u>

If smart phones and GPS rule the world - why am I hunting a magic compass to save the planet?

Austin Detective Maggie Parker has seen some weird things in her day, but finding a surly gnome rooting through her garage beats all.

Her world is about to be turned upside down in a frantic search for 4 Elementals.

Each one has an artifact that can keep the Earth humming along, but they need her to unite them first.

Unless the forces against her get there first.

<u>**AVAILABLE ON AMAZON AND IN KINDLE UNLIMITED!**</u>

CONNECT WITH THE AUTHORS

Martha Carr Social
Website:
http://www.marthacarr.com
Facebook:
https://www.facebook.com/groups/MarthaCarrFans/

Michael Anderle Social
Website:
http://www.lmbpn.com
Email List:
http://lmbpn.com/email/
Facebook:
https://www.facebook.com/LMBPNPublishing

Made in United States
Troutdale, OR
10/12/2023

13640654R00169